A Dead Cousin
Jessica Huntington Desert Cities Mystery #5

Anna Celeste Burke

A DEAD COUSIN

Copyright © 2018 Anna Celeste Burke

www.desertcitiesmystery.com

Independently Published

Cover Design by Anna Celeste Burke
Public Domain Photo from Pixabay

ISBN: 9781723817540

DEDICATION

To my husband. The bravest man I've ever known.

Books by USA Today and Wall Street Journal Bestselling Author, Anna Celeste Burke

A Dead Husband Jessica Huntington Desert Cities Mystery #1
A Dead Sister Jessica Huntington Desert Cities Mystery #2
A Dead Daughter Jessica Huntington Desert Cities Mystery # 3
A Dead Mother Jessica Huntington Desert Cities Mystery #4
A Dead Cousin Jessica Huntington Desert Cities Mystery #5
A Dead Nephew Jessica Huntington Desert Cities Mystery #6 [2019]
Love A Foot Above the Ground Prequel to the Jessica Huntington
Desert Cities Mystery Series

Cowabunga Christmas! Corsario Cove Cozy Mystery #1
Gnarly New Year Corsario Cove Cozy Mystery #2
Heinous Habits, Corsario Cove Cozy Mystery #3
Radical Regatta, Corsario Cove Cozy Mystery #4 [2019]

Murder at Catmmando Mountain Georgie Shaw Cozy Mystery #1
Love Notes in the Key of Sea Georgie Shaw Cozy Mystery #2
All Hallows' Eve Heist Georgie Shaw Cozy Mystery #3
A Merry Christmas Wedding Mystery Georgie Shaw Cozy Mystery #4
Murder at Sea of Passenger X Georgie Shaw Cozy Mystery #5
Murder of the Maestro Georgie Shaw Cozy Mystery #6
A Tango Before Dying Georgie Shaw Cozy Mystery #7 [2018]

A Body on Fitzgerald's Bluff Seaview Cottages Cozy Mystery #1
The Murder of Shakespeare's Ghost Seaview Cottages Cozy Mystery #2
[2018]

Lily's Homecoming Under Fire Calla Lily Mystery #1 [November 2018]
Love Under Fire Romantic Suspense Box Set

CONTENTS

ACKNOWLEDGMENTS

Thanks to Peggy Hyndman for another speedy and thorough editing job on the manuscript for *A Dead Cousin*. I'm grateful, too, for her feedback and all the suggestions that made this a better book.

Another big thank you for the readers who support and encourage me—especially my "ARC Angels" who read my books before they're published. I appreciate the feedback many provide while I'm writing as well as their cheerleading. Some have even granted me permission to name a character after them! In this book, Harry Mik, Michele Bodenheimer, Carmel Schneider, Kay Sarginson, and Renee Collins all loaned me their names. Thank you!

1 A FRANTIC PHONE CALL

Trouble always seems to find me when I least expect it. Is it just me or does that happen to calamity magnets everywhere? Not all trouble is created equal though, is it?

After a late night of celebrating with my Cat Pack friends, I planned to sleep in Saturday morning. Three months without a new trauma had been reason enough to celebrate, but that Mom was on the mend had added to the festive feeling. When my handsome detective friend, Frank Fontana, informed us that the law had finally caught up with my ex-husband's despicable trophy wife, the mood turned jubilant. Life behind bars would put a welcome damper on the tantrum-prone Hollywood diva's ability to make a scene and get me unwanted media attention as the jilted ex-wife.

Frank had even more good news. The French Connection, a big undercover operation centered in and around Perris where he lives, was finally over. Frank, who'd been in a funk for months, was almost giddy with relief. His mood was contagious, and I'd let my guard down. I should have known better since the hallmark of life in my mid-thirties has been a blitz of improbable events. Most involved murder and mayhem, and only a few of those events could be attributed to problems for the clients in my law practice.

Anastasia, a charming standard French poodle orphaned in the wake of one of those improbable events, must have been pooped. She usually serves as my alarm clock these days. This morning, my phone woke me instead. I struggled to find it in a semi-conscious state.

"Hello," I said in a raspy voice.

"Jessica is that you?"

"Yes."

"It's Evie."

"Good morning, Evie."

"No, it's not!" Evie exclaimed and then began to sob. "Some men came to the house to see Dad. I was upstairs, and I heard him use our secret word that means I'm supposed to hide. They took him away."

I gasped as I sat up and sleepiness gave way to panic—a disorder I still battle at times. My heart raced. I couldn't breathe. Somehow, I flew into action anyway. I retrieved the jeans and t-shirt I'd worn the night before from the back of a chair near my bed where I'd tossed them. *No, no, no! Not Frank! Not Evie!* I shrieked inwardly. *Frankie! What about Frankie?*

"Where's Frankie? Is he with you?" I asked, as I dressed in record time.

"No. Frankie spent the night at a friend's house. Dad and I were going to pick him up and take him to breakfast," Evie replied in between sniffles.

"Tell me where he is, okay?" Evie gave me the name of Frankie's friend and the address where he'd spent the night. I checked the time on my phone, surprised to see how early it was. Normally, it was too early to call and arrange for someone to pick up Frankie except that they must have been expecting his dad to drop by before breakfast.

"I'm on my way and I'm sending help. What's the code word that everything's okay?"

Evie gave it to me. I'd already composed an email to one of Frank's colleagues, Detective Rikki Havens. Once I had that code word from Evie, I hit send. Rikki could expedite a 911 emergency dispatch sending help to Frank Fontana's address in Perris. I warned her to be careful since there might still be a crime in progress—the kidnapping of Frank Fontana, and maybe his daughter, if Evie was mistaken and the abductors were still around.

"My friend, Rikki, who works with your dad, will get there before me. Stay put until she gives you the code word that it's safe to come out. I'm going to call your grandpa and grandma, too."

"I know who Rikki is. I was going to call Grampa, but I didn't want to give him a heart attack." Evie's voice broke. Rikki responded to my text immediately.

"Don't worry, sweetie. I'll be careful. Besides, your grandpa's a tough cop. Rikki just texted me that she's on her way and bringing help." I heard a beeping sound on the line. Rikki was trying to call me.

I slipped on my shoes, grabbed my purse, and headed down the hallway toward the kitchen. Anastasia suddenly bounded my way. I gave the happy poodle a pat on the head and hollered for Bernadette. She came running from the wing of the house in which her suite is located and met me in the kitchen.

"Bernadette and I will get there as soon as we can. Don't hang up. I want you to tell Bernadette what you told me, please, honey?"

"Okay."

"Where's your phone?" I asked as I handed mine to Bernadette. She pulled it out of a pocket. "Keep her talking, will you?" Bernadette nodded as we completed the phone switch.

"Coffee," Bernadette said, pointing to the pot with a mug sitting next to it.

"What's going on, Evie?" She asked in a sweet, gentle voice. Her eyes widened as she listened to what Evie had to say. Anastasia's leash was hanging on the back of a bar stool in the kitchen.

"Has she already been out?" I whispered as I pulled a travel mug out of the cupboard for my coffee. Bernadette nodded. "Her breakfast, too?" Another nod. I brushed Bernadette's sweet face with a grateful kiss. The moment I grabbed her leash, Anastasia went on alert.

"Let's go!" I said, as I took a couple of sips of coffee, and then ran with Anastasia to my car in the garage. I called Rikki on Bernadette's phone as I put Anastasia in her harness. In two or three minutes, Rikki and I had worked out a plan for what to do when she arrived at Frank Fontana's house. I prayed with all my heart that help would get there in time and that we'd find Evie and Frank unharmed.

"This can't be happening!" I muttered a few minutes later as I merged onto I-10 West. Bernadette didn't say a word until she ended her call about ten minutes later. By then, I was racing at top speed, and had already almost reached the San Gorgonio pass leading out of the Coachella Valley.

"You'd better slow down. I want to know what's going on, too, but we won't get to Perris faster if you're in a wreck or get pulled over by the police." A glance at the speedometer told me Bernadette was right. Pushing the speed limit's one thing, flying at over ninety miles an hour is just plain crazy.

"Evie's so scared," I said, trying not to tear up at the memory of her sobbing.

"Rikki's with her now. Evie's tough and smart. She did just what her dad told her to do in an emergency."

"I know." I slowed down as I hurtled past a line of semis as though they were standing still. "Uh-oh. Too late!" The flashing lights were almost on my bumper before I heard the siren. I pulled off the highway onto the berm. The police officer jumped out of his SUV and almost ran to my window.

"Great! This guy can't wait to ticket me!" I moaned. Anastasia who'd been as quiet as a mouse since I'd put her into her doggie harness, whined.

"That's what you get for driving so fast in a hot car—como alma que lleva el diablo!" I huffed at Bernadette's chiding tone. Maybe I was driving like a soul fleeing the devil, yes, but my Bimmer convertible is more a sedan than a roadster. A rap on the window kept me from arguing with Bernadette.

"Ms. Huntington," the officer said when I rolled my window down. I cast a puzzled glance Bernadette's way. She shrugged. He must have run my plates before pulling me over to have my name already.

"Yes."

"I've been tailing you with my lights on for a few miles. You were moving!"

"I'm sorry. I have an emergency on my hands. If you don't give me a ticket, I promise I'll cool it. I really need to get back on the road."

"I'm not going to ticket you. Detective Havens with the Riverside County Sheriff's Department says I'm to provide you with an escort. Let me get ahead of you, okay? We'll ease out onto the highway and then we'll hit it!"

"Thank you, uh, I…" That's all I could say before he hustled back to his car. He had the siren and lights on in seconds, and was back on the highway waiting for me before I even had my foot on the accelerator.

"It's a good thing it's Saturday and there's not much traffic. That doesn't look like easing it to me!" Bernadette harrumphed and gave her seat belt a little yank to make sure it was secure.

"Aw, come on, I thought for sure you'd tell me God just sent us a guardian angel."

"Let's roll!" She exclaimed. When we edged past ninety, Bernadette crossed herself. Keeping up with the Sheriff's deputy was harrowing, especially once we'd made the transition from I-10 to State Route 60 heading toward Riverside. That highway winds through a hilly pass before reaching the turnoff that leads south to Perris.

By the time we pulled into the gated community where Frank Fontana lives, I'd considered the possibility that our escort was more of a demon than an angel. He didn't stick around once we reached Frank's house. That could have been because two squad cars, a rescue vehicle, a security patrol car, and the unmarked car Rikki drives were already parked in the driveway and on the street. Neighbors were milling about, too.

Evie hollered as soon as we pulled up and I opened my car door. She was sitting in the back seat of Rikki's car.

"Gracias a Dios! Frankie's with her." Bernadette sprang from the car. I'm half her age and it took me longer to exit the driver's seat.

My excuse is that I'd stiffened up after gripping the wheel and willing the car to stay on the road travelling at break-neck speeds. Our ninety-minute drive from Rancho Mirage to Perris had taken less than an hour. Anastasia woofed, reminding me that she didn't want to be left behind. "Let's take her to the kids. She'll keep them calm."

"Good idea," I said, as I put the sweet, lively poodle on her leash and let her pull me toward Rikki's car. When we got there, Evie was out of the back seat. She threw her arms around my neck.

"Jessica, thank goodness you're here. You'll find Dad, won't you?" I wanted to say something reasonable like "I'll do my best," but Evie was looking for reassurance, not a judicious adult response.

"You know I will. Please don't worry."

"Why shouldn't she worry?" Frankie asked. He was out of the car now, too, and in his teenager hard-case mode. "Those weren't nice guys and they've been gone for more than an hour. What if they missed some of those guys when they did that big round up last week? They could be in Mexico by now with their drug cartel thugs."

"Wow, you know about that?" I asked.

"Of course, I do. I'm no dummy. It was all over the news. Dad watched every minute of it. He said it was over, but it doesn't look like it, does it?"

"Don't say that, Frankie!" Evie yelled, stomping her foot. Anastasia took the foot-stomping as a call to action. She woofed and then wiggled toward Evie. Nuzzling Evie's balled up fist, the friendly poodle didn't give up until Evie relaxed her hand and petted her. Then Evie knelt, hugged Anastasia, and buried her face in the poodle's soft fur.

"It's not likely they're already in Mexico," Rikki Havens asserted as she stepped next to us. She'd been in the middle of what appeared to be a serious phone conversation when we arrived. "Your next-door neighbor gave us good information about the car they were driving, so if they'd shown up at one of the border crossings in it, we would have nabbed them."

"Unless they changed cars," Frankie argued. I'd been tempted to respond in the same way, but was still trying to avoid being brutally honest about the desperation of the situation. Rikki eyed Frankie, pausing as if not sure what to say next to the detective's savvy son.

"They did, but we've got a lead on that vehicle, too. I hope you're right and they're on their way to Mexico. We've got the escape route covered no matter where they try to cross the border." I peered at Rikki trying to decide if she was as confident as she sounded or was playing the reassurance game with the kids, too.

"Please, Frankie, I understand you're anxious about your dad. We are, too. Thanks to Evie's quick action, they only got minutes, not hours of lead time. Rikki and her colleagues are on it," I said as I reached out and gave him a reassuring pat on the shoulder. He stiffened at my touch, but teared up, too—playing the tough guy—a chip off the old block.

"Don't listen to Frankie. Those weren't Mexican cartel guys. They spoke English without any accent. I don't have any Latino friends named Barney, do you, Frankie?" She stomped her feet again. Anastasia imitated her, which forced a smile from Evie despite her irritation with her brother.

"Barney? Does that mean one of them called the other by his name?" I asked Rikki.

"Well, there weren't just two of them, and that may have been more like name-calling than a personal form of address."

"You mean slang, like surfer lingo?" Brien Williams, my wannabe surfer pool boy turned security associate had told me Barney is used as a snide term for a newbie surfer.

"Something like that." Rikki glanced at Evie and Frankie who were staring at us. "Let's have a look around and I'll fill you in."

2 GOOD COP, BAD COP?

Bernadette must have sensed the furtiveness in Rikki's demeanor. Something was up. That was Bernadette's call to action.

"I was afraid you two might not have eaten, so I brought treats. I bet Anastasia could use one, too, after our wild ride from Rancho Mirage. Let me tell you about it." Bernadette waved us off. The offer of food got through to Frankie. Teenage angst and attitude in a thirteen-year-old boy is only exceeded by the desire to eat—according to his dad anyway.

"He eats every hour on the hour. It wouldn't be so bad if he cleaned up after himself, but the kitchen's a wasteland after one of his assaults." My heart twisted remembering that conversation. Frank loves his kids and has done his best to show them how much since he and their mother divorced several years ago. Frank's dark eyes were tender and pensive even as he griped about his son. A rueful smile on his lips had moved me to kiss him, reassuringly. He'd returned the favor with more than reassurance on his mind.

"I'll try to get back to say goodbye before your ride gets here. If not, I'll see you tonight at your grandparents' house." Evie rushed forward to give me one more hug.

"This is hard, I know. Hang in there," I said, holding onto her tightly.

"I'd rather stay here, so I know what's happening."

"Your mom is on her way to your grandpa and grandma's house. I bet she's going to beat you there. You don't want to make her wait too long, do you?" Evie shook her head "no."

"You'll give us an update tonight, won't you?" Evie asked that question in her best imitation of a stoic, adult voice. Her lip quivered, though, betraying the scared child within.

"Will do!" I hope I have some good news for her by then. As Bernadette put an arm around Evie and led her back to Rikki's car, I battled with my emotions. I couldn't face the possibility that I might have to deliver bad news.

How could Frank put us through this? I groused silently. He could be so open and candid at times, it was touching. On the other hand, like his dad, Frank sometimes kept too much to himself. If he'd been more forthcoming, he might not be in the trouble he was in— whatever that might be. Even though I'd sensed for weeks that something was bothering him, I couldn't get Frank to come clean no matter how much I pried.

Last night, when he'd confided that the French Connection operation had ended, his relief had been palpable. Or so it had seemed. Had he been wrong, or had he deceived me? At this point, I wasn't as convinced as Frankie that the undercover operation had anything to do with Frank's disappearance. The coincidence blared at me, though, like the siren on the police car that had led us here.

"Thanks for the escort. Your pal doesn't mess around."

"He said the same thing about you—once he caught up with you." Rikki smiled. "When is Peter March getting here?"

"Soon. He doesn't have an escort, but he does have one of those rooftop lights and a siren like you and Frank use for police emergencies."

"How did he score that?" Rikki asked.

"You'd know more about what that requires than I do. Peter's roots run deep into the underbelly of law enforcement—more military than civilian. I'm sure he's still got good security clearance since the bigwigs who hire him in the desert are often connected to one government agency or another."

"As in spy vs. spy?" I shrugged noncommittally in response to her query. Peter's another man in my life who keeps a lot to himself. Rikki shook her head. "How anyone can handle the black-ops and spook stuff is beyond me. Speaking of the underbelly of law enforcement, though, we think that Barney term Evie heard is cop lingo—a smartass reference to a small town cop."

"Ah, I get it! Like Mayberry's Barney Fife, right?"

"Yes. Evie's clever. She had her window open. Even though she was supposed to be hidden behind the false wall in her closet, she eavesdropped on the conversation as the men took Frank with them. I'm pretty sure there was another cop with the group, too, because Evie asked me if her dad was working on a gambling case. She heard someone speaking in a different voice say something about 'bingo.' It's likely to be more name-calling if what they said wasn't 'bingo' but 'bingo cop.' That's another cut at small town cops, or it could be a slur against a member of the tribal police." I nodded as I tried to make sense of what she was saying.

"So, what you're saying is that cops hauled Frank off. Good cops or bad cops?" I asked.

"I'm trying to sort that out. Internal Affairs claims they didn't send anyone to pick him up." Alarms went off in my head at the mention of IA. There was an uneasiness in Rikki's manner, too. "I don't see any reason good cops, no matter who sent them for Frank, would have ditched the car they were driving and switched to another one."

"Not even if they're working undercover?" I asked. Rikki stopped and stared at me as if wondering where that question had come from or perhaps she was uncertain about how to respond.

"I've contacted everyone I can think of and put out a request for information about any active undercover investigations. Nothing helpful has come in so far."

"What about the French Connection?"

"Frank told you about that?" Rikki asked. Her eyes narrowed as she gazed at me with suspicion.

"Just enough to make sure we didn't trip over the investigation while we were trying to determine what happened at my ex-husband's house in Bel Air. I'm sure you've heard by now that Cassie Carlysle-Harper's handler, William Hargreaves, was mixed up with the drug ring they busted here in Perris."

"Her dead cousin, you mean? Murdered by the lady in orange—not that I believe she'll wear that colorful jumpsuit for long. Her wily lawyer's already working hard to make the Hollywood heartthrob out to be the victim of a dirty cop."

"Dead, yes. Cousin, no—unless by that she was referring to kissing cousins. They've got that cop she's blaming in custody, too. The nanny says he was at the house and she saw him arguing with Hargreaves earlier that day. Maybe that'll give Cassie's lawyer the wiggle room she needs to help her client get away with murder."

"I'm sure your ex-husband's lawyer has told you there's physical evidence linking Cassie to the deed, too. And not just her fingerprints on the murder weapon."

"Yes. Paul's over the moon that Jim's off the hook for murder, although my scumbag ex-husband is still facing other charges. Serves him right for trading me in for the trophy wife from hell. The shady cop, who claims Cassie killed Hargreaves, has plenty of reasons not to want to be charged with another crime—especially murder. Given the officer's alleged involvement with the drug ring, Paul's lucky they've got more than his testimony to use against Cassie."

"That's true. From what I've heard, the guy they're holding is a ruthless S.O.B. He'd use Cassie or anyone else as a 'get out of jail card,' without giving it a second thought," Rikki said, scowling. "If Cassie's case goes to trial, it's going to be quite the show. The powers-that-be are doing everything they can to keep a lid on the cop's involvement in the mess in Bel Air. I'm sure they'll pull strings to get Cassie a plea deal, if she'll accept one. In the meantime, she's on a campaign to clean up her image, isn't she?"

A wave of revulsion swept over me as I adopted the scowl Rikki still wore. We started walking again. When we reached the sidewalk leading to Frank's porch, we stepped around a uniformed officer taking pictures. Hearing the click of his camera, a montage of exploitive photos flashed through my mind.

"I take it you've seen the photos and video footage of Cassie and her beautiful baby, Destiny, that are plastered everywhere. It's the best acting Cassie's ever done! She lays it on thick, playing the role of devoted mother clinging to her child during visitations while sitting in jail charged with murder. Jim's fighting for sole custody, but he and Paul are on the same wavelength you are. They'll be amazed if she doesn't get the charges reduced to manslaughter and a light sentence. The fact that's she's not out on bail is a miracle."

"Despite her fame, her fortune makes her a flight risk. Besides, she's got a history of violence including that attempted assault on her husband in the courtroom. What self-respecting judge could ignore that?"

"You'd be surprised by the kind of pressure Hollywood can bring to bear on Cassie's behalf. Although nothing like what the government agencies can do that want to keep details about a cop involved in the French Connection from going public. You probably know more about this than I do, but Paul also mentioned that the charges against the cop are being challenged based on a procedural error. He might get out of jail before Cassie does."

"If he does, the DEA will be waiting to pick him up." When Rikki said nothing more as she walked up the steps to Frank's porch, I sighed and shut up. I mulled over the shocking possibility that the men who'd taken Frank might be cops. *Good ones or bad ones—how did Frank get himself into this mess?* I wondered once again.

"It's not just procedural errors that muck things up," Rikki said with one hand on Frank's front door handle. "In an undercover operation like the French Connection, the line between good cop and bad cop isn't always clear. Boundaries get blurrier the longer a cop is undercover. Even a great cop like Frank can slip up." I reached out and took Rikki by the arm, pulling her around to face me. I wanted to look her in the eyes.

"What are you saying—that Frank crossed a line? What do you know that I don't?" My heart raced as I asked that question, especially when Rikki avoided making eye contact. "Come on, he's a Boy Scout. You haven't known him long, but you must have figured that out. Would he do anything to jeopardize the wellbeing of Evie and Frankie?" Rikki had a miserable expression on her face when she finally looked me in the eye. Then, after checking to make sure the officer taking pictures was no longer close enough to overhear her, she spoke almost in a whisper.

"I told you I don't get it when it comes to spy games. I'm not sure I understand enough about what's happening with the French Connection to confirm whether the operation is closed or not. The Sheriff's Department cooperated with the agencies running the sweep to round up suspects. We weren't privy to all the inside info—not me anyway. I can't tell you much about Frank's role or what he did 'in character' as an undercover operative. I don't know if he committed some indiscretion or an out and out breach of the law."

"Please quit being cagey with me. If Frank's accused of doing something wrong that might be related to his disappearance, I want to know what it is." Rikki glanced from side to side again before going on, speaking so quietly I could barely hear her.

"There's money missing. Whose money is it? I can't tell you that for certain—maybe cartel money—maybe money the DEA or ATF put up to buy drugs as part of a sting. I've got permission to find Frank. Otherwise, I've been told to butt out. I'm going to do my best, but what if Frank doesn't want to be found?"

I felt as if I might faint. A commotion at the curb was a welcome relief. Even in my dazed condition, I recognized Peter's black SUV immediately. He hustled over to Rikki's car where Bernadette and the children were waiting just as two identical SUVs pulled up alongside Peter's vehicle.

My disorientation didn't completely recede until I saw Peter's hulking form walking toward us. It was quite a sight to see the six-foot-eight, muscle-bound man sporting his usual grimace, striding toward us with my fluffy white standard poodle leading the way.

Brien, who now works for Peter's firm, was on his heels. A shorter, blonder version of his boss, Brien scanned the area around us, looking every bit like the security guard he was training to become as one of Peter's associates. Peter and Brien carried themselves with purpose—men on a mission.

They may have warned Rikki to butt out, but let them try to do that with Peter March and Brien Williams, I thought. *Or me.*

3 GO BAG

"I'm supposed to return her to you," Peter said, handing me Anastasia's leash. "I have a team taking Evie and Frankie to their grandparents' home in the desert. Bernadette's going with them."

I turned and waved as Bernadette and the children yelled goodbye. Bernadette ushered Frankie and Evie into a black SUV that was double-parked in the street. The flinty expressions on the faces of Peter's men told me they were concerned about more than just getting a parking ticket.

"That's great. They'll be as comfortable as they can be while waiting for news about their dad. I heard Jessica tell the children that their mother's going to meet them there. You seem to be intent on making the transfer a safe one," Rikki said as the SUV took off with a second vehicle almost on its bumper.

"Until we have a better understanding of what went on here, we can't rule out the possibility that members of Frank's family are targets."

"I understand completely. Hello, Brien."

Brien nodded in acknowledgement of Rikki's greeting. He appeared remarkably professional in his black slacks and a matching t-shirt stretched tight over his well-developed chest. Maybe he struck me that way because he hadn't uttered a "yo" or a "dude"—no surfer lingo greeting at all—even in response to Rikki. In fact, he was about as somber as I'd ever seen him.

"Thanks so much, Peter. Mary can negotiate with Don and Evelyn about where they should stay until Frank's back," I offered.

Brien did a surreptitious sweep of the area where we stood. I felt increasingly uncomfortable as his eyes roamed the line of the rooftop. My anxious mind suddenly leapt to the possibility that he and Peter were concerned about someone conducting surveillance of the crime scene, or worse even—a sniper.

What if Rikki was wrong and cops hadn't taken Frank? Maybe this was an attack on local police as payback for the raid on cartel stash houses. Rikki and the other first responders had been here for over an hour. What were they waiting for, though, if the plan was to abduct Frank and then shoot the law enforcement personnel who arrived to investigate his kidnapping?

Why wasn't Rikki more worried about it? I did a little surreptitious scanning of my own as she and Peter spoke. She was as tightly-wired as I'd ever seen her. How much was Rikki keeping from us?

"They can't go wrong either way since Don's a cop and Mary's married to one. I told them what you said, Jessica, about keeping my guys on the job around the clock, too, wherever they end up. Bernadette promised not to let them talk their way out of it."

"I guess we know who's going to win that one," Rikki muttered. "If Bernadette threatens to withhold the cake and cookies, the opposition will fold like a lawn chair."

"I doubt Bernadette will have to resort to threats. Even Don will see the wisdom of taking extra precautions to keep the kids safe. He's proud and stubborn, but a smart cop with decades of experience."

"Do you want to do a walkthrough, now?" Rikki asked.

"Sure, although it doesn't sound like there's much to see."

"You're more familiar with this place than I am," Rikki commented. There was something in the way she used the word "familiar" that implied intimacy. "You might notice something odd or out of place that we missed."

Rikki opened the door and stepped into Frank's house. As I followed her into the house, I scanned the foyer leading to the great room and kitchen. Nothing jumped out at me as missing or disturbed. Frank must not have put up a struggle or he left before the men had entered his home.

"Frank's a good friend and I've been here a few times, if that's what you mean when you suggest I'm 'more familiar' with the place than you are. It's not like I've had the run of the house or know where Frank's secrets are hidden." As I said that, I suddenly remembered trailing after Frank one afternoon as he removed his gun and placed it in a wall safe. "Unless they're in the safe in the closet of his den."

"Show us." That was a directive, not a request from Rikki.

"Don't get too excited. I have no idea what he used as a combination."

"That's not a problem," Peter asserted. "Technically speaking, anyway. If you need to see what's in that safe, I can make that happen."

"Go for it! This is an emergency, so we don't need a warrant. If there's any chance the contents of Frank's safe can reveal more about the situation he's in, we can't pass it up," I said.

Peter spoke to someone using a mic he wore. In a flash, another of his associates entered the house with a small kit and then left as quickly as he had come. Anastasia and I led the way to the den. I opened the closet door and pushed hanging items out of the way, revealing the panel in the wall where Frank's safe was hidden. Peter and Brien went to work.

Anastasia and I were standing out of the way in the den. She was exceptionally quiet, as if she sensed the tension in the room. When I heard Peter say "Yes!" in a soft voice, my heart jumped into my throat.

"You want to check out the contents, Detective? Or do you want Jessica or one of us to do it?" Peter asked, as he and Brien stepped out of the closet.

"Let Jessica do it. I'll be right back," Rikki replied as her phone rang. "Put these on," she added, handing me a pair of latex gloves before stepping out of the den and into the hallway to take the call.

"Here," I said, passing Anastasia's leash to Peter again as I slipped on the gloves. "She's being such a good girl. I don't want her getting into anything that might matter to the police."

"I'll bet she'd be happier outside. You want to take her for a quick walk?" Peter didn't wait for Brien to respond before giving him the leash. Anastasia wagged her tail when she heard the word walk, but then looked at me for reassurance.

"It's okay, Anastasia. Go with Brien." Anastasia wagged her tail and nuzzled Brien. He smiled for the first time since he'd arrived.

"Come on, dudette. Let's blow this popsicle stand. Your doggie momma's gotta find Cousin Frank. I don't want to see Tommy until she's got good news for him, do you?" Anastasia woofed when Brien mentioned Tommy's name. Tommy's one of her favorite humans.

Brien was right. Frank's actual cousin, Tommy Fontana, was going to be frantic when he learned about Frank's disappearance. Rikki, still on the phone in the hallway, stepped out of the way as Brien led Anastasia from the den.

"Gun!" I hollered seconds later when I peered into Frank's safe. "He doesn't have it with him—it's here. Badge, too!" I pushed aside the holstered gun and a box of bullets that sat beside his badge. Then I pulled out a stack of colorful file folders that were leaning upright against the side of the safe. Each one was neatly marked in Frank's handwriting: KIDS, HOUSE, CAR, HEALTH CARE, TAXES— files that I quickly determined contained important papers—birth certificates, Social Security cards, car title, mortgage loan documents, insurance declaration pages—nothing out of the ordinary.

As I returned those file folders to the safe, I felt a little guilty going through the "valuables" Frank had stashed in there. I recognized the engagement ring tucked into a little black velvet box. It had belonged to his grandmother. I'd seen Mary wearing it years ago, so she must have returned it to him when they divorced. I also found the watch Frank's dad had given him when he graduated from St. Theresa's Catholic High School two years ahead of me. Behind that was a clear plastic container that held a single CD even though it was deep enough to hold several. I fought tears as I opened the container to find that the CD had been marked in a felt tip pen: "wedding, births, family events." When I shut the container, something rattled. I found Frank's wedding ring and a key beneath the CD.

"What does that key unlock?" I jumped about a foot off the ground when Rikki asked that question.

"Have a little mercy on me, will you?"

"Sorry. I thought you heard me come in here a few seconds ago. I heard the message you shouted out about the gun and badge. What else did you find? What's with the key?"

"I don't know. It was in a container with a CD that says it has family stuff on it. His wedding ring was in the container, too. Maybe the key's a keepsake that has sentimental value to him. I suppose it could be the key to a storage unit where he has more family stuff stashed, but why wouldn't that be on his keyring? Now that I think about it, he and the kids have a ton of camping equipment—canoes, too. There's not room to keep all of that gear in the house and garage."

"A storage unit's as good a guess as any. The kids can tell us where it is. I'll ask."

"Do you want the key?"

"No, it must be an extra. A set of keys was hanging in the kitchen and it there's a small key on it like that one. We can always get the operator of the facility to let us into the unit if the key doesn't work."

"If Frank is suspected of stealing money, wouldn't whoever's investigating him have checked for a storage unit and searched it as a hiding place?" I asked as I returned the wedding ring to the container and snapped it closed. I held onto the key. If it did open a storage unit, I wanted to check it out for myself, and Peter could locate that unit as fast as Rikki could. More importantly, he'd be able to help me figure out what else the key might open if it didn't fit a lock at a storage facility.

"Who knows? I told you, I'm in the dark when it comes to what they have or haven't done to investigate Frank. The information I got came second hand. Yes, as in cop gossip. You've used information gathered that way from Don Fontana and other cops, so don't look aghast!" She paused and glanced around even though we were alone in the closet. "I find it as hard to believe as you do that Frank would do anything underhanded. As I already told you, however, when I tried going directly to Frank's boss in the Sheriff's Department this morning about IA, I got shut down quick..." Rikki's voice trailed off and her eyes widened as I slid the contents of an unmarked padded envelope into my gloved hand. The envelope had been pressed up against the back wall and I'd only noticed it when I returned the CD to the safe.

"Is that a go bag?" Rikki gasped.

"A what?"

"The essentials you need, all in one place, if you have to make a fast getaway."

"Are you saying Frank knew someone was coming for him?" I asked.

"That's one reason he would have put a go bag together," Rikki replied.

"A what?" Rikki and I both jumped this time as a voice came out of nowhere. It was Peter speaking as if echoing my previous question. The walk-in closet suddenly felt claustrophobic with his bulk looming over us. It's a testament to his stealth that we hadn't noticed his approach until he'd spoken.

"You can probably answer that question better than we can. Do you want to see for yourself?"

"Sure. Hang on a second." He donned a pair of gloves he pulled from a pocket. I handed the envelope and the items in it to him. Items that included, among other things, a stack of neatly-bundled cash.

"It sure could be a bail out bag," Peter muttered as he glanced through the items.

"Just like I said—a go bag."

"Go bag, bail out bag, bug-out bag, quick run bag—same thing. You'd need more safety and first-aid equipment to hide out in the wilderness. The plane ticket to Rio says Frank had a more urban escape in mind." Peter stopped to show us the ticket.

"That's not his real passport or driver's license," I said, stating the obvious as Peter examined them. There were pictures of Frank's face on them, but the name, Frederick Fletcher, and other information with it wasn't his.

"Good fakes," Peter said. Without asking, he snapped photos of them from a camera located on the headset he wore. "He was working undercover, wasn't he? Maybe, the name's the one he used then—is there any way to know that?"

"Frank wasn't even straightforward with me about working undercover, why would he have given me a name?" I gazed at Rikki hoping she knew more than I did.

"Don't look at me, I've already told you I wasn't in the loop either. I only learned Frank had a role to play in the investigation when we moved in and made arrests. I'm going to need to take those materials into evidence since they could be the work of a man planning to run for his life because bad guys were after him. They might also be construed as evidence that he was intent on becoming a fugitive from the law. Maybe the stack of cash is part of the missing money." Rikki sighed, although I couldn't fathom what was behind the sigh.

"Are you kidding?" I snapped.

"Come on, Jessica! A fake passport, a bunch of money, a plane ticket..."

"And sheets of paper with numbers on them," Peter added, interrupting Rikki after he'd given that padded envelope another shake. He slid the rest of the items he held in his enormous hands back into the empty envelope.

"What kind of numbers?" Rikki and I asked almost simultaneously.

"At first glance, I can't tell you that. They're handwritten on pages torn from a journal or a ledger or some other old-school record book like that." He smoothed out the crumpled pages on the flat surface of the envelope to get a better look at them, taking a photo of each page. "These have been folded more than once or crumpled as if someone threw them away or hid them in a hurry."

"Are those initials and dates?" I asked.

"That's my guess. The figures in the last column are dollar amounts."

A sudden chill swept over me as if the hand that had written those numbers had reached into the closet and disturbed the air around us. The script bore a hard edge with a cold precision as if written by a heavy hand using a sharp pointed pencil.

"Really old school if those erasure marks mean the information was recorded in pencil," I muttered.

"Pencil in some places. Pen elsewhere," Peter added as he looked through the pages again. "Someone was studying these pages carefully by the look of the coffee ring on this one." Peter showed us what he meant by that, and I took the pages to scrutinize them more carefully.

"That must not have been Frank. He wouldn't have handled them so carelessly or set a coffee cup on them," I said, quickly scanning the initials. Several sets appeared more than once, but I couldn't find "FF" on any of the pages. A little sigh of relief escaped my lips. "Could they be records of drug transactions?"

"Not very big ones given that the largest amount I saw was around twenty-grand. I've made copies. You can look them over." I heard a whoosh sound as Peter sent them to me.

"Maybe they're dollars brought in by runners on the street. Those wouldn't be that large depending on how often they turned over the cash," I mumbled.

"True, but I don't see why Frank would care about what was going on that low down in the food chain, do you? When they wrapped up the French Connection, they collected a bunch of little hustlers, but the top dogs were the real targets. Let's put these pages back in the envelope with everything else and I'll get the lab to look for physical evidence on the pages themselves while we see if we have any luck figuring out what the numbers or initials mean." Rikki held the envelope open as I added the ledger pages to the other items that Peter had already returned to it.

"It's too bad the pages have been handled as much as they have been. There might have been fingerprints that could have revealed who kept the records," Peter said.

"Don't worry. If the crime lab can lift prints from the pages after what they've been through, we'll do what we can to identify the owner." Rikki looked worried. "Frank's prints are on file."

"Good grief! The papers were stashed in his safe. Why wouldn't his prints be on them?"

"Don't jump all over her, Jessica. Frank's an excellent detective. As you pointed out, it's likely he handled those pages with care. I'm as doubtful as you are that he's the one who left that coffee ring on them. He had a much better idea than we do about what he was squirreling away in here and its value," Peter said.

I could tell Peter was getting antsy. Despite his murky past in Special Forces black-ops and his lightning quick action when there was trouble afoot, Peter often grew uncomfortable when interpersonal exchanges became unpleasant. Perhaps he was more annoyed and impatient than uncomfortable. In any case, he was ready to move on, and so was I.

"I hear you, Peter. I agree that Frank had them hidden in here for a reason. If those papers have some bearing on who's taken Frank or why, we've got to figure it out."

"Tucked in along with the other getaway stuff, you mean? It's possible our detective pal was keeping them as insurance to ward off the bad guys if he made it to Rio." Rikki shrugged as she said that, and then turned to shut Frank's safe. A similar thought had occurred to me, but I wasn't going to let Rikki know that. In my preferred version of the story, Frank was hanging onto them long enough to fix the mess he was in, even if it meant he had to hide out in Rio. My stomach churned at my own screwy logic.

"From what you've said, Rikki, the thugs who took him from his home this morning are the bad guys—bad cops, maybe. If Frank's just another cop gone bad, why not go off with his buddies? Why give Evie that warning?"

"If he's on the run, the warning to Evie could have been a ploy," Rikki replied. I rolled my eyes in my desperation, wanting to rant at her. Still, Frank hadn't been himself for weeks—at least not until last night. I couldn't let go of my conviction that Rikki was wrong about Frank being up to no good. I felt quite certain, though, that the pages in that envelope had something to do with the trouble he was in. Another certainty struck me, too.

"He wouldn't use his daughter as a pawn in a game knowing how much that warning would terrify her!"

"Hang on, you two. I've got a call," Peter said as he turned and left the closet.

"Me, too," Rikki added as her phone rang again.

"Anastasia's found something," Peter said as Rikki and I emerged from the closet trailing after him.

4 ANASTASIA'S FIND

As Rikki stopped in the hallway to speak to her caller, Peter and I dashed past her to the front door. Peter's surprisingly quick on his feet for such a big guy and he got there first. When we stepped out onto Frank's large, covered front porch, Anastasia spotted me. She woofed and wiggled with excitement from the yard below us.

"What did you find, you good girl?" I asked as I walked down the steps. When the young woman sporting a county crime lab jacket held up the clear plastic evidence bag, I was bewildered by what I saw.

"I gave that to Frank," I said. I'd given him the small laminated card not long after he'd chided me about my diatribe on untrustworthy men. The phrase on the card had come from Father Martin, although it hadn't originated with him. The priest, who I seek advice from, even though he's often irritating, said he understood my reluctance to trust easily. The series of misadventures in my life had all started with my ex-husband's infidelity. I'd passed that card along to Frank in jest. The words didn't sound so funny now.

Don't trust anyone. The devil was once an angel.

"Where did you find it?" I asked.

"Uh, the dog and her handler found it in the dirt, here at the foot of the steps leading from the porch. I don't believe I would have seen it. It was almost hidden in what's probably an indentation made by the heel of a shoe."

"Found what?" Rikki asked as she almost dove down the steps to the sidewalk where we stood.

"A card I gave Frank months ago. Anastasia must have sniffed it out—maybe because I'd slipped it into a tin of Bernadette's cookies when I gave it to him."

The CSI waved it at Rikki, who paused long enough to read it.

"That's poignant—unless it's a confession." My mouth popped open. Before I could chastise her for bringing up the Frank's gone bad idea again, she spoke to someone on the phone. "Great! I'm on my way." Then she turned and gave us the news.

"So much for finishing our walkthrough—you can do it if you want to. We've found a body near the location of the abandoned car Frank was seen leaving his house in. The car was found more than an hour ago. Someone had rolled the dead man into a ditch, so no one discovered the body until a drug-sniffing canine arrived at the scene." Something like an electric shock passed through my brain and I must have blanched. "Not Frank, but it is a cop. What's your guess—devil or angel?"

"I don't know, but I intend to find out," I responded without waiting for Rikki to invite me to follow or warn me off.

"Keep up if you can." Rikki said something to one of the CSIs and then ran to her car. Peter ran too, shouting commands into the mic he wore.

"Come with us, Jessica. We won't lose her." He pointed and beeped at his SUV parked across the street and the engine came to life.

Neighbors who were still milling about darted out of the way as we all bolted in different directions. I was holding Anastasia's leash again, and she was delighted at the game we were playing. At my command to "heel," she ran alongside me.

By the time we reached Peter's SUV, Brien had the back door open for us. In seconds, he'd rigged a seat belt and child's restraint to work as a harness for Anastasia. We hopped in as Peter slid into the driver's seat and hit the siren. We had no trouble keeping up with Rikki who wasn't breaking any speed limits. I could understand that. Whoever it was who'd met his end alongside the road, wasn't going anywhere.

"Rikki had it right when she concluded that the men who took Frank were police officers," I commented.

"That's one explanation for the silence, too. It's unusual that there's not more of an uproar given that a police detective may have been abducted and another officer's dead in a ditch beside the highway. There's not a peep out there about an attack aimed at law enforcement. There would have been more of a response by police at Frank's house if Rikki had reported his disappearance as an abduction. She must have called it in as a missing person."

"No one gets too excited about those for days," Brien commented.

"I don't like it," Peter asserted. "Their caution is understandable if they're treating this as a dispute among bad cops."

"At what cost? More of the 'keep a lid on it' response rather than mobilizing to find him won't save Frank's neck!" I exclaimed angrily.

We lapsed into silence as Peter tailed Rikki back toward Riverside and then followed her onto 215 North toward San Bernardino. *Not south toward Mexico,* I noted. The latest wave of adrenaline induced by the terror I'd felt when Rikki announced they'd found a body finally fled. A dull sense of dread settled in instead as my wish for a quick rescue faded, too. Without even realizing it, I'd hoped the jerks who'd taken Frank were heading straight into the waiting arms of law enforcement at the border.

A sentence from an article I'd read about abductions flashed through my mind—"*after seventy-two hours, we start looking for the body.*" It hadn't even been three hours yet since Frank was snatched, and the police already had a body on their hands. Not his, thankfully, but these murderous thugs were wasting no time. I leaned forward a little, trying not to hyperventilate. Anastasia, sensing my distress, pawed at my arm. Apparently, Peter noticed too.

"Jessica, I've got this. Rikki Havens is locked in on my GPS. Even if she picks up the pace, wherever she goes, we go."

"That's great, Peter. I'm not too worried about this crime scene—it's the next one—the one we haven't found yet—that's making my scalp tingle and my skin crawl."

"If their plan was to grab Frank and put a bullet in his head, it would be his body lying on the side of the road. These guys are up to something else."

"What?" I was asking myself that question, too.

"If I had to guess, I'd say Frank has been caught with his hand in the cookie jar. These guys want their cookies back before they decide what to do with him."

"As in the stolen money? Please don't tell me you believe Frank would have put his life as a cop and his kids' lives in danger over money. Dirty money, most likely."

"No way, man!" Brien suddenly exclaimed.

"I agree with both of you, but Frank might have taken the money rather than let it fall into the wrong hands."

"As in dirty money going to dirty cops?" I asked Peter. "Something like that occurred to me when we found the list of initials, dates, and dollars. What if they're payouts to cops who were on the take—maybe tied to the French Connection somehow? Frank was so happy and relaxed last night. I felt certain he'd solved whatever problem had been bothering him before that operation ended."

"Maybe he thought he had—and put his trust in the wrong place." That was Brien speaking with such insight.

"I hear you." I felt sick as I considered the message Frank had left behind. "His 'don't trust anyone' message was a warning for us, wasn't it?"

"Yes and an invitation to find him, Jessica, although I'm not sure how he knew that card would turn up the way it did."

"You're right about the card being hard to find. I walked by the spot earlier and didn't see it. That dog's got powers—like

Bernadette."

Ah! That's my buddy, Brien, I thought. *Dogs with superpowers!*

"Invitation or not, the card is a clue from Frank about the situation he's in. The CSIs would have eventually found the card," I suggested. "Of course, in that case, we might not have heard about it for another day or so until we got our hands on the evidence log. Presuming we can get it given the paranoid effort at control surrounding this investigation. So far, Rikki's been cooperative, but I keep waiting for her to slam the door in our faces as our detective pals all seem to do at one point or another." I fumed as I considered the possibility of being shut out.

"She won't have much luck doing that if Don Fontana starts putting the squeeze on authorities to let him in on what they know about his missing son. I'll be surprised if he hasn't already been on the phone trying to break through whatever wall Rikki banged her head against. He won't let it go even if they try to cover up Frank's role in the French Connection."

"Uncle Don may already be way ahead of us on that front. Evelyn was as worried as I was about Frank's odd moods over that past few months. His dad kept reassuring both of us, so maybe Frank confided in him. When we pick up Bernadette, Don's going to want a report from us, and I want one from him."

"Uh, Jessica, I don't want to be a dope, but what about Rikki? Can you trust her?"

"You're no dope, Brien. I've been wondering the same thing. She seems quick on the draw when it comes to believing Frank's dirty. Rumors that he's suspected of taking money could explain that, but where did she hear it if she's so out of the loop on Frank's undercover work? She says it's 'cop gossip,' but I'm not convinced."

"The card Frank left says 'don't trust anyone,' so I'm with him on that. I'll try to find out what I can about the French Connection and any leftover trouble for Frank or anybody else by using my network among the feds."

"We can do a background check on Rikki, too, right?" Brien asked.

"Yep. I'm already on it. I sent her name to the staff on weekend duty at my office. I also spoke to the guard on duty at the front gates here. They gave me information about the make and model of the car the neighbors saw leaving with Frank in it. I know they've abandoned it, but maybe a surveillance camera picked up a photo that shows who was behind the wheel. The guard at the gate said they'd review the footage to see if the camera caught any images of the men in the car. It's too bad Evie didn't see them. She's sharp."

"She is, Peter, but I'm glad she followed her dad's instructions as well as she did. Evie took a few too many chances as it is. Maybe the police can come up with a sketch based on descriptions from the neighbors," I offered.

"Kim can help us find out about Rikki. She's got her own methods—almost as mysterious as Bernadette's superpowers."

There he goes again! I thought. Bernadette's supposed superpowers are almost an obsession for Brien. Superpowers, as in ESP, which, according to Brien, stands for Extra-Sensatory Precipitation. He was so intent on being helpful that I didn't chastise him about his repetitive references to superpowers. Besides, he was right that Kim Reed has skills.

"Good thinking, Brien. No one's better at sniffing out dirt if it's reached cyberspace than Kim is. Until now, I've taken Rikki at face value when it comes to explaining the reasons for her move this past year from wine country to our valley. It's time to take a closer look at Detective Havens and how she happened to join Frank's team at the Sheriff's Department with a big operation like the French Connection in the works. Let's find out who asked for her transfer and when."

"I'm sure Kim can do that," Brien responded. "Maybe cop gossip's been passed along through social media about dirty cops or a secret undercover operation—the French Connection or something else. If it's out there, Kim will find it!"

"I agree. It's time to keep all of this just between us for now, too—eh, Dude?" Peter asked.

"No one's who's not a Cat Pack member is going to hear anything about anything from me," Brien said, doing a little zipping motion to his lips as he spoke. "I've gotten better at keeping my mouth shut, haven't I?"

"No doubt about it," Peter responded. As he said that, he slowed down. Once we'd made the transition to I-215 North, Rikki had poured on the speed—until now. Up ahead, I could see the flashing lights of police cars pulled off onto the shoulder of the roadway. A county van was sitting there, too. Since we'd crossed the county line, this one was from San Bernardino County.

"Good luck keeping a lid on this mess as more cops get pulled into the investigation," I griped. "It doesn't seem like a smart move by the dirty cops with Frank to bring another Sheriff's Department into the mix. Killing one of their own isn't smart either, is it?"

"They needed to make the switch quick and this spot isn't far from Perris. The guys who snatched Frank may also be counting on screwing things up or at least slowing them down by crossing jurisdictional lines," Peter commented as he pulled off the road.

"Involving more jurisdictions won't make coordination and communication easier. I suppose more cops in more jurisdictions might help us, too. It's got to weaken the control over the investigation from the top." I shut up as Peter maneuvered his SUV into a spot behind Rikki's car.

Would it help Frank was the bigger question. I thought. That his kidnappers were in a hurry was an understatement. The men who grabbed Frank must be in a pressure cooker trying to wrap up whatever mission they're on. Whoever was trying to control the situation from the top was under the gun now, too. The debacle hadn't hit the airways yet, but it was only a matter of time.

"A ticking time bomb," I whispered under my breath as I stepped out of Peter's SUV and into our second crime scene of the day.

5 BARNEY'S FATE

"Why here?"

"What?" Rikki asked. I was a little puzzled by her question since, in my anxious stupor, I wasn't even aware I'd spoken those words aloud. The last thing I recalled before falling into the pit that had opened in my mind, was Rikki being directed toward the CSIs after checking in with a uniformed officer at the scene.

"What's going on?" Rikki had asked a tall, black middle-aged man she must have regarded as the CSI team leader. Perhaps because he was entering information into a tablet he held in gloved hands. He responded quickly and succinctly to the detective's question.

"We've got one man, dead. The first responders missed him because he was shot back in that line of trees, and then his body rolled into the culvert below. He landed a few yards from the railroad tracks. The victim appears to be in his mid-thirties, medium height and build, with dark hair cut close almost military style. He had a bloody lip as if he'd taken a punch not long before he was killed. What else can I tell you about him, Detective Havens?" She hadn't introduced herself, so they must have met before. I was certain that was the case when she addressed him by his first name.

"Thanks, James. I'm ahead of you when it comes to the victim's description and identity. We were able to make an identification the moment you faxed in his prints. According to my colleagues in the San Bernardino Sheriff's Department, he's Randall Roberts—a member of the local police force in the small town of Banner Falls. That's about forty miles northeast of this location." Rikki looked at me when she mentioned the small town.

"Our Barney, huh?" Rikki nodded at me.

"How did he die?" I asked, still focused on the conversation.

"The ME will have to put it in writing before it's official. Off the record—it's clear to me that Officer Roberts was killed by a single gunshot to the back of the head, fired at close range. Given the mess his head's in, I'd say a large caliber handgun—like lots of cops carry. His weapon's not on him, so maybe he was shot with his own gun and the killer took it or tossed it into the brush. Our K-9 officer will find it if it's still in the area."

"Maybe it's in the car," Peter offered. The CSI looked up at the huge man who had joined us and now towered over him.

"We didn't spot it when we went through the car before they towed it to the lab. It's possible it's concealed somewhere. If that's the case, we'll find it. We've got people going over the car with a fine-toothed comb. There's blood in the car. Not a substantial amount, so it's possible the fight that caused the victim's lip to bleed took place in the car. Not all the blood in the car matches the victim's blood type, though—so we've got two bleeders."

Rikki suggested the blood might have come from Roberts' assailant. James nodded and may have said more, but that was the point at which I'd dropped into the abyss. It was like falling down a well. I fought not to stay there, determined not to let my anxiety problems allow me to miss something important. I came around with that "why here?" question in my mind and on my lips. I asked it again.

"Why did they make the switch here?" In a way, I was returning to the conversation Peter and I'd started in the car. Both Rikki and James appeared to be puzzled by my question.

"Who knows? When we catch up with them, I'll ask," Rikki responded.

Apparently, "why here" didn't matter much to her. She wandered off with James. He opened the rear door of the county van, perhaps signaling that they were getting ready to haul the body off to the morgue. Rikki was on her phone again. Peter finally responded to my question after peering at the activity going on below through a small pair of binoculars.

"If the men with Frank crossed the railroad tracks after they did away with one of their partners, there's a split in the fence on the other side. They could have had a vehicle parked on the roadway down there," Peter said.

I took the binoculars Peter offered and scanned the area. I spotted the body bag a few yards on this side of the railroad tracks. A wheeled stretcher sat nearby. Beyond that, I could see the span of tracks and the chain link fence. The split wasn't evident until I stared at it a bit longer. Someone must have tried to put it back together because the gap wasn't visible except near the bottom. I swept the area again, searching higher up this time.

"Rikki said they caught the vehicle used in the switch on a camera. If you're right, and the car was parked down there, did you see a surveillance camera along the track or on the posts across the road?" I asked.

"No, I didn't. I'm not sure what she's talking about. Maybe a passing train picked up something." When I handed the binoculars back to Peter, Rikki was still on her phone. She was also watching us like an Irish setter on point.

"Geez, Rikki looks as if she might tackle us if we head closer to where the CSIs are still working. I'd like to find out if there's a camera we can't see from here, but I don't want to do anything to get the door slammed shut on us."

"I hear you. We can get off at the next exit, take the frontage road, and check it out that way."

"Good idea," I said. "The view will be less obstructed by the trees from that angle, too." I paused for a second, taking in the scene one last time. "Trees hid them when they murdered Roberts—if that was part of their plan."

"Being able to get out of the sight of passing motorists quickly as they moved to a second vehicle might have been a reason to select this spot with all the trees. Especially, if they had Frank in cuffs or constrained in some other way. I doubt bumping off their comrade here was in the plan, though. Why confirm Rikki's suspicions that this is a cop on cop crime when they could have kept her guessing by killing Roberts somewhere else?"

"The body almost eluded discovery, didn't it?" Peter nodded, but didn't appear to be convinced. "I get what you're saying. Something seems spontaneous about his murder to me, too. Maybe it's the fact that Officer Roberts was punched in the face before someone shot him. A fist fight couldn't have been in their plans given the rush they had to be in to get into that second car and keep moving."

"I agree! I don't think we're going to learn anything more hanging around here. Let's go look for a camera."

"Okay. I'll touch base with Rikki and remind her to send us copies of the police reports as they become available—including the pictures she has of the second vehicle. If she balks, I'll know it's time to sic Don Fontana on her when we catch up with him later."

When I turned around, Rikki was no longer looking at us, but waiting as a uniformed officer approached with a German shepherd. Peter took a step toward his SUV where Brien and Anastasia were waiting. Brien was talking on his cellphone, sitting in the passenger seat. The door was open, and he'd let Anastasia out on her leash. It dawned on me that we had our own K-9 companion with us. Why not put her to work?

"Peter, since there's no police presence on the frontage road, I don't see why we can't inspect the gap in the fence. We'll let Anastasia help us check out the area and the roadway where the vehicle could have been parked."

"Why not?"

"Any luck?" Rikki hollered at the officer handling the dog. The K-9 had paused to sniff the ground.

"I'm afraid not," he replied.

As I hustled on over to play nice-nice with Rikki, I could tell I needed to keep it short. She clearly wasn't happy that Officer Roberts' weapon was still missing.

"At least you know Frank's gun wasn't used to kill Officer Roberts since it's still in his safe," I said as I reached her side. As soon as the words were out of my mouth, I realized it had been the wrong thing to say.

"Don't look so smug. Frank's not off the hook. Anyone in that car could have killed Barney with his own gun, execution style. Someone got into a fight with Roberts before shooting him. Maybe a punch in the mouth wasn't enough to shut the guy up, and Frank shut him up permanently."

Rikki eyed me with wariness. That was appropriate since I was fighting the urge to grab her by the shoulders and shake her. Why bother? There were so many holes in her reasoning, so why point out what a stupid argument she was making? When I let out a huge sigh, she picked up the conversation.

"What's up?" She asked.

"We're leaving. I'll finish my walkthrough at Frank's house tomorrow—after the CSIs have completed their work. I'd like to see what they come up with once they're done there, and here, too, and with the examination of the car. I'm sure Frank's dad can get copies of the reports as they become available, but I hope you'll get them to me first. If there's bad news in them about his son, I'd like to be the one to break it to him. Don Fontana's a good cop, but he's an old man, and has already lost one family member in an ugly way."

"Yeah, I know. I heard you and Frank worked a cold case last year that involved his cousin, Kelly Fontana, who was murdered when she was basically still a kid."

"So, you also know that even though she was killed years ago, it's as if it happened recently given that Frank's family members had to relive the whole ordeal last year. They're a tough bunch, but another incident so soon is brutal. I'd like to soften the blow if I can by getting in the loop ahead of Don and other family members."

"Hey, I've already cut you in on this investigation—against my better judgement given how much trouble you can get into. I expect you to share and share alike, and not to do anything to compromise the process. That's true even if you find evidence that Frank's crossed a line. And don't tell me he's just a family friend, either. I'm not blind…" Rikki paused and peered at me, tilting her head to one side, "… although you might be." She shook her head.

I shrugged, unwilling to acknowledge to her or to myself that I'd let Frank cross a line with me despite my efforts to limit my involvement with him or any other man. Paul Worthington's handsome face and engaging smile flashed through my mind, but without raising the same fears. Maybe because until recently he'd been my boss at the law firm, I'd taken more care not to let him trespass on my still damaged heart. Not that any of this was Rikki's business. I didn't trust myself to speak. It was her turn to let out an enormous sigh.

"I'll do my best to get stuff to you before Don Fontana sees it." She might have had more to say, but, thankfully, her phone rang again so I could take my leave. I was right about the "more to say" bit. As I walked away, Rikki answered her phone and then called out after me.

"Attorney Huntington," she said. When I turned to respond, she had her phone pressed against her chest covering the speaker.

"Yes?" I asked, bracing myself for what was coming.

"If you mess with me, I will get the DA to prosecute you for obstruction of justice. Talk about putting on a show. I doubt your boss, Paul Worthington, would appreciate seeing one of the firm's associates charged with a crime, even if you don't get as much press as Cassie."

"Detective Havens, I don't want to bring my firm bad press any more than you want to do that to the Riverside County Sheriff's Department. I'm also confident that you want justice as much as I do. Since Frank's innocent until proven guilty, my plan is to do everything I can to get a good cop out of a bad situation. What's yours?" I didn't wait for her to reply.

When I got to Peter's SUV, he was in the driver's seat with the engine running. Brien had put Anastasia back into her harness. He was riding "shotgun" in the front seat, and I took my place in the back seat beside Anastasia. I slammed the door too hard.

"Whoa, you're ticked off," Brien said.

"You've got that right! We've arrived at the point where our detective friend is warning us to stay on the right side of the law or face the consequences. She's flinging around that obstruction of justice crap. Ironic in the current context where dirty cops are shooting each other." I gritted my teeth and made growling sounds as I fastened my seatbelt. Anastasia pawed at me and whined ever so slightly. My anger fled. It's hard to stay angry when a dog's around to soothe the soul.

"It's okay, Anastasia. I'm not growling at you. She nuzzled me and gave me a kiss when I put an arm around her. I felt the wave of near-panic that had engulfed me subside as I buried my fingers in her soft fur. Tommy Fontana sure had it right when he'd referred to Anastasia as my service dog.

Tommy was going to need a little "Anastasia time" of his own once he heard about Frank's disappearance. I dreaded the thought of Frank's family members hearing such news. As troubling as it would be for them to handle Frank's disappearance, the rumors that he was suspected of wrongdoing would be worse. Don knows his son far better than I do and would fight back, but the idea would still bother him.

"Let's go, Peter. You've got to be right about where these guys had their getaway vehicle stashed. If our detective friend had been in a more accommodating mood, I would have brought it up and asked more questions, maybe even asking for permission to search the area. Under the circumstances, it's better to ask for forgiveness later, don't you agree?"

"Until we have a clearer picture of who we're dealing with, I believe we should avoid seeking Rikki's permission to do anything unless there's no way around it."

My scalp tingled again as Peter uttered those words. Of all my fellow Cat Pack members, Peter's ability to smell a rat is as keen as my own. Why had she cut me in on the investigation—especially given the nasty tone that went with her threat to bring me up on charges? Why keep us in the loop? A quote from Michael Corleone in the Godfather movie suddenly popped into my mind, sending a chill down my spine.

"Keep your friends close, but your enemies closer." Were we friends or

enemies?

6 A DETOUR TO NOWHERE

"Forgiveness for what?" Brien asked. As Peter eased off the shoulder of the road and merged into the flow of traffic on I-215, I filled him in about our destination and why we were interested in the spot. We didn't have to travel far before Peter reached the next exit and made a right turn onto the frontage road that runs parallel to the highway. Detour signs popped up almost immediately. We had to make a series of turns to get back to the point we were trying to reach in the first place.

"That was weird," Brien said as we pulled up across from the spot we wanted to inspect.

"What was weird?" I asked as Anastasia and I disembarked.

"A detour to nowhere," Brien replied. "There's no roadwork or anything going on around here."

"Maybe the signs and roadblocks are left over from an old job," Peter suggested. "The road crews don't always remove things right away."

"Are you suggesting something else?" I asked.

"I guess so. Cops would know how to post detours and roadblocks to keep traffic away from this area if they wanted to leave a car around here ahead of time." Brien was doing one of the things he does best—eating. Even a gruesome crime scene's no match for his appetite, but his observation was a good one.

"Hmm," I murmured as we crossed the road. "Kim can check out the surrounding area and see if there's roadwork that was recently completed or scheduled to begin soon. She can tell us where this road leads and what towns are nearby. After killing one of their companions, they must have been under pressure to get out of sight fast. That makes me wonder if they've got a hideout that's not far from here."

"If they have pictures of the vehicle, do they know in what direction it was headed once they made the switch?" Peter asked as he examined the gash in the fence. He'd put on a pair of latex gloves and had barely touched it when the split in the fence opened wider.

"I don't think so. Rikki didn't speak to me directly about the second vehicle. I overheard her telling someone on the phone that they're looking for a white unmarked paneled van seen near the exit we just used to get here. I don't know if by that she meant it was parked here or en route somewhere. If they have information about where the van's heading, she didn't share it with whoever was on the line at the time. When she spoke to Frank's kids a while ago, she seemed to believe it was possible that the men who grabbed Frank were on their way to Mexico. We were headed north when we pulled off the highway, so why alert law enforcement at the border south of us? Maybe someone reported seeing the van heading south. My guess is the authorities don't have a clue where the van was going."

"Maybe you'll get more details from the police reports. If not, Don can find out more, can't he?" Brien asked as we watched Peter.

"I'm sure he can. I made a heartfelt appeal for Rikki to keep us in the loop, so we can stay ahead of Don. She agreed, but even if she intends to honor her agreement, it won't be easy. Don's crafty and he's got way more contacts with local law enforcement than Rikki or the rest of us all put together. Once I pick up my car at Frank's house, I'm going straight to Don and Evelyn's house and see what Sergeant Fontana's dug up." Peter interrupted our conversation.

"This gap in the fence has been here for a while. These aren't fresh cuts." He pointed out a couple of places where rust or dirt had accumulated on the links where the cuts had been made.

"So, are you saying it's been used for other things than as an escape route for murderous dirty cops?" Anastasia and I roamed along the edge of the road near the fence while I waited for Peter to respond.

"Something like that," Peter replied, and went back to working on the gap in the fence.

As Anastasia and I walked north along the road toward the exit we'd taken from the highway, I searched for cameras. I stopped abruptly when I spotted what could be one. A box mounted inconspicuously on a telephone pole on the other side of the road could house a camera. It wouldn't be obvious unless you had a reason to look for one.

"You see that?" Brien asked. "It's a camera, although someone's tried to camouflage it by making it blend in with the pole it's mounted on. Peter's shop can do stuff like that. Do you want to take a closer look?" Brien asked as he crossed the road and handed me a pair of binoculars. He'd been walking in parallel. He did a complete three-hundred-and-sixty-degree turn, surveying the lonely stretch of road we were on.

"It's a camera all right." I handed the binoculars back to Brien.

"A detour to nowhere and a camera aimed at nothing!" He exclaimed as we walked back toward Peter.

"Because the road doesn't get much use makes it a perfect place to leave a second getaway car. Still, we can't be the first ones to have stumbled across an opening in the fence alongside a restricted area."

"Railroad security must inspect this stretch on a regular schedule. They could have discovered it. If they'd asked Peter, he would have told them to repair it right away. Maybe they wanted to nab whoever's been using it and installed the surveillance camera, instead." Brien shrugged.

Peter was still working on the breach in the fence. I searched the ground nearby, not sure what I hoped to find. It didn't matter since I didn't see a thing. Nor did Anastasia react or do anything other than happily wag her tail.

"If the van was parked here, the police must have already collected any evidence left behind. Otherwise, don't you think Rikki or someone else would be hurtling toward us objecting to our presence?"

"Yep, or they didn't leave anything. I don't see any footprints or tire tracks. The surface isn't good here for leaving anything like that, though. If they'd torn out of here in such a rush that they burned rubber, they could have left marks." Brien scanned the crime scene on the other side of the railroad tracks no more than a couple hundred yards away.

"The body's gone, but the CSIs are still there gathering their equipment and packing it up. One of those dudes could run us off if they didn't want us here."

"It's possible our detective friend hasn't spotted us from where I last saw her. You have to walk to the edge of the tree line where the ground slopes down toward the tracks to be able to see us." I checked using the binoculars as I said that, but no one was watching us.

"Good point," Brien said. Anastasia woofed as if agreeing with Brien's statement. Or maybe Peter's movements set her off. To my surprise, despite his enormous bulk, Peter had squeezed through the opening in a flash and stood inside the fence. He was examining the area that led away from the fence and took a few steps toward the railroad tracks.

"Brien and I think we've spotted a camera. Odd, given how little traffic this stretch of road must get. Unless you have more to say about how the gap in the fence has been used before."

"This area has seen more foot traffic than that made by the men who passed through here today. You can see where the skimpy fresh growth has been stomped on today, but there's not much growing around it. The whole area's been well-trampled. See?" I stepped in through the gap and made sure Anastasia followed me without getting snagged on the fence. There weren't any footprints. I had to strain to see what was so apparent to Peter. I trusted his judgment given that in his former life as a member of a Special Forces unit, he must have trailed fugitives in more desolate and remote areas than this one.

"Why so much traffic?" I asked.

"Moving contraband is my guess."

"As in people, drugs, counterfeit goods, or what?" Brien asked, as he maneuvered his muscular body through the opening in the fence to get a closer look.

"Take your pick—maybe all of them. Most likely drugs, if Frank's current trouble is somehow tied to the French Connection operation and his pals are familiar with this location. They could use it as a place to move product from one vehicle to another, the way they moved Frank today. If trains stop here for some reason, they could also move product that way."

"That's an interesting idea," I said as I began running through my family's business associates, wondering if any of them might have inside information about rail transport. "If trains do stop here, maybe someone's been pilfering legitimate goods transported by railways. Theft would be a reason to post a camera. I'll call Dad and see who among his cronies is familiar with railway operations in this area."

The Huntingtons were once insiders in the railroad industry, but that was decades ago. In fact, my father, Henry "Hank" Huntington, was named for a distant relative—Henry E. Huntington who owned the Pacific Electric Railway at the turn of the twentieth century. Anastasia, who'd tugged at her leash until I let out more lead, suddenly woofed. Then she whined and backed away from the low brush she'd been inspecting.

"Anastasia, did you poke yourself?" I stepped closer to her and leaned down to check her snout for stickers or brambles. Even this far north of the Coachella Valley, stubby shrubs, and cactus are commonplace. Closer to her eye-level, a brightly colored scrap of trash caught my eye. The red, white, and green colors weren't the only reason I noticed it. I'd seen it before.

"Yo, what is it?" Brien asked, peering over my shoulder into the scrubby bush. "Whoa! Don't touch it. I bet that's blood." I squinted at the wadded up cocktail napkin on the ground near a dried skeleton of a plant. A good gust of wind would turn it into a tumbleweed. My sharp-eyed friend was right. One corner was discolored with what could have been blood—the deep wine color certainly wasn't tequila.

"Frank's left us another bread crumb to follow," I said, standing up straight. "That's a cocktail napkin from Rosalina's Tequilería in Marina Del Rey. Frank and I visited the place often while Mom was in a Malibu rehab center."

"We'd better catch those CSIs before they take off." Before Peter could holler, Brien put his fingers into his mouth and produced an ear-splitting whistle. The investigators who were still at the site looked up. We waved at them to join us. They made no move toward us, but one of them pulled out a cellphone and placed a call.

"Argh! I'm never going to get back to the Coachella Valley to speak to Don, am I? We can't be more than a few hundred yards away. Why not just come running?"

"No one wants to buck protocol, or drop the ball on this case. If the lead investigator or Rikki is still up there, why risk ticking anyone off by acting without getting clearance first?" Peter made a good point. Especially considering our previous discussion about multiple jurisdictions with divergent interests in this case.

"I'm sure you're right. Whoever missed this bit of evidence is going to get a tongue-lashing from Rikki no matter what." As if on cue, Rikki appeared above us, one hand on her hip. I felt cornered and stepped away from the place where Peter, Brien, and I stood huddled together. Anastasia and I wandered away just as my phone rang.

"What now?" Rikki asked.

"Anastasia found a wadded up cocktail napkin your CSIs should get over here and collect. I think it's another message from Frank since I've seen one just like it before. I'm not sure why Anastasia found it so interesting unless it smells like food, or like the card that she found earlier that earned her so much praise. This isn't Anastasia's first exposure to murder and mayhem, as you know. It's possible she reacted to the scent of blood, but..."

"Blood!" Rikki exclaimed, interrupting me. "We'll be right there." I saw her hustling down the slope, hollering to the CSIs who darted toward us as she pointed them our way.

Peter waved his arms, directing them to where he stood as Anastasia and I meandered along the tracks. I wondered about the blood on that napkin. Was it Frank's? Had he been injured or was it blood belonging to Randall Roberts? I stopped abruptly, hoping to keep my brain from spinning needlessly out of control.

The best thing I could do for Frank was to get to Don's house and compare notes with him. Maybe he knew something that would help us put the pieces of the puzzle together in a way that could help us figure out what to do next.

"Let's go see how soon we can get away from Rikki once and for all, okay?" Anastasia's tail wagged furiously. She loves it when I talk to her as if she's a person.

When I turned around, I noticed a large metal box that we'd walked past moments earlier. It wasn't the box that caught my eye, but a damp area next to it. Nothing remains moist for long in the dry California air and relentless sunshine. Whatever caused it couldn't have happened very long ago.

"What do you suppose this is?" I muttered, causing Anastasia to woof in reply to my question. The metal box was marked with official looking letters and numbers. It was large enough that it could house some kind of railway equipment or machinery. I stepped closer and examined what must have been a puddle of liquid. Some drops had hardened in the surrounding dirt as if someone had poured water from a bottle onto the ground and it splashed.

"Good grief!" I exclaimed aloud. Had the investigators missed something else left behind as the occupants of the abandoned car switched to the van? If someone stopped here, they'd taken a detour from the escape route through that split in the fence. Why take the time to do that? I bent down closer to the damp spot. This time I smelled urine. "Well, that answers one of my questions," I said as I stood up. I pulled my cellphone from a pocket where I'd stashed it and took a couple of pictures.

Urine isn't a good source of DNA, so I'm not sure what could have been learned by collecting evidence of its presence here. Still, I was angry and would gladly step in for Rikki and chew somebody out about the oversight. I kicked the ground, scattering dirt and a few pebbles. When the debris from my mini-tantrum hit the metal box, the padlock moved. Anastasia must have interpreted my actions as an invitation to play a new game. She began digging furiously in front of the box. As the rocks and dirt flew, it pummeled the metal container, and the padlock not only moved but suddenly came undone. I snapped another picture.

"How do you like that? A locked box that isn't locked at all." Anastasia was delighted at the news. "Peter!" I shouted. He was on the run, sprinting toward me. Brien was on his heels.

"Have you got another pair of those latex gloves?" I asked when Peter reached my side seconds later, pointing at his still-gloved hands.

"Sure," he said. "Someone left this open, huh?"

"I don't believe they meant for anyone to know that." As I put on the gloves Peter gave me, I quickly explained how I'd found out the box wasn't locked. The tantrum part was a little embarrassing to share, although neither man appeared surprised by my disclosure.

"The padlock's damaged," I added as I removed a piece of the lock preventing me from opening the top of the box. Brien, who had leaned in as I opened the lid, uttered one word when he saw what was in it.

"Whoa!" Then he let go another of those shrill whistles.

7 OVERLOOKED CLUES

This time when Brien whistled, one of the CSIs came running. He'd already made his way onto this side of the railroad tracks. His coworker and Rikki weren't far behind.

"Gun," I said calmly when he was at my side.

"I see," he responded. Before he could do anything, Rikki and the other CSI had joined us. Rikki was breathing hard and sweating, too. When she saw the contents of the box, she spewed a stream of epithets. I tried to use my words in a more useful way.

"How is it possible that you missed valuable evidence in this area?" I asked the CSI.

"We didn't miss anything. We weren't instructed to check this area at all," the CSI responded. "The Sheriff's Department called us in after the K-9 officer found a body. They were getting ready to tow the car when we arrived. James had us search it for a weapon, but we had no reason to extend the search past the edge of the railroad tracks since the dog didn't go beyond that point."

"Didn't anyone identify this as a possible exit route for the fugitives who abandoned the car along the highway and murdered one of their companions?" Peter asked.

"You can ask James about that, but I don't believe we were given much background about the car, who was driving it, or any information about an exit route. We were called to process the scene where a body had been found not far from an abandoned vehicle. Period." He shrugged. I studied Rikki who stood there with her hands on her hips again, biting her bottom lip. She finally shrugged before speaking.

"I suppose it's possible the situation got handled as if it was an unrelated incident rather than being connected to the abandoned vehicle," Rikki offered. "I got a call that a body had been found near the location where the car we'd been trying to locate was found, so I assumed the connection had been made. I also can't be sure anyone made the connection to the van if it was parked on the frontage road. I haven't seen the photos yet, but my understanding is that the van was closer to the ramps leading to and from the highway, not here."

"Why didn't you ask them to search the area leading from the murder site to the frontage road?" I asked, trying to keep my question from sounding like an attack. That wasn't easy because I was at the point I'd reached earlier where I wanted to shake her.

"I assumed it had already been done once the dog was brought in." I was about to shriek at her when Peter spoke.

"That's one of the problems we're going to have until you track these guys down. As the fugitives continue to move across jurisdictions, it's going to be harder to connect the dots with new honchos calling the shots about how to handle the investigation at each crime scene." An expression of bitterness and misery stole over Rikki's face. She folded her arms across her chest in a defensive way.

"Too many chiefs," Brien added, using this know-it-all nod he adopts that's way too much like a bobble-head doll for me to take him seriously. Rikki bristled and almost hissed between her gritted teeth.

"You think I don't know that?" She turned to the CSIs who were standing as if paralyzed by the situation. "Photograph the scene, bag the gun, and let's get it to your county lab ASAP, please."

"Sure," the guy who'd arrived on the scene first said. He let out an enormous sigh as he went to work.

"Please don't miss anything else like drugs or money or a note from the killer with his telephone number or address telling us where to find him, okay?" He looked puzzled, but nodded as if he understood. Rikki had looked askance at me as she made that request. I knew it was meant for me. I played dumb.

"What did that mean?" I asked as Rikki motioned for the second CSI to follow her as she walked back toward the location where we'd found the wadded up cocktail napkin. When Rikki didn't respond, I kept moving toward the fence. Rikki paused to get a glimpse of what we'd found near where the CSI had set out an evidence marker. As he photographed it, she hustled to catch up with me. I watched as the CSI picked up the napkin and examined it. The tequilería's logo was clear now, as was the bloodstain. Rikki stepped closer to me.

"It makes me uneasy that you and your dog keep finding these little love notes from Frank," Rikki snapped.

"Really? It makes me uneasy that no one's got a grip on this investigation. Have the big dogs running this operation, while also trying to keep a lid on it, cut you out of the loop? It doesn't appear to me that you or anyone else is making a coordinated effort to save Frank's neck."

I wanted to fix Rikki with a withering glare as her fists clenched and steam poured from her ears. Angry tears welled up in my eyes, so I bored holes into the ground at my feet instead. When I regained my composure, I spoke again.

"I already said I won't do anything that forces you to make good on the threat to go after me for obstructing justice. You must be desperate if you're suggesting I somehow got my hands on the murder weapon and left it in that box for you to find. What a clever trick! Maybe you've decided Frank's not just a bad cop, but a supervillain as well. Did he teleport it to me from his bat cave or fortress of solitude?" I took another step toward the gaping hole in the fence—an apt metaphor for the shape of the investigation thus far. Rikki ignored my ridiculous question and resorted to a new threat.

"Trespassing on railroad property's not very convincing if you want me to believe you intend to uphold the laws you're sworn to defend."

She had a point. I wasn't sure what to make of the detective with an edge I'd found annoying from the moment we'd met. Why hadn't she had us arrested? Frank had referred to her as a straight shooter with a penchant for following the letter of the law—crossing t's and dotting i's. We could use more of her persnickety need for control focused on finding Frank rather than harassing us. Was she deliberately screwing up the investigation while pointing fingers at me or just proving to be inept? I stopped and stared directly at Rikki, making eye contact, as another possibility suddenly occurred to me.

"You know what, Rikki? If I were you, I'd be trying to determine if the failure to search this area was because of miscommunication or an attempt to set up a nosy detective who's been given titular permission to find her colleague when the real message is to back off. At this point, I wonder if they're planning to charge you with collusion or incompetence."

"Titular? My, my, Attorney Huntington, you do have a way with words, don't you?" Despite her bravado, I could tell I'd touched a nerve. Her body tensed, and it was her turn to stare at the ground. Brien and Peter, who'd stayed behind to watch as the CSI retrieved the gun, caught up with us.

"If you have nothing more to say about my vocabulary, I'm going to go talk to Frank's dad and try to find some reassuring words for him, his wife, and their grandkids."

Rikki said nothing. Instead, she turned, raised her hand in a dismissive wave, and stomped back toward the guys from the crime lab. They were standing like statues, holding the evidence they'd collected in bags that now bore tags.

"Our work is done here, don't you think?" I asked Brien and Peter, my tone still huffy.

"Yep. I bet they're praying theirs is, too," Brien replied, nodding toward the CSIs that still hadn't moved. Our detective friend was on the phone again. "Rikki's going to have a reputation before this is over."

"So true," I responded as Anastasia and I followed Brien, cleared the fence, and stood on the roadside. I felt as if I'd been let out of jail. "What kind of a reputation remains to be seen."

"I'm going to let the detective secure the scene as she sees fit," Peter said, staring at the breached fence once he'd joined us outside.

"Let's hit the road before she decides to have us arrested for trespassing."

"You heard that, huh?"

"Yes."

"Did you also hear what I said about the prospect that she's being set up?"

"I did, indeed," Peter replied. "That possibility, along with the fact I don't completely trust her, is the reason I took this." Peter flashed a scrap of paper concealed in the gloved palm of one of his enormous hands.

"What is it?" I asked. I had to take two steps for every step Peter took as he almost ran to his SUV. Once we were all inside his vehicle, Brien and I watched as Peter photographed the scrap of paper. I heard a telltale whoosh as he sent the photo somewhere before slipping the latest overlooked clue into an evidence bag.

"Take a closer look," he said, passing it to me in the back seat as he fastened his seatbelt and started the engine.

"It's another page from a ledger!" I gasped. "Part of a page, to be more precise."

"That's what I thought when I saw it. There were a few more scraps in the bottom of the box. I palmed one of them before making sure the CSI bagged them, in addition to the gun."

"This scrap is more weathered than those in Frank's safe. The writing's so faded; I can barely make it out." I turned the bag over to examine the other side. There wasn't any writing, but it had the faint lines common to record books.

"If it's another remnant from the same ledger it could have been damaged on purpose. Or weathered is right and it degraded fast because it was more exposed to the elements in that box than the pages stored in Frank's safe. I wish we'd kept one of the pages Frank had stashed away. We'd be able to make a better comparison to this one than we can make using the photos we have," Peter said as he pulled onto the frontage road.

"There's a distinctive squarishness to the numbers, though, isn't there? That suggests the same person penned the numbers whether or not the pages came from the same source."

"Squarishness—how do you spell that?" Brien asked as he pulled out a little note card he carries with him. He's on a kick to build his vocabulary, noting new words so he can learn to use them. "That's a new one to me—like titch-u-lar." After enunciating each syllable, he wrote the word down. I could only imagine how he was spelling it. He didn't ask, so I let it pass.

"Et tu, Brute?" I muttered under my breath.

"I'm not working on my Spanish vocabulary yet. Brute will have to wait!" Brien remarked with enthusiasm.

"It's Latin, not Spanish," Peter said. Brien shrugged. Peter went on, speaking to me this time. "I understand what you mean by squarishness."

"Which I still don't know how to spell..." Brien interrupted.

"Which you don't need to know how to spell because I probably should have left out the 'ish' anyway. Square, okay? There's a square shape to the letters in this sample that's strikingly similar to the lettering on the pages now logged into evidence." Brien gave up and slipped his vocabulary card back into his pocket, along with the tiny pencil he carried with him.

"If that's where they ended up given the bumbling we just witnessed," Peter commented as he navigated his way around a roadblock without bothering with the detour. We drove in silence as I ruminated about the possibility that those pages might be gone.

"Frank warned us not to trust anyone, but it's stupid to make those pages disappear. We saw them and have pictures to prove they exist. Rikki was there when you sent them to me, so she knows we have photos. Plus, presuming it's a match, we also have this little snippet of paper which I'm sure you photographed in situ, right?" As Brien reached for that card in his pocket, Peter spoke.

"Latin, it's more Latin, Brien—meaning in the place where we found it. And yes, I've got pictures."

"Okay, I get it. I don't know how you're going to explain how we ended up with it," Brien added. "It's obstruction of justice to abscond with evidence."

"An excellent point, although I'll argue that it's not obstructing justice since we're trying to preserve the evidence given our concerns about the chain of custody. Intentions matter. Not that we know anyone's absconded with the pages from Frank's safe, or any other evidence yet. At least we'll have something we need to explain even if those other pages aren't around." I paused and patted Anastasia who had dozed off slumped against me.

"The trick at this point is to figure out who's trustworthy enough for a game of show and tell." I spoke in a quieter tone of voice, hoping not to wake the sleeping poodle. I needn't have bothered. Anastasia heard the approaching siren before I did. Her head popped up and her eyes opened. When the car was almost on our bumper, Peter slowed and pulled off the road.

"It could be show and tell time whether we like it or not," Brien said.

"Not a word, remember?" Peter asked once he'd put the SUV in Park, still idling. He used the same zipped lips pantomime Brien had resorted to earlier. It's as if a lightbulb went on in Brien's head and he nodded solemnly.

The back door of the police car that had pulled us over opened even before the car came to a complete stop. I couldn't believe it when the occupants sprang from the back seat. My brain struggled to make sense of what was going on as another improbable event unfolded right before my eyes!

8 SURPRISE PARTY

"No way! It's Tommy and Jerry!" Brien gasped as he jumped out of the passenger seat to greet them. Anastasia yipped at the mention of Tommy's name. I slid out of my seat and stepped onto the shoulder of the road as incredulous as Brien was by the surprise party now assembled alongside the highway.

"Whoa, dudes, how did you score a police cruiser?" When a uniformed officer emerged from the driver's seat, Brien switched to a whisper. "Did you do something to get the cops on your case? He looks like he's ready to shoot you."

"Nothing illegal," Jerry replied. "Don's pal, here, has reached his limit with Tommy's alternating commands to speed up and shrieks of terror when he did."

"Can I help it if my senses are on hyper alert? Cousin Frank's been kidnapped. Uncle Don and Aunt Evelyn are basket cases. Mom and Dad aren't doing much better. This is a disaster!"

"Can you please finish this family reunion elsewhere? This is no disaster, but it isn't safe." The officer had to bellow to be heard as a semi blasted us with its horn and the percussive force as it passed. Peter's extra heavy, fortified SUV shook.

"We've been trying to catch up with you since Bernadette and the kids showed up at Don and Evelyn's house. Don sent us to find you," Jerry said.

"We're envoys," Tommy whispered, leaning in close to speak to me. As he did that, he lifted a bag he carried in one hand. He glanced at the police officer sporting Palm Springs PD emblems on his shirt shoulders. The officer made no indication that he'd heard or cared that Tommy had just shared a secret with me. Brien heard—or thought he'd heard Tommy.

"Two vehicles won't make us a convoy. You can follow us, though. We're going back to Frank's house, so Jessica can pick up her car."

"Convoy?" Tommy asked, blinking his eyes as he tried to figure out what the heck Brien was saying.

"We're not going to follow you. Officer Pickens' job is done now that he's delivered us to you. You've got plenty of room in the SUV, don't you?" Relief swept over Officer Pickens' face as I nodded yes in response to Jerry's question. Not giving anyone else a chance to disagree or change the plan, he slid back into the driver's seat and took off. Anastasia woofed in delight as Tommy dove into the back seat next to her.

"Bernadette sent you a care package." Tommy whipped water and food for Anastasia from the bag along with bowls, too. "She knew your doggie mommy would get into a mess and you wouldn't get food or water." Anastasia snapped up a treat Tommy offered and then lapped up the water he poured into a bowl.

"Oh, stop it, Tommy. It's not even lunchtime yet." Jerry shook his head.

"Hey, I could eat if Bernadette sent us something," Brien offered.

"Sorry, Brien. I've got a special delivery for Jessica, but it's from Uncle Don, not Bernadette. Get in the car and I'll hand it over," Tommy said. My heart raced wondering what Tommy had brought me.

"You've got the longest legs, Jerry. You take the front seat. Jessica and I will sit in the third-row seats." Brien and I squeezed into the seats behind Anastasia and Tommy.

"Why didn't Frank's dad just have Officer Pickens deliver

whatever you've brought me?" My mind had flashed immediately to the card Frank had left for us—I wanted to hear what Don had to say about it. Jerry responded to my question as Peter eased the SUV back onto the highway.

"For the first time in almost thirty years on the police force, he doesn't completely trust his own guys. Don's really upset about it."

I let out the breath I'd been holding. Jerry's words confirmed my worst fears. Losing his son had to be hard on Frank's dad, but to suspect that his coworkers at the Palm Springs PD were involved in Frank's disappearance had to be another devastating blow.

"That's what I figured. Did he say why?" Peter asked.

"Don said Frank came to him a few weeks ago concerned about an informant's murder. The guy had told Frank he was in big trouble. When Frank asked him why, he said he'd accidentally picked up the wrong backpack during the last visit to his supplier," Jerry explained.

"Yeah, right," I said. "Loaded with dope, no doubt. What a horrible accident."

"The guy was a low-level street dealer and a user, too, so Frank thought the same thing. From what Don told us, Frank didn't take him seriously and didn't even ask what was in the backpack. When the guy was beaten to death a few days later, Don says Frank kicked himself for caring too little, too late."

"That sounds like Frank," I said softly, remembering how preoccupied he'd been. "I could tell something was bugging him for weeks."

"Yeah, Uncle Don said Cousin Frank was kind of a mess about the dead guy and said he should have known better. That's not all that had him freaked out," Tommy added. His voice broke. I could see the side of Tommy's face and neck flush—a clear sign he was getting upset. He shut up and reached out to pull Anastasia toward him. Jerry picked up where Tommy had left off.

"A few days after someone killed the informant, a key taped to a card with an address on it showed up in a letter mailed to Frank at home." I sucked in a gulp of air when he mentioned that key. Peter glanced at me in the rearview mirror.

"What does the key unlock?" I asked Jerry.

"A locker at an SRO where homeless men stay after they leave rehab."

"Let me guess what happened next," Peter said. "Frank opened that locker and found the backpack."

"Yes, along with a few pieces of raggedy clothing and other junky possessions that belonged to the dead guy, according to Don."

"Whoa, good guess, man!" Brien exclaimed. "Was it dope like Frank thought?"

"An ounce of meth and a small quantity of black tar heroin that could have belonged to the informant. There was money, too. Lots of it—several hundred thousand dollars."

"That's a lot of moolah!" Brien said. "No wonder the dude was scared."

"That wasn't all," Tommy added, sniffling a little now. "There was a record book in there." I gasped. Peter's foot shifted just a little—enough to make the SUV hesitate for a second.

"What? You know about that, too?" Jerry asked.

"We found pages from a book like that in Frank's safe this morning. A small key was in there, too," I replied. "Where's the book now? Do you have it with you?"

"No," Jerry replied. "No money, either. Give her the letter, Tommy." Tommy passed a small, sealed envelope to me. My hand shook as I took it from him. Jerry began to speak again as warring urges surged through me. On one hand, I wanted to rip that envelope open. Another part of me wanted to shove it into a pocket and avoid the possibility that Frank had written the note to say goodbye because he knew someone was going to kill him. Jerry went on with his rendition of the conversation he and Tommy had with Don.

"The worst part of the story is what happened *after* Frank found the stuff the dead informant left behind. Frank told Don he started getting threats at home and at work. He got hustled almost immediately, too, by several guys he'd met while working undercover."

"The French Connection?" I asked.

"Don didn't call it that, but I assume it's the same operation Frank mentioned last night. If that's what you're calling the French Connection, that must be it. Don thought the same thing we did—that the trouble was over. In fact, Frank told him he could throw away the letter he'd left for you. Don said he'd planned to do that today." Jerry's voice dropped as he finished that sentence.

"Frank couldn't have been working undercover on more than one operation, so he had to be talking about run-ins with men he'd come into contact with doing whatever he was doing for the French Connection," I said. "They didn't refer to it as the French Connection in the news coverage when they conducted the sweep last week. Lots of agencies were in on it—DEA, ATF, and Homeland Security—as well as local law enforcement in Riverside and several other counties. The operation focused on busting up a ring of dealers moving drugs from Mexico and stashing them in gated communities throughout the Inland Empire, including Perris. From there, they distributed the drugs more widely via the I-10 corridor."

"Perris—as in Paris! The French Connection—I get it!" Brien exclaimed.

"Even though he didn't use the name, Don told us the same thing. He also said Frank had tried his best to keep us from stumbling into the middle of the operation since a dirty cop involved in the drug ring was also mixed up in the trouble at Jim's house in Bel Air. You already knew that, too, didn't you?" Jerry asked.

"Yes. The dirty cop's the guy in custody playing let's make a deal with what he claims to know about how Cassie murdered her handler, Bill Hargreaves. He's not the only reason she's been arrested for murder, but an important one. Now that I think about it, I wonder if Cassie's out on bail because she's in danger. What Rikki Havens told us today is that there are big shots trying to keep the dirty cop from testifying against Cassie."

"Why?" Tommy asked. "She deserves to wear orange if she killed someone."

"Because playing let's make a deal with the dirty cop involved in Cassie's case runs the risk of opening a whole can of worms about the French Connection investigation, doesn't it? Even if that operation is over, it's going to take months to get convictions," Jerry said.

"She's lucky they're keeping her in protective custody. Killing Cassie would solve problems for the good cops and the bad cops," Peter suggested, making my skin prickle.

"I wondered why Paul called us off when we were running down background about the cop," Jerry said.

"Does that mean you have his name?" I asked. "That's more than we know at this point."

"Yes, it's Devon James. If you're right and Cassie's life is in danger, we don't want to add Paul or anyone on her defense team to the list—or us."

"What are you saying, Jerry?" Tommy exclaimed. "Frank's in big trouble! If this dirty cop is important to finding out who's got Frank and why, we've got to dig up everything we can about the weasel."

"Stay cool, dude. Jerry's not saying we shouldn't investigate him. He's just urging us to be careful. It's obvious that cop's not the only weasel on the force."

"So? When have we ever worried about getting in the way of weasels? Why do you think Don's so weirded out about who to trust among his law enforcement colleagues? Don was clear that some of the men who made threats against Frank were cops. They lied and tried to set Frank up, too!" Tommy was hyperventilating as he spoke.

"What's he talking about?" I asked.

"Frank's cover was arranged to make it appear that he'd be willing to join the ranks of the dirty cops. Someone began spreading rumors that he'd done just that."

"It's worse than rumors!" Tommy exclaimed. "Frank told Uncle Don that someone reported him for stealing money and drugs. It's got to be the guys who grabbed him this morning, right? Who else would do it? If we find out who they are, maybe that'll help us figure out where they took Frank and why."

"We do have the name of one of the guys who picked Frank up this morning. A cop, but he's dead, so he's not going to help us find his dirty coworkers." I filled them in about what had happened to Randall Roberts, the abandoned car, and the escape route we'd discovered, as well as the items we'd uncovered at that site.

"Devon James is dirty. Maybe he knows who the other rats are. There's got to be a way to find out what he knows. Make Paul talk to him, Jessica. He'll do anything you ask him to do! Even if he might be happier to have Frank out the picture, Paul's got principles." Tommy was almost pleading with me at this point.

"I'll speak to Paul, but the French Connection was a big, complex operation, Tommy. Devon James is in a different county than Frank. Who knows if his law enforcement networks intersect with Frank's in the Inland Empire where the nerve center of the drug ring was located? There's a reason Paul instructed his team to back off investigating Devon James. Rikki got the same message this morning. She was told in no uncertain terms to stay away from anything having to do with the French Connection."

As I spoke, I flipped the envelope over and stared at Frank's handwriting. *"For Jessica"* is all he'd written on the outside of the envelope. My heart ached for Frank and his dad. No wonder Rikki's confused about Frank's situation with all the rumors about Frank and the warnings to butt out. "It's not the weasels we're asking Paul to go against." I recalled what Peter had told me earlier.

"You know guys, Frank's been leaving us messages, trying to tell us what's going on, and that he's still alive. Maybe he can help us figure out who's a good guy and who's not. Is Don aware that Frank's still under suspicion?" I asked.

"Yes," Jerry responded in a dismal tone.

"He also knows it isn't true!" Tommy exclaimed. "Uncle Don says Frank was being set up because he wouldn't hand over the stuff the dead informant stole."

"What made them think Frank had the goods?" I asked.

"From what Don told us, there are lots of ways that could have happened. Maybe they saw Frank pick up the guy's stuff. Even if they didn't, he and Frank could have been seen together at the SRO since Frank had stayed there over the past few months. Part of Frank's cover was that he was a cop who'd gone through rehab and was intent on keeping the force from knowing he was abusing drugs."

"So, are you telling me he went undercover as Frank Fontana?" I asked, even though I found that impossible to believe.

"No, but he told Don that given his backstory, no one thought it would be a bad thing if they outed him. Trying to evade detection as a police officer with a drug problem by using a fake name in rehab would just make him appear to be more credible as a corruptible creep even if someone discovered his real identity." I couldn't speak.

"He never gets to tell us not to do stupid things in pursuit of justice ever again," I muttered blinking back angry tears. I fought the temptation to fling Frank's letter out the window without reading it.

"Uncle Don chewed him out about it. He said Frank apologized yesterday when he believed this mess was finally over." Tommy started to sob as Jerry spoke. Anastasia pawed at Tommy, and then looked over the seat as if asking me to do something to help. I leaned forward and ran my fingers through Tommy's hair, making it stand up on end.

"It's beyond stupid. They know about his kids, his parents, and his ex-wife. Everyone's been left exposed. Why?"

"Uh, come on, you must get it, dudette," Brien said, slinging an arm around my shoulders like he was a big brother laying it on the line to his kid sister. "These are bad guys. Like the crud music producer who had Kim under his thumb. You walked right into his office—alone—and pretty much called him a killer. That wasn't just because you wanted to make him pay. He had to be stopped. Frank must have felt the same way."

"Yeah, but I was a fool—Frank's told me that more than once." As I said that, I slid a fingernail under the edge of the flap on the envelope and opened it. When I removed and unfolded Frank's handwritten note, a smaller sheet fell, fluttering as it settled into my lap.

Jessica, if you're reading this...

As I read Frank's note, tears streamed down my face. It was so quiet in the car I imagined everyone could hear my heart pounding out of my chest. When I'd finished reading the note, I picked up the sheet of paper. Frank had written a list of names on it.

"What is it?" Tommy asked as he twisted in his seat to gaze at me. His eyes were reddened by tears that had left his freckled face streaked. The flush had faded, leaving a ghostly pallor in its wake. "Don't keep us waiting! Tell us what he said. Why are you crying?"

"He asked me to find him!" I replied. There was more, but I kept it to myself.

"Whoa, that means he's counting on us to get him out of this. He's no fool and knows you're not one either, Jessica!"

"He needs someone he can count on, that's for sure. You wanted to know who turned on Frank, Tommy. Here's a list of a dozen crooked cops Frank identified. Their initials are in the ledger. We were right when we guessed the pages in Frank's safe came from a record of police taking money from the drug cartel. Frank doesn't say what they were paid to do. I don't know who's who yet, but a couple names sound familiar." I paused for a second to catch my breath. "If I've heard their names, I doubt they're low-level members of law enforcement."

"Oh, no. That's not good for Frank," Tommy moaned.

"No, it's not. Officer Randall Roberts is on the list. Maybe Kim can help us find information about his connections to others on this list. Or maybe one of his buddies not on the list will talk to us about him now that one of his cruddy confederates has killed him."

"If they're not too scared to talk now or don't close ranks to protect his reputation as well as their own." My stomach twisted, hoping Jerry was wrong. He sighed. "This won't be easy, but we've got to start someplace."

"Devon James isn't on this list. Have you run across any of the other names on it?" I asked, handing the paper to Tommy who passed it on to Jerry.

"Not that I recall. Sorry."

"There were more than two dozen sets of initials on the pages we found," Peter reminded me. "Cops not on Frank's list could have been in the group of men that took him this morning."

"Frank said almost the same thing when he wrote this note. 'Be careful, since I haven't figured out who else ought to be on my list.' I don't believe Frank would have been so relieved last night unless he'd found a way to identify the other names and someone assured Frank they'd round them up. If it was someone with the feds, who could have given him assurances like that?"

"I've already called my connections at DEA, AFT, and Homeland Security. I'll try to get the answer to your question and find out why no one made good on the promise to Frank."

"Frank couldn't have known anything was wrong until this morning. He was so happy and relaxed with us, and his dad said they spoke last night about his problems being over," Jerry added.

"Why didn't they protect Frank until they could keep their promise?" Tommy's sorrow had turned to anger.

"They could have made him that offer, and he refused it," Jerry said. "It's hard to believe he'd do that given that his kids were at risk, too."

"It's clear the plan went off the rails somewhere. If your hunch is right, Jessica, and names on the list aren't just rank and file members of law enforcement, that adds to Frank's problem. With a complicated conspiracy like this one, it's a political as well as a legal matter. Rikki's already told us that. Who knows what deals had to be cut before they could round up all the men Frank named?"

"His handler should have at least warned him," Brien added. "It would really help to know who that slacker is!"

"It's possible we can figure that out by going through Frank's phone records. If he spoke to the feds or some bigwig in local or state law enforcement that might give us a lead—especially if they spoke recently or on a regular basis."

"Rikki must have asked for Frank's phone records already. I'll have her send us a copy. Frank was so hush-hush about all this that I won't be surprised if they kept their interactions secret."

"That's possible. If his handler was someone he interacted with anyway, that wouldn't have aroused suspicion," Peter added. "Let's review his calls. The key to all this seems to be the ledger. I wonder where it is."

"I can tell you where it was when Frank wrote his letter to me. He gave it to someone he trusted for safe keeping."

"Great! Let's go get it! We won't have Frank's sense of who's who, but if we work at it, maybe we can figure out who else should be on the list Frank gave you," Tommy said. "Who has it?"

"The same person who took the pages from Frank's file into evidence this morning."

"Rikki Havens?" Brien asked.

"Yep."

"Her name isn't on the list Frank gave you," Jerry observed after scanning it again.

"I know. Obviously, Frank trusted her. He placed his trust in the wrong person somewhere along the line, though, didn't he?"

"What about the money?" Peter asked.

"He didn't say, but he made a point of telling me he's not a dirty cop; didn't steal money or drugs and has never been on the take no matter what anyone claims."

"He could have given the money to Rikki, too, if it was in the same backpack with the ledger," Brien suggested.

"If Rikki has the ledger, the money, or anything else Frank gave her, she's not telling. She appeared to be as surprised as we were to find those ledger pages in his safe."

"What if Frank gave her the ledger and the money, but didn't tell her what he'd asked her to hold for him?" Jerry asked.

"Maybe. She claims she didn't know that he was involved in the French Connection until they made all the arrests aimed at busting the drug ring, so it's possible she didn't understand what she was holding for Frank. It's not like Frank, though, given the risk it entailed."

"Getting rid of the missing money and the ledger would explain why he was so stoked last night. Whether she knew what it was or not, Frank must have asked her to hold it for him until he was ready to turn it over to the authorities as part of the discussion that led him to believe his troubles were over."

"Your reasoning makes as much sense as anything I can conjure up," I said.

"Rikki seemed genuinely surprised to find pages from a ledger in Frank's safe. Either Jerry's right and she didn't know what Frank gave her to hold for him or she wasn't sure how much to reveal to us if she'd promised to keep Frank's secret," Peter offered. "She may not be sure who to trust at this point either—including us."

"Or she doesn't trust us because she's an untrustworthy snake in the grass and what surprised her was finding out Frank had pages from a ledger she figured was long gone. Rikki doesn't just mistrust us, Peter, she flat out accused us of aiding and abetting a fugitive from justice when we found a go bag in his safe."

"A go what?" Tommy asked.

"A fugitive from justice?" Jerry asked, speaking over Tommy.

I explained what Rikki meant by a go bag and detailed the items we'd found in Frank's safe along with pages torn from a ledger.

"Yikes. Frank sure needed assurances from someone with clout to get out of this without his reputation being ruined," Jerry commented.

"Or going to prison," Brien added. "That passport, plane ticket, and other go bag stuff would have made him look like a real dirty cop. Especially if it had turned up somewhere other than in his safe. Frank must have found the incriminating evidence before they could use it to set him up."

"Brien, you're a genius. Of course, that must be what happened. Frank told his dad he was being set up. Maybe when he got wind of the setup, he found the documents, and hid them in his safe!"

"Unfortunately, now they're in the police evidence room, where whoever set him up intended for them to end up in the first place. It's odd that he didn't hand those items over, too. Maybe he wasn't as certain as he appeared to be when he told his dad and the rest of us that his problems were solved." Peter was right. At any other time, the truth of what he'd just said would have sent me spiraling into senseless panic. The urgency of the situation took over, though.

"If I'd only kept my mouth shut, we could have gone through Frank's safe without making it so easy for Rikki to get her hands on everything in it."

"And opened yourself up to the charges she's threatened to make against you," Peter said, interrupting me.

"I know, I know. So far, by trying to stay on the right side of the law, we appear to have played into the hands of the people in Frank's life who've crossed the line. We can't keep doing that, which means we've got to go on the offensive and I.D. the culprits, quick!"

"I agree we need to be more proactive. If you're right and Rikki's not on Frank's side, we've lost the advantage of surprise. She's well-aware of the fact that we're running an independent search and rescue effort," Peter added.

"If we pick up the pace and quit spilling our guts to Rikki, we can get some of the advantage back. Let's go get my car. Tommy and Jerry, you can ride with me to Don's house. We'll pick up Bernadette and set up a situation room at my house in Rancho Mirage. We'll have dinner and then work all night if we need to."

"Surprise!" Tommy exclaimed. "Bernadette's a step ahead of you. Kim and Laura are planning to join us at your house by dinnertime. Bernadette's ordered food from the amazing caterers you use. That's if we can get back in time for dinner. What's going on?"

When we reached the outskirts of Riverside, we hit a traffic jam almost immediately. We were still crawling south toward Perris but at a snail's pace.

"How do I know? Traffic on weekends isn't usually this bad." I'd visited the area often enough to know that much.

"It's lunch traffic," Brien added. "We could pull off and get some lunch, until the traffic clears out."

A siren screamed from somewhere ahead of us. In the opposite lane, coming toward us since the sound was growing louder. Northbound traffic was at a dead stop.

"There's an accident," I said, sighing deeply as we crept along. "At least we're still moving."

"People can't seem to resist gawking," Jerry said doing a little gawking of his own. "Once we get past the accident site, the pace will pick up again." We fell silent for a few minutes as we inched forward. When we drew closer, I could see the flashing lights of police and rescue vehicles. Eagle eyes, Brien, was the first to react when we spotted the car crumpled against the concrete barrier that ran along the median.

"Yo, that's Rikki Havens' car, isn't it?"

"It is," Peter responded. "Single car accident. Female driver transported to Riverside Community Hospital with serious injuries. A member of my crew picked up the report from a police dispatch. No one has said anything about a police officer being involved in the incident. When my team saw a picture of the car taken from a TV news helicopter, they recognized Rikki's vehicle from a photo I sent them earlier."

"Wow! You're becoming a clairvoyeur like Bernadette!" No one responded immediately as Brien butchered another word despite his efforts to improve his vocabulary.

"I'm not clairvoyant," Peter said with emphasis on the "ant." "I am taking Frank's message seriously—trust no one."

9 WRECKING CREW

Jerry was right. As soon as we moved passed Rikki's car, the traffic slowdown ended. When we finally arrived back at Frank's house, I couldn't stop wondering about what happened to Rikki. Her accident struck me as one too many improbable events for today—even for someone with my track record.

What if her accident was no accident? I wondered as we pulled up in front of Frank's house. Nothing made sense to me at this point. If we could get home and spend the evening organizing and sifting through the bits and pieces of information we had, perhaps a clearer picture would emerge. The moment I climbed out of Peter's SUV, I could tell something was wrong.

Peter was on the phone trying to get an update on Rikki's condition, so I didn't want to interrupt him. Besides, I couldn't say what bothered me. As I took a few steps toward Frank's house, it became clearer. Someone had moved the furniture on Frank's porch. The investigators who'd collected evidence earlier could have done that, except that one of the side tables was overturned, chair cushions were on the ground, and dirt was spilled from a potted plant.

"Hang on to Anastasia, please?" I asked, handing her leash to Tommy.

"Sure, but I'm going with you. Your crud detector's going off, isn't it?" Tommy turned and whispered. "Jerry, come!" Anastasia looked at him and cocked her head as if wondering whether that command was meant for her.

Jerry joined us without hesitation as we walked up to the porch. I had a bad case of goose bumps as I climbed the steps. When I reached the porch, I froze. Frank's door wasn't shut completely. Someone had forced it open, and the area around the door handle was damaged.

Jerry stepped in front of me and listened before giving the door a little tap with his shoe. The door swung open. We didn't have to go inside to see that Frank's usually comfy, orderly home was in shambles.

I suddenly heard thundering footsteps behind me as Peter and Brien stormed up the steps together. Peter blew past us, went into the house with a gun drawn, pointing it one way and then another as he moved through the foyer. He signaled Brien, who stopped, turned to face us, and posted himself in our path.

"Clear!" Peter hollered moments later from the back of the house.

"Stay here, will you? I want to see if I can tell what went on without Anastasia stepping into any mess whoever did this left behind."

"No problem. We don't want to step in any mess, do we?" Tommy asked. Anastasia wagged her tail in apparent agreement with Tommy. Jerry had a different reaction.

"Sorry, Tommy, but I'm going to tag along with Jessica and take lots of pictures."

"Suit yourself," Tommy said shrugging. "They've left us on guard duty, haven't they, precious?" Anastasia woofed as Tommy strutted like a toy soldier.

"Uh, I'll stay with you to supply more muscle in case we need it," Brien added, stepping from the house back onto the porch and taking up a post with his arms folded. Anastasia must have liked that idea. She jumped up and spun on her hind legs in happy poodle fashion.

I couldn't find anything to be happy about as Jerry and I made our way through the devastation. It was clear someone—perhaps more than one person—had been furiously searching for something. Drawers weren't just left open, but pulled out, dumped, and then dropped onto the floor. The intruders trashed the place by emptying the contents of the fridge, freezer, and cupboards, before emptying the garbage can. The result was a goopy mess of broken eggs, smashed jars of jam, bottles of condiments, milk, and juice. A sickening smell arose from the vile mixture splashed on the counters, cupboards, walls, and floor.

A pantry door in the kitchen had been wrenched loose and hung by a single hinge above the floor that was littered with flour, cereal, and other contents from the pantry. A peek into the laundry room that reeked of bleach was all it took to see that intruders had created havoc in there, too. The marauders had poured bleach over clothes tossed onto the floor and shoved other cleaning items from a cupboard or shelf onto the floor as well. The door to the dryer was dented as if it had been kicked or pounded with a heavy object.

"I can't believe no one heard what was going on over here. This is almost as bad as the damage left in Laura's house after Roger's murder."

"They wanted their money back, didn't they?" Jerry asked.

"Do you suppose that's what someone was looking for today?" I asked as Jerry and I moved into the family room off the kitchen where the vandals had slashed the couch cushions and pillows, and ripped family portraits from the walls. I felt a new surge of anger at the damage done to the room that Evie and her grandma had taken such delight in redecorating last year.

"Why not? Burglars will break in hoping to grab a TV and a few pieces of jewelry. Imagine what someone would do to get their hands on several hundred thousand dollars?"

"Frank's paying a price for those rumors, isn't he?"

"Jessica!" Peter called from somewhere at the back of the house. Jerry and I dashed toward him as quickly as we could without stepping on or tripping over the debris in our way.

"Where are you, Peter?"

"Den!" As Jerry and I ran into the den, Peter emerged from the closet. "It's a good thing we got to Frank's safe before the wrecking crew went through here. They cleaned it out. By the destruction in here, I'm assuming they weren't pleased about the fact they didn't find what they were after."

"Is that urine I smell?" Jerry asked, wrinkling his nose.

"Yes, it is," Peter replied.

"Not again," I said. I explained to Jerry how an idiot who'd relieved himself near where Randall Roberts was killed had inadvertently led us to the likely murder weapon—the small-town cop's service weapon.

"Is it possible the same guy who left his calling card near the railroad tracks did this?" He asked.

"It's possible one or two of the guys who took Frank doubled back and returned here after they made the switch to the van. Maybe Frank told them about the safe." I gulped, wondering what they'd done to Frank to get him to give them information.

"Then why hack into it?" Jerry asked. "I mean hack in the old school sense of the word. It's as if someone pried it from the wall and then took an ax to it to open it. If they forced Frank to tell them about the safe, why wouldn't he have given them the combination, too?"

"Good point. Whoever did this must have come up with the information some other way or stumbled onto the safe by accident." I wanted to believe Jerry was right. I let go of just a little bit of the worry that Frank had been beaten to within an inch of his life to give up information about the existence of his safe. "If they believed what they were looking for was in the safe, why search and destroy the rest of Frank's house?"

"If they were after the money Frank's informant stole, why look for it in the refrigerator? Urinating on the floor and trashing the house was as much an act of vandalism as it was a burglary," Jerry said.

"Jeff Baker," Peter said. "It's likely the informant's name was Jeff Baker. One of my guys called to tell me they dug up his name from an incident reported about ten days ago about the beating death of a drug dealer suspected of being a 'snitch.' Sorry to interrupt, but I thought you'd want to know."

"Thanks. Names are useful," I said, sighing heavily. "One down and who knows how many more to go before we get to the bottom of what's going on."

"We've got the names Frank's already given us. Let's hope we don't have to track down too many more. We don't have time to identify all the cops whose initials are in the ledger."

"I'm with you, Peter. If we can ever quit running into new crime scenes, we can get to work trying to find Frank using the information we already have. That would be a start and one way to determine what else we need to know."

"What I don't understand is why Baker didn't just tell whoever beat him up where he'd left the backpack before they killed him," Jerry said as he snapped pictures of the damage done in the closet and den.

"From the way this place has been trashed, some of the people mixed up in this mess obviously aren't too tightly wrapped. Anyone that out of control could have used too much force too soon and killed Baker before he told them what they wanted to know," Peter shrugged. "It happens."

"A person like that in law enforcement must have a history of complaints or may even have been investigated for excessive use of force. Some of those complaints get filed with the feds," I offered.

"We can find that kind of information. Let's start with the names Frank's given us and see what turns up," Jerry suggested.

"Frank's safe was well-concealed, so I doubt the intruders found it by accident. How did they find out about it?" Peter rubbed his hand over his bristly buzz cut.

"Speaking of accidents, what about Rikki?" I asked. "I'm not saying she told anyone about Frank's safe since she seemed surprised that he had one. She was on his team and worked with him every day. Maybe she has some idea of who he met with around the time he asked her to hang onto the ledger—even if she didn't know what Frank gave her to hold onto for him." I'm not sure if what I was saying was even making any sense. Apparently, it didn't matter anyway.

"We're not going to get any info from Rikki any time soon. I couldn't find out much in the way of details about her injuries. It doesn't sound good though. She's in intensive care and about to undergo emergency surgery."

"Not good is an understatement," I murmured. "I suppose the medical staff is being cautious about revealing what happened to her. Or only providing details to family members—if she has any."

"It's not just that. Authorities have thrown up a wall of secrecy around her—maybe to protect her if she had a little help plowing into the median. We got nowhere when we tried to get the Sheriff's Department and the Highway Patrol to tell us how the accident happened."

"Eventually, they'll have to file accident reports. We'll find a way to get them. Jeff Baker's name sounds familiar to me. Let's find out if that SRO Frank visited to pick up Jeff Baker's backpack is in Riverside County or elsewhere." I suggested.

"Downtown Riverside," Peter replied instantly. "It was listed as Jeff Baker's last known address."

"Okay, well, I've got someone local who can help give us the scoop on Jeff Baker. I'll call Dick Tatum. As a court appointed public defender, he's dealt with lots of the local offenders with drug problems who do a little dealing on the side. Maybe Dick mentioned Jeff Baker at some point or I ran across the informant's name in one of his files and that's why it sounds familiar to me."

"That's a great idea. Chester Davis' lawyer must know every low-level dealer in town—even if he hasn't represented all of them," Jerry said as he looked at the upheaval surrounding us in the den. "Not finding the money in the safe or in here could explain what triggered the thugs to ransack the rest of the house. They must have started in here or there'd be flour or coffee grounds tracked down the hall and on the carpet in here."

"I agree. That means they started by looking for the safe, hoping whatever they were looking for was in it. Maybe this isn't just about the money. If the intruders' initials are in the ledger, they could have been trying to retrieve it—before the police got to it. If we hadn't shown up and pointed it out to Rikki, I doubt it would have been emptied today," I said.

"The timing sure makes this seem like an act of desperation. Staging a break-in on the same day Frank disappears was definitely risky." Jerry shook his head. "If it wasn't a member of the group that picked up Frank this morning, maybe it was the police activity that triggered someone to act."

"I think it would have taken more than that to take the kind of risk you're talking about Jerry. Something motivated the rage and desperation behind what went on here. We'll get the lab team back out here to see if they can find prints or any other physical evidence that can identify who did this."

Good luck, I thought as I imagined the poor schmucks assigned to this job searching for a needle in a nasty haystack of filth.

"Hey, you know what? If the wrecking crew drove the van, maybe a neighbor spotted it!" I exclaimed. "That's one way to determine if Frank's pals doubled back hoping to find something in his safe."

"I doubt they'd just park it in the driveway or on the street. They would have had to come in through the front gate, though. The security camera ought to have a photo. I can check that out," Jerry offered.

"Here's the guy we spoke to earlier," Peter said. "The phone number for the guard gate, too. You can check while I call and report the break-in to the police."

"It's not likely they'd let an unmarked van in through the gate unless someone in the neighborhood authorized their entry at the guard gate." I gulped. "Frank could have done that if he was with them."

"Hey, this is a long shot, but I'll check it out," Jerry said already entering numbers on his phone.

"If they don't know, don't worry. We're already trying to get their security service to share the surveillance footage with us. I'm sure the police are on it, too." Peter grabbed his phone to place a call to the police. Jerry and I wandered back outside as he called the guard gate.

"Yeah, but that'll take time," I muttered. Time we couldn't afford to lose. Especially since we'd lost any advantage we had based on the deal I'd cut with Rikki to keep us in the loop. Without her as a point of contact, we'd have to jump through more hoops to get the reports she'd promised. Don still had an "in" with law enforcement, if he could decide who he could trust.

The thought of standing around waiting for the police to arrive had me antsy as soon as I returned to the porch. I took Anastasia's leash from Tommy, walked down the steps to the front lawn, and started to pace when I got an inspiration. Several of them, in fact.

10 FRIENDS AND NEIGHBORS

"Laura," I said as soon as I heard someone say hello.

"Jessica, thank goodness you called. What's going on? Have you found Frank?"

"Not yet. We're working on it."

"Then why are you calling me? Go find him. I'm going to meet you at the house for dinner. You can answer all my questions then."

"Unfortunately, we're tied up for a while longer in Perris. Someone broke into Frank's house and searched it with a vengeance. Not in the way your house was almost dismantled, but with the same kind of ferocity. The kids can't come back here any time soon," I said, surprised to hear my voice waver a bit.

"That's going to be hard on them. It's good their school year is almost over. They can stay with their mom like they do most summers," Laura added and then paused. "That's not why you called, though, is it?"

"No. There's been an accident."

"Oh, no! Not you, right? Who? Where? How?" Laura was clearly as wigged out about all this as I was. I'd tripped a wire. I took a deep breath, hoping if I spoke in a calm voice, she'd settle down.

"Not me. Not any of us. I can tell you who and where but not how." It took me very little time to share what we'd learned about Rikki's all too coincidental highway accident. "What I'm hoping you can do is find out more about the accident and her condition. We've been told she's awaiting emergency surgery. Do you have friends or colleagues who work at Riverside Community Hospital?"

"Of course, I do. Do you remember Carmel Schneider from St. Theresa's?"

"Sure. We had angsty heart-to-hearts about our parents' divorces. Her experience was even worse than mine was in some ways since her dad was dead set against the divorce her mother wanted. Ninth grade was rough on both of us."

"Hey, you don't have to tell me that. I was there, too, dealing with Mom's illness. Anyway, Carmel and I kept in touch after high school since she went through nursing school with me. She works at RCH now and she's an operating room nurse. She ought to know what's going on. If not, she'll find out. Let me see if I can track her down and get the scoop before I see you tonight."

"That would be terrific—if we can use a word like that about anything on a day like today."

"I should have asked how you're holding up, given that it's Frank who's missing. You two seemed to have made up last night after all the time you spent being angry and worried about him the past few months."

"Now I know I was too quick to forgive him! I can't decide what I'm going to do when we find him—throw my arms around his neck and kiss him or wring it for him for not telling me how much trouble he was in."

As I spoke, my mind drifted back to the letter Tommy had delivered from Frank. Frank had apologized. There was more, too, that had touched me deeply. I'd kept things from him, too. I was mad at myself about not being able to admit how important he was—is— to me.

We've both made mistakes, I thought. *Please, please don't' let it be too late to fix them. We will find Frank!* I chanted inwardly and gave my shoulders a little shake to rid my mind of other possibilities. Anastasia loved my shoulder shake and imitated me by shaking her entire body like she does after swimming with me in the pool.

"Either way, it means you're convinced you'll have him back soon enough to give him whatever you decide he deserves," Laura's voice settled down almost as if she'd taken up the "We will find Frank" chant with me.

"Convinced isn't the word I'd use, but I'm intent on finding him. We've got lots of leads we're working on. Rikki was working on some too… maybe," I said, my voice trailing off. Laura picked up on the suspicion in my tone.

"Let me see if I can find out what's up with Frank's inscrutable colleague. A colleague who manages to get into a serious car accident on her way back to the office after leaving the scene of an abduction involving her team leader sounds dodgy to me. I'll tell Carmel to keep this between us. Talk to you tonight," Laura said and hung up before I could correct the conclusion she'd reached about the sequence of events prior to Rikki's accident.

Where had Rikki been going? She must have left the crime scene where Randall Roberts was killed not long after we did. That was odd. I would have expected her to be at that site for at least another half hour or longer, if she'd decided to ask the CSIs to take a closer look at the area where we'd stumbled across such important evidence.

Even if she'd left soon after we did, how had she caught up with us? Being pulled over by the officer transporting Tommy and Jerry detained us by twenty minutes or so. Maybe that had given her enough time to catch up—and pass us as we sat on the side of the road.

"Rikki must have been in a big hurry, Anastasia," I muttered. Maybe in too much of a hurry if rushing had caused her accident. Had she been called back to Frank's house in Perris to investigate reports of a break in? If so, the call hadn't come through regular police dispatch or Peter's men would have alerted us. Not to mention the fact that the police would have been at Frank's house when we arrived, and Peter wouldn't have had to report the crime. That couldn't have been what led to Rikki's sudden departure.

Why hadn't we seen her as she flew by us? Brien and I were out of the car talking to Tommy and Jerry, but Peter was still at the wheel. What on earth was she doing in the northbound lane when she'd had the accident? All good questions to ask Rikki once she was stable enough to answer them.

Out of the corner of my eye, I noticed the blinds move in a window of the house across the street. That's where I planned to go next. My second inspiration was to ask Frank's neighbors if they'd seen anyone at his house recently. By that, I meant in the past couple of hours because we hadn't been gone much longer than that.

I'd seen an older woman going in and out once or twice after the house was sold a few months ago. Unlike the neighbors who live on either side of Frank, I'd never met her. I put my phone away, just as Jerry joined me on the lawn.

"No sighting of a white van, according the guard at the gate. He knows Frank Fontana and heard there was a problem at his house this morning. The guy says he'd remember if Frank had let anyone in through the front gates no matter what vehicle they were driving. He pointed out that the front gate's not the only way into the community for residents." Jerry noticed the direction in which I'd glanced. When he followed my gaze, someone closed the blinds.

"True. I've exited using one of two other gates, but to get in you need a keycard or a transponder. If they brought Frank along, he probably had his keycard with him."

"Or a cellphone with a mobile app that opens the gate. A passcode you can key into the pad will also open the gate, or you can buzz a resident, and they can let you in. Too many ways someone can get in according to the guard I spoke to at the front gate."

"He has a point." I shook my head. "If Frank was with them and helped them get into the community, why would they need to hack the safe to bits and trash his house?"

"It wouldn't be easy to talk Frank into cooperating. I don't like to think about it, but maybe their efforts to get him to cooperate went too far—like what Peter says may have happened to Jeff Baker. What if they killed him before they got into his safe? That might account for the fury unleashed on his house."

"I understand what you're saying. Leaving his body in the wreckage would have been as good a place as any if they were finished with Frank one way or another." I said that with conviction, forcing myself to believe it. "Frank's kidnappers have at least one hothead among them—the one who punched Randall Roberts before blowing him away. They had no trouble leaving the body behind, though. I don't think it was the same crew, do you?"

"No. Despite the loose cannon in their midst, they seem more methodical. They've got a plan to implement given the advance work required to make the transfer from the car to a van."

"Too bad we don't know what that is. If they're not behind the break-in or if Rikki's accident wasn't an accident, that means we have at least one or two other loose cannons out there." My eyes wandered across the street again. "While we're waiting for the police to arrive and go through their routine, I'm going to see what the neighbors have to say—starting with the curious one across the street."

"I was about to do the same thing. The neighbors are going to love having more strangers asking them questions. It's worth a try. Tommy's waiting for security to come by and document the new problem here."

"Good. Let's make the best use of the time as we can," I said. "Right now, we're drowning in crime scenes and suspects. We need a break to get our heads above water."

I quickly crossed the street with Anastasia on her leash, rang the doorbell, and waited for someone to respond. The woman who answered the door was the one I'd seen before. She only opened the door part way and didn't smile as she grunted out a one syllable greeting.

"Yes?"

"I'm sorry to bother you, but I'm hoping you can tell me if you've seen anyone enter the Fontanas' house across the street recently?" She scanned me with suspicion.

"Besides you, the two big guys with you, the lady detective, and a swarm of people in uniforms this morning?" She appeared as if she was ready to shut the door on me until Anastasia stepped closer, wagging her tail in a friendly way.

"Yes. That's what I'd like to know. Peter and Brien are over there again," I responded calmly. She opened the door a bit wider and reached out to pat Anastasia's soft head.

"I can see that." She peered over my shoulder as she spoke.

"They're hard to miss," I added, hoping to keep the conversation going.

"You can say that again—especially the seven-foot one. The tall, handsome new addition to your entourage is a standout, too."

"That's Jerry. I'm afraid I don't know your name. Forgive me for not introducing myself right away. I'm Jessica Huntington and this is Anastasia."

"I know who you are. Nice to meet you. I'm Michele Bodenheimer. I've seen you before and the redhead pacing around in the front yard, too. You're much harder to miss now that you've got this princess with you." Anastasia sat down and offered a paw to the woman who stepped out onto her porch and shook it.

"You're a family friend and not with law enforcement, right? Well, that's not quite true, since lawyers are part of law enforcement." Michele shrugged a little when I cocked my head to one side, wondering how she knew I was a lawyer and what point she was trying to make.

"You're a keen observer, Ms. Bodenheimer. Resourceful, too, to figure out who I am."

"I don't have to be very observant or resourceful to notice a friend of the Fontana family whose face pops up in the media time and time again. I'll accept the compliment, though. It's been like Grand Central Station over there since early this morning with police and rescue people coming and going. How could anyone miss the county's van sitting there with people wearing gloves and hauling away who knows what from the house? I don't know them as well as you do, but the Fontanas seem like a nice, normal family. The kids are noisy sometimes. Kids are kids," she said shrugging.

Then, she leaned in and lowered her voice as if to avoid being overheard. I tried to see over her shoulder wondering if someone was in the house. I sensed rather than saw movement behind her. I strained to see what appeared to be a figure hidden in the shadowy foyer.

"I know Frank Fontana works for the County Sheriff's Department—is his disappearance work-related? An officer who stopped by this morning just said they were trying to locate him and asked if I'd seen him leave this morning. I took that to mean he's missing, but the officer didn't explain why they were concerned about it."

"As you can imagine, I'm not able to say much about an ongoing police investigation," I stammered wondering who was doing the interview. "I have heard that Frank's neighbors were cooperative and incredibly helpful. They must mean you."

"Another compliment. Thanks. I did my best to describe the car parked in the Fontanas' driveway this morning, but I'm afraid I didn't see the occupants." I was tempted to press her about her use of the plural. Had the police told her Frank left with more than one person or was she being evasive? I didn't want to risk ending the conversation before I got the information I'd come for in the first place.

"I'm not sure when things quieted down since they were still collecting evidence when we left. Did you notice when that happened? I'm even more curious to find out if you saw anyone over there after the police investigators cleared out."

"Well, I thought they were done when I left to go grocery shopping around ten thirty. I'd planned to get up and go early, but with all the chaos going on I waited. I was glad when it cleared out enough that I could back my car out of the garage. When I returned a little while later, there was another car parked in the driveway. It wasn't one I'd seen earlier in the day."

"How long ago was that?"

"A little before noon." That wasn't too long before we'd arrived—we must have just missed the culprit!

"Can you recall what kind of car you saw?"

"One of those unmarked police cars in a silvery gray color with a row of lights in the back window."

"Did you see who was driving the car?" My heart had sped up at the prospect that the last person in Frank's house was another cop.

"No, I'm afraid not. The only other thing I noticed was that some of the numbers on the license plate were the same as my wedding anniversary. Silly, huh?"

"Not silly at all. What numbers?"

"Eleven twenty-two as in November 22nd—the same date as the JFK assassination, too. Those numbers were just behind the letter S. There were more numbers and letters, but I don't remember what they were. Sorry."

"There's no need to be sorry. This is great information. Did you notice anything else going on across the street after you returned home?"

"I'm afraid not. I wasn't all that surprised the police were back. Besides, I had groceries—ice cream—in the car. I pulled into the garage and went straight into the kitchen with the groceries I needed to put away."

"Is there anyone else at home who might have seen something you missed?" Her body went rigid. A distressed expression stole over her face and quickly turned to anger.

"No! I live alone—not that it's any of your business." My eyes shifted just a little at another flutter of movement. This time, Michele Bodenheimer noticed where I was looking. She backed up a step.

I wanted to ask her with whom she celebrates her memorable wedding anniversary if she lives alone. I couldn't think quickly enough about how to ask without sounding abrupt or insensitive. She could be divorced, but it's my divorce anniversary date that's more memorable to me now than my wedding day. If she's a widow, her wedding anniversary might still hold sentimental value for her. Why lie to me if there was someone inside the house? I must be imagining things.

"I've got to go. Nice meeting you." She didn't sound like it was nice to meet me as she turned away from me. Time to go. I suddenly remembered another loose end.

"Just one more thing, Ms. Bodenheimer. When the police asked you about the car you saw parked in Frank Fontana's driveway early this morning you said you didn't see the occupants—as in more than one person. What made you believe more than one person was in that car if you didn't see anyone?" She appeared to lose her composure for a split second.

"Occupant—occupants—what difference does it make? I'll tell you again what I told the police already. I didn't see who was in the car—coming or going." With that, she went into the house and shut the door behind her. I heard the lock click.

"Geez, at least she didn't slam it," I said, making Anastasia's tail wag. "Maybe her ghostly companion saw the men with Frank and mentioned there was more than one. What do you think?" Anastasia woofed. I took that to mean she agreed.

I knocked on a couple more doors on the same side of the street without anyone responding. I hoped Jerry, who was working the opposite side of the street, was having better luck. I decided to try talking to the neighbors on the other side of Michele Bodenheimer's house. At one house, I could hear laughter coming from the backyard, but no one responded even after I rang the doorbell.

I should be happy that the Bodenheimer woman had given me as much information as she had before bidding me goodbye. Jerry was probably right about the neighbors not relishing more strangers on their doorstep asking questions. They may also have put off errands because of the unwelcome intrusion into their community on a usually peaceful Saturday and were gone now.

There would be more questions whether they liked it or not. We'd get copies of the police reports as soon as they finished knocking on doors again—one way or another even though Rikki was out of the picture. I turned around and headed back to Frank's house. I picked up my pace when I saw a patrol car parked behind my car. That's when I heard a 'yoo-hoo,' seconds before someone called me by name.

11 MILLIE'S HUNCHES

"Hello, Millie," I said, turning around to greet the smiling woman. "How are you?"

"Better than the Fontanas, I guess. Is there more trouble or did you just come back to pick up your car before the police towed it?" The petite, older woman asked a little breathlessly as she almost ran to close the distance between us.

Anastasia was delighted, touching noses with "Miss Mini-Penny," Millie's adorable miniature pinscher. Anastasia and I had run into Millie Nordstrom on several occasions while visiting Frank. Since I'd become a dog owner, we'd had several delightful conversations when we both happened to be out walking our dogs at the same time.

My fondness for her has nothing to do with the fact that her last name is the same as one of my favorite shopping haunts. Despite the strides I've made toward vanquishing my shopping addiction, I felt a sudden desperate urge to binge shop my way out of the dread that gripped me about Frank's disappearance. Old habits are hard to kill. Thankfully, Millie didn't wait for me to answer her question and interrupted my tailspin into a shopaholic delusion.

"I'm so glad you're here. I was going to call you, but I couldn't find your phone number. Of course, I couldn't tell Frank anything about it since the police officer who visited me said no one was sure where he was. When I saw him leave with a carload of men this morning, it never would have occurred to me to be worried about anything until the police showed up."

"You saw Frank leaving?"

"Yes—just for a second. I was getting ready to walk Miss Mini-Penny. I saw Frank getting into the back seat of a car with two men. As I told the police, I was sure there had to be two more in the car. I could see a man sitting in the front passenger seat which meant it was only logical there was a fifth person in the car because someone had to be driving, right?"

"It's sound logic to me. Did you get a good look at any of the men?"

"I'm afraid not. I was trying to get Miss Mini-Penny to stand still and let me hook her leash to her new collar. She was so excited about it. Red is such a good color for her, don't you agree?" I tried not to sound anxious even though I wanted Millie to get on with it!

"Red is her color," I said. "You were about to tell me what you remember about those men. From what you're saying, you only caught a quick glimpse of them."

"Two glimpses. The first time, what I noticed is that both men getting into the back seat with Frank were big. I told Miss Mini-Penny I sure hoped they didn't have too far to drive because it had to be a tight squeeze with all three of them in there."

Hmm, not Randall Roberts, I concluded. The lead investigator, James, had described him as medium height and build. To the tiny woman, though, big might mean something different than it does to me.

"By big, do you mean tall—like Peter?" I asked, pointing to the giant towering over the uniformed officer taking his statement.

"Tall, yes, but not like him. He's a giant! Around six feet, I'd say. They weren't nearly as muscle-bound as your friend is either. I'd describe them as big like Russel Crowe when he put on a little weight for a movie role. Now what was that part he played?" I'm pretty sure the question was directed to herself, not me, so I moved on.

"How about anything else about their age or hair color? Did they wear glasses or any clothing you noticed?"

"The polite, young officer who came to my door asked me almost the same question. One of the big guys—the black man—had on a baseball cap and was wearing sunglasses. I'm not good with sports, so I can't say what team was on the cap, but it was a dark color with a red letter 'A' on it. I thought that maybe that's why they were getting together—to go to a sporting event. The driver wore sunglasses and a cap like that, too."

Uh-oh, I thought as her story took a confusing twist.

"I'm sorry, Millie, but didn't you say you didn't see the driver?"

"I said I glimpsed them twice remember? I was right that there was a fifth person in the car. When I had Miss Mini-Penny all ready to go, I stood up. The car was leaving, and that's when I noticed the driver was wearing a baseball cap and sunglasses, too!"

"I get it."

"The driver had a big, chunky ring on his hand, too. I wondered if that had anything to do with the sports team, you know? Don't sports teams hand out rings if you win a big game like a World Series Bowl or something like that?"

"You know about as much as I do about sports. I'll do my homework, though, I promise. I trust your hunches." Millie smiled.

"Did you hear that, Miss Mini-Penny? She trusts my hunches and she's going to do her homework." Apparently, both dogs loved the idea because Millie's question set off a duet of happy yips and woofs. She spoke a little louder to be heard above the ruckus, redirecting the conversation back to me.

"I'm sure whatever you do will be better than what the police will do. He was polite, but I'm not sure the officer believed me about the ring since he laughed when I told him about it. Did Frank go missing at a ballgame?"

"Honestly, we're not sure what happened. From what I've heard, he didn't go to a ballgame. The men with him are missing, too." To be more precise, three of them are missing given that Randall Roberts was lying in a morgue by now. "Why were you going to call me?"

"Oh, yes! It doesn't matter now. I was going to call about your car. I told the police officer who came by a little while ago not to worry about your car." I went on alert.

"Are you sure he was a police officer?"

"Oh yes. He wasn't wearing a uniform, but he was writing down your license plate number. I didn't want him to give you a ticket or have your car towed, so I came out and talked to him. I told him you were a close family friend and the Fontanas always let you park nearby. Security leaves you alone, too, since you're registered at the gate. I said he could check with the guard if he didn't want to take my word for it."

"Did you give him my name?" Dread filled me even before she replied. I trust my hunches, too. I don't like the idea that my name had come up within hours of Frank's disappearance. Still, if Rikki was working for the dark side, it didn't really matter what Millie had said. Besides, it wouldn't have taken the officer more than a couple minutes to run my plates and get my name that way.

"Sure, I did! What a grouch, though. I thought he was going to have your car towed anyway. He said you shouldn't be surprised if your car gets impounded when it's left at a crime scene. That's when I said there wasn't anything I could see that made it clear this was a crime scene. I asked him for his name and badge number."

"Did he give them to you?"

"Yes, but he rattled them off so fast, my head did a spin." Miss Mini-Penny must have recognized Millie's last word and did a little spin. Anastasia loved it and followed with a version of her own. "I told him I needed to get a pen and paper, so I could write it down. It didn't take long at all, but when I got back, he was gone! A grouch, I tell you."

"Thanks for looking out for me." As Millie and I walked back toward Frank's house, I knew when the police left this time they'd make it clear this was a crime scene. "Millie, you said the officer wasn't wearing a uniform, how did you know he was with the police?" I expected her to launch into a description of the car he drove and hoped it would be close to the one Michele Bodenheimer had given me.

"Sergeant Ellison has visited Frank before." I came to a halt in front of Michele Bodenheimer's residence.

"You knew his name?" I asked, a little confused. "Why did you ask him for it?" Millie giggled at my puzzled expression.

"Oh, no, I'm sorry to get you so mixed up! I'd seen him before, but I never met him. So, I asked for his name. Simple, huh? Except, I needed to write it down to make sure I spelled it right. And, I wanted his badge number, too. That way, I could report him if he had your car towed. After all, he'd parked in almost the same spot in his cherry red Mustang more than once. He had some nerve picking on you!" Another wave of dread washed over me. This time it was for Millie.

"Did you happen to mention you'd seen him before?" She paused for a second before responding.

"I'm sure I did—probably when I got his name."

"Let's cross the street here. I want you to meet my giant friend, okay?" I stepped from the sidewalk to the curb.

"I'd love to meet all of your friends." Peter was the one I wanted her to meet so he could help me keep Millie safe for the next few days. If Sergeant Ellison was the person who took Frank's house apart, I didn't want him returning later to have another chat with Millie. At least, not without one of Peter's security associates keeping an eye on her.

Anastasia woofed and strained on her leash—trying to pull me from the curb toward the house we'd visited earlier. Michele Bodenheimer was watching us from the window and made no effort to hide this time. I waved in a friendly way, even though she wasn't smiling. I got a perfunctory wave in return.

"Let's go," I said, stepping from the curb and crossing the street. "Michele Bodenheimer said she saw lots of vehicles in front of Frank's house today. She didn't mention a red Mustang, though."

"The sergeant wasn't driving his personal car today. The car he parked in Frank's driveway was a gray one. It wasn't in tip-top shape like his Mustang. The hubcaps were missing and there was a scrape near the back bumper. It's sad the police drive junky looking cars like that, but I could tell it was an official car even though it wasn't marked. It had police lights in the back window, and I could hear a police radio."

"Your neighbor described a car she saw in almost the same way. Do you have any idea when it arrived?"

"You're lucky Michele spoke to you. She's not very neighborly—not toward me anyway. I hardly even wave anymore. If she does wave back, it's a weak little 'don't bother me wave' like she just gave you. To answer your question, I'd say Sergeant Ellison got here an hour and a half ago. He didn't stay long. I usually take Miss Mini-Penny to the dog park earlier, but when we went out for our morning walk, we returned home right away because of the unusual circumstances. We didn't want to miss what was going on, did we Miss Mini-Penny?" The tiny pooch replied instantly.

"Okay," I sighed. I tried to imagine how one man could have done the damage we'd found in Frank's house. If Sergeant Ellison hadn't done it, why hadn't he reported it? "I'm sure Miss Mini-Penny was dying to show off that gorgeous new collar."

"That's exactly what we did as soon as Sergeant Ellison left. I shouldn't be so hard on him. He must have been in an awful hurry to leave before he put his crowbar and gloves back into the trunk of his car. Maybe he got a call on the police radio about an emergency."

"Crowbar? What crowbar?"

"The one Miss Mini-Penny and I put on my porch for safekeeping until he comes back for it." I couldn't stop myself from hugging Millie. Then Anastasia and I took a step up the sidewalk toward Frank's porch. Miss Mini-Penny was following us with Millie holding her leash.

"Where is everyone?" I asked a uniformed officer posted on the porch.

"Inside, but you can't go in there. It's a crime scene—a disgusting one."

I've seen worse, I thought. At least there wasn't any blood or, thankfully, a dead body. I hadn't intended to enter the house with Millie and our dogs, but I did want to talk to Peter.

"We don't want to go in there. I would like to speak to my

colleagues if you can let them know I'm out here."

"Sure. They must be finished by now."

"Are the CSIs on their way?" I asked.

"Yes." As he said that, he opened the door and stepped inside, almost running into Peter. Tommy, Jerry, and Brien were a few paces behind. A police officer followed them out.

"When they arrive, they need to go next door and pick up a couple of items Millie Nordstrom has on her porch. A crowbar and gloves left by someone in a hurry. They should be taken into evidence." Peter was listening intently.

"Sure. I don't know how soon they'll get here with all the calls that have come in today."

"See? What did I just say? That must be why Sergeant Ellison left so abruptly." Millie sighed and then twisted a little, gazing at the house across the street.

As she took a few steps down the walkway, Tommy walked with her and introduced her to Brien and Jerry. While she was busy, I explained to Peter and the officer how Millie came into possession of a crowbar and a pair of gloves. I also made it clear that Sergeant Ellison had been in Frank's house, and had either done the awful deed or failed to call it in.

"The neighbor across the street, Michele Bodenheimer, can corroborate Millie's story. She saw the car and described it in a similar manner. She doesn't claim to have seen a driver of the vehicle, but she does recall part of the tag numbers."

After a couple more minutes with the officer, he assured me he'd have someone interview Millie Nordstrom and Michele Bodenheimer. He seemed to grasp the importance of questioning Sergeant Ellison, too. I wasn't sure how seriously he considered the possibility that a police sergeant had broken in and vandalized Frank Fontana's property. I hoped the physical evidence would be convincing even if all they found were the crowbar and gloves. When I finished my conversation with the officer, I asked Peter for his help.

"I'm concerned Millie's been a little too helpful for her own good. Do you have anyone you can spare to watch out for her? Just put it on my tab." Peter knows better than to argue with me about money at this point. Footing the bill for extra security is a small price to pay to keep the people I care about safe, including a helpful friend like Millie. Her amiability stood out in such stark contrast to Michele Bodenheimer's pique.

I couldn't stop myself from staring at the house across the street. From this distance, I couldn't be sure, but I thought those blinds moved again. The shadowy form was much bulkier than the homeowner was. Why lie to me about living alone? Millie caught me staring and had more to say about her neighbor.

"Maybe I shouldn't be so hard on Michele," she said when Peter and I joined her. "Her life can't be pleasant now that she's got that awful brother of hers living with her."

"A brother? What's so awful about him?" I asked.

"He's not very attractive—unlike Frank and the other men in your circle of friends. They can't all be hunks, though, can they?" Millie said, leaning over and lowering her voice to a whisper. She smiled and raised both eyebrows a couple of times as she asked that question. Without waiting for me to reply, she continued. "Michele's brother is even grouchier than Sergeant Ellison. It's not just that he's so unattractive; he has an ugly personality, too. Josh is a rude, overbearing bully!"

The mention of the man's name set off a series of yelps and a snarl from Millie's feisty, pint-sized dog. Anastasia stared at her pooch pal, tilting her head one way and then the other. My large, standard poodle puppy that weighs at least five times as much as Miss Mini-Penny, took a step closer to me.

"Oh, Anastasia, she's not mad at you! It's that bully we don't like." I was beginning to wish I hadn't been so curious about Michele Bodenheimer's brother. If he was as bad as Millie described, maybe Michele hadn't wanted to provoke him by asking him to speak to me. Millie was wound up now and rushed on with her story.

"Miss Mini-Penny and I dropped by last week to give Michele a letter the postman delivered to me by mistake. When Michele opened the door about half way, I explained why we were there. Miss Mini-Penny is so friendly, that she stepped right into the house. The next thing I knew, this nasty man swung the door wide open. He snatched the letter from my hand and told us to scram as if we were a couple of alley cats!"

"What did Michele do?"

"She looked shocked, but just stood there. I grabbed Miss Mini-Penny before he could kick her or slam the door on her. It was traumatic. I couldn't understand why Michele would tolerate such behavior until a neighbor at the dog park told me he's her brother. People will put up with a lot from family, I guess."

"That's true. Maybe he'll leave soon."

"I hope so. Michele hasn't been the same woman since he moved in a few weeks ago. They almost never go anywhere together. I don't blame her since he's got that scruffy, unshaven look and tattoos. It's hard to imagine how they can be brother and sister." She shrugged.

"Millie, I don't feel good about all the trouble going on at the Fontanas. I hope you'll let my friend, Peter, send someone to look out for you. At least for a few days."

"Someone like him?" She asked, pointing to my handsome surfer dude pal, Brien. "Will he be my bodyguard?"

"From a distance," Peter said. "He'll come by and introduce himself. I want you to let him in your house when he gets there in a little while. He'll want to have a look around and then he'll have a few ideas about how to make your place safer."

"That'll be good to know so we'll be safer even when our bodyguard's gone."

"That's it exactly!" Peter said emphatically. "While he's on duty, he'll keep a low profile. You shouldn't even notice he's around—unless you need him."

"How will he know?"

"He'll have a device you can use to signal him. That probably won't be necessary since he's likely to know you need his help before you do."

"This is so exciting! Isn't it Miss Mini-Penny? I'm practically

Mrs. Pollifax in one of those Dorothy Gilman spy-mystery novels. I suppose we should keep this to ourselves, shouldn't we?"

"That's a good idea," I replied.

"Can I invite him in for lunch or tea?"

"Once a day. He's going to have a schedule to maintain and won't go hungry. If he needs to take a break before his shift ends and a new security person takes over, he can always call for backup. For the next few days, someone will be watching you around the clock." I gave Millie a hug and said goodbye as she walked to her house chattering with Miss Mini-Penny about bodyguards, backup, and stakeouts.

I was so grateful Millie didn't object. I wanted to keep her safe, but it also seemed worthwhile to have surveillance on Frank's house and Michele Bodenheimer's place, too. Millie's hunch that something was amiss with Michele's mean, ugly brother had piqued my curiosity. If Sergeant Ellison paid Millie another visit, I wanted to know about it. If we could catch up with him, I'd like to hear what he was looking for and why he'd turned into a rampaging vandal when he didn't find it.

12 AN OLD FRIEND AND NEW FOE

Somehow, we managed to get home before dinnertime despite the delay caused by Rikki's accident and the latest havoc wreaked at Frank's house. We also stopped, as planned, to pick up Bernadette and check in with the Fontanas. We had pitifully little to tell them, although they took heart from the fact that Frank had left messages for us to find. As soon as we finished our brief update, the kids' mother and grandmother hustled them off into the kitchen to make homemade pizzas for dinner. I got another one of those sweet, desperate hugs from Evie before she left.

"Don't stop 'til you find him, okay?"

"I won't. When we get home, we'll work all night if that's what it takes to make progress." As I said that, I heard the seventy-two-hour clock ticking in my head.

"Thank you. I don't care about what happened to my stuff at home—that's just stuff, but Dad..." Evie said giving me another squeeze as her words gave out on her.

"Hold on a little longer, okay?"

"I will. Cops have tough kids, you know."

"I do know. That's only one of the many reasons I find you so loveable." I hugged her as tight as I could—drawing strength from the words of this stoic twelve-year-old girl. "Remarkable, too!" That evoked a shy giggle from Evie that instantly reminded me of her dad.

He often responds to compliments in the same aw shucks way. I was glad she and the rest of Frank's family were hanging in there. It was going to be a long, stressful weekend.

One reason we had so little new to share when we finally arrived at Don's house was that I'd had a third inspiration while waiting for the police to respond to Peter's report of a break in. I texted Don about the trouble at Frank's place and Rikki Havens' accident and told him we needed a new, reliable source of information about the investigation.

Because Don wasn't sure who to trust among his colleagues, I'd suggested he contact a mutual friend for help—Detective George Hernandez with the Cathedral City Police Department. Like the other detectives I'd encountered in my short career as an accidental sleuth, it was sometimes stretching it to call George Hernandez a friend. Don's quick response to my text made it clear he had no reservations about Hernandez' trustworthiness or their friendship. Apparently, Detective Hernandez hadn't hesitated to help.

George was still at Don's house when we arrived. He even had a few updates for us. Fortunately, because George had done much of the work for us, it meant we didn't need to stay long.

"Hello, Attorney Huntington. It's good to see you," he said as we followed Don into the den where we could speak without worrying the kids any further.

Bernadette was in the kitchen helping and had taken care of Anastasia before letting her out into the backyard to romp with Mary's spunky Jack Russell terrier she and the kids had named Zip. The name was a good one given that Zip was always a bundle of energy.

"It's good to see you, too," I responded. "I wish, once in a while, we'd run into each other under better circumstances."

"Anytime Bernadette's baking cookies, I'm in! Especially if you'll make coffee to go with them."

"It's a deal—as soon as we get Frank home. Thanks for your willingness to help us now that Rikki Havens is out of the picture."

"Don and Frank are excellent cops. I'm as anxious as you are to find Frank and sort out the trouble he's in. Rikki's hasn't been around long, but Frank spoke highly of her." A screwy look must have flashed across my face because the detective paused and furrowed his brow. "What? You don't agree with his assessment?" I shrugged. He confirmed she was in a local hospital with serious, but non-life-threatening injuries. Who would step in to take her place as lead investigator wasn't clear yet.

"Maybe it's not such a bad idea that someone else will be stepping in. I don't know what to believe about her or anyone else in Frank's circle of law enforcement colleagues. Right now, it's hard to know who's a friend and who's not. The issues we ran into with Sergeant Ellison today don't make that any easier," I said.

"The police in Riverside County are trying to locate him for questioning. I'm not sure how quickly they'll find him or what they'll learn that will make it easier to understand who's a trustworthy cop or who isn't—especially if he lawyers up." He smirked a little as he mentioned the lawyer angle.

"Lawyers can complicate matters, I'll admit it. Apparently, Don's struggling with the good cop-bad cop issue too."

"He said that when he called and asked for my help. Don's good at picking up signals when something shifty is going on. He doesn't miss a thing."

"Tell me about it. Evelyn's never been able to pull off a surprise party for him since they married. You know how hard Frank and I tried to keep it from him when we began reexamining the cold case involving his niece, Kelly Fontana."

"I do remember that," George replied. "He was on to you two almost immediately. What's bothering him right now didn't require much effort on his part to discover. Someone searched Don's office at work. Nothing was taken, but he's concerned now that they were trying to find money or a ledger Frank had acquired from a dead informant."

"I take it there was no sign of a break in."

"Nope. That's why he suspects it was an inside job carried out by a colleague."

"Does he have any idea who did it?" I asked.

"Who did what?" Don inquired as he walked into the den where George and I were chatting. "George, here's your beer. Do you want one, Jessica?"

"No thanks, Uncle Don. I promised Evie I'd go home soon so we can try to get our investigation organized. So much happened today, we have tons of information that needs to be reviewed. That includes the names Frank gave us in the letter Tommy and Jerry brought me."

"Are any of them my colleagues?" He asked as he motioned for us to grab a seat around a bar in what Evelyn referred to as his "man cave." When he'd stashed the rest of the beer in a small built-in beverage fridge, he slid onto a bar stool next to me with his drink.

"A couple names on the list sound familiar. It's possible that's because I ran into them at one of your backyard barbeques or you've mentioned them. I don't know yet. George says you suspect that an uninvited visitor went through your office. That's the 'who did it' you heard us talking about."

"Yes, and right now, I'm paranoid and suspicious about everyone. After what went on today, I'm almost certain the search had something to do with Frank. I guess I should be grateful the rat didn't ransack my office like someone did at Frank's house. I could tell you quickly if you have the list with you. Maybe the dirtbag will help us find Frank."

"Hang on a second and I'll dig it out. Peter's got people running background checks. Randall Roberts' name was one of them. What would really be helpful is to determine not just who they are, but how they're interconnected with Frank and with each other." I handed the list to Don who scanned it as George spoke.

"They're all linked somehow to have ended up in that ledger. Drug rings are like old mob families. Gang members do lots of the grunt work—lots of them got picked up in the sweep. If they go outside the family, they rely on referrals from an insider who's putting his head on the block if he invites the wrong person into the syndicate."

"How do you like that?" Don asked. "I knew there was

something off about this guy the minute he came on board. George, I believe we need to go find Jimmy Dunbar and have a chat with him first thing tomorrow."

"Who is he?" I asked.

"He's a new hire. New to Palm Springs PD—not to the force. He transferred less than a year ago from Hemet."

"*I'll* find Jimmy Dunbar and ask him a few questions. You need to stay put and watch over your family. They're counting on you."

When we'd arrived, Peter had made an appeal for everyone to hunker down for a few days. To my great relief, Mary had accepted the invitation from Don and Evelyn to make it a long weekend. Evie and Frankie were relieved, too, when their mom had rearranged her schedule to remain with them through Monday. I reminded Don that he'd agreed to do the same.

"You promised Peter and me, as well as the kids, that you'd hang out here with them." Don rubbed both hands over his face before he gave in.

"Oh, okay. Let me know what you find out, will you, George?"

"Of course—I'll call you and Jessica as soon as I've heard what he has to say. There's no legal action we can bring against him just because his name is on a list Frank made up. You don't have any evidence that he's the one who searched your office and nothing of value was taken, right?"

"Right. I'll probably have to continue to work with the rat, won't I? I won't hold my breath waiting for him to come clean, but maybe he'll let something slip that will be helpful when it comes to finding Frank."

"It ought to rattle him that we're questioning him about Frank's disappearance and that his name is on a list Frank got by going through a ledger, documenting payouts to dirty cops. That might scare him enough to spill his guts—especially if he doesn't already know the guy who kept the ledger was murdered. I'll put a tail on him and let's see what he does after we let him go. Maybe he'll help us out if he runs to a friend who also happens to turn up on Frank's list."

"Thanks, George. Wouldn't that be great? Maybe he'll lead you to his dirtbag pal and he'll be the one holding Frank. That's probably too much to hope for, isn't it?" Don appeared to age right before my eyes as his hope fled. It had been a long day. Stress and fatigue were taking their toll. As if on cue, Peter joined us. Before he could say anything, I tried to offer Don another reason to hope.

"We're checking him out, too. Even if he doesn't give anything away to George or lead us to Frank, there must be something in his background that connects Jimmy Dunbar to Randall Roberts or one of the other creepy characters on Frank's list. You've given us a great lead." I put my arm around him and hugged him awkwardly.

"Are we ready to go, Peter?"

"We are. I made the rounds and checked in with the team and everything is secure. Evelyn knows that if she needs anything, she should ask one of my guys to get it." Then he glanced at Detective Hernandez.

"Unless you object, Don, Evelyn has also given us permission to eavesdrop on your phone conversations. I doubt this is a typical kidnapping for ransom, but if Frank or anyone else contacts you, we'll be listening."

"They may not be after ransom in the typical sense. These slugs may want you to give their money or the ledger back," George suggested.

"If I knew where either one was, I'd offer it to them in a flash. It would make me sick to help them get away with what they did to Frank's informant, but I'd do it anyway if I was sure they'd let Frank go."

"I understand. I don't think you'll get a call like that. If you do, Peter and I will know about it."

"It's okay to ask to speak to Frank, but otherwise, just listen carefully. If they want the ledger or money, slow them down. Get them to give you the details about what they want—when, where, and how the exchange for Frank will happen. Then, tell them you'll need a little time. If you can get them to go over the details again, do it."

"In other words, ask for proof of life, keep them talking as long as possible, and then stall about giving them what they want so they have to call again," Don said.

"Yes, Uncle Don. It's hard to teach a cop new tricks, isn't it?"

"True. Unfortunately, some of the guys who took Frank are cops too. They know the ropes and won't be fooled easily."

"I don't expect them to call. If they do, we'll track the source of the call. Unless these guys are really sophisticated, and their tricks include rerouting the phone call several times, we should be able to get a fix on where they are. We'll know more than we do now, even if we can't pinpoint their exact location."

"Then let's hope they want money and they call. What do I say if they want the ledger?" Don had asked.

"Tell them you don't have it, but you know how to find out who does," I replied. Don nodded in agreement.

"Stall on that, too, huh? I guess Frank told you where to find it in that note he left for you?"

"Sort of," I said. "I'm working on it." I hopped off the bar stool, ready to leave. Don slid out of his seat and stepped closer.

"Pick up the pace, will you?" With that, the usually reserved man reached out and embraced me. "We've got to get the man we both love back in one piece. You know how much he loves us—he'll do everything in his power to help us find him." I blinked back the tears that welled up in my eyes. Had he peeked at that note from Frank?

"Frank's got more tricks up his sleeve than any of those dirty cops with him," I said with conviction. I hugged Don as hard as I could. He felt fragile in my arms despite the height and weight advantage he has over me. "We'll check in with you in the morning. Promise you'll get some sleep and let us do our work." He nodded and wished us well.

13 THE SITUATION ROOM

"The situation isn't good, is it?" Tommy had asked anxiously after we'd gone through a quick overview of the day's events to make sure we were all on the same page. We reviewed the information we'd gathered which was too much and too little, at this point.

"The situation isn't good," I replied. "But it could be worse."

"You mean, because I don't have a dead cousin, yet? That could be because the dirtbags who took him haven't killed him, or maybe they have, and we just don't know it!" As Tommy spoke, the volume and pitch of his voice rose. Jerry put an arm around him and tried to calm him down.

"Come on. We have so much to do, and it'll go faster if we stay positive. That's our best hope of getting Frank out of the trouble he's in."

"How are we going to beat these people? They're ruthless, way ahead of us, and not afraid of anyone. If Laura's nurse friend is right, and these cruds took a potshot at Rikki, what chance do we have to save Frank? They ran a police detective off the road in broad daylight and got away with it!"

"¡Ay, Dios mío! Listen to Jerry. What's the point of having someone in your life who loves you and gives you good advice if you don't take it?" Bernadette stood up and put her hands on her hips, spreading her arms out like wings in full-blown mother hen style.

"Uh, he has a point. These psychos have badges to hide behind."

"¡Cállate!" Bernadette snapped. "What part of 'so much to do' and 'stay positive' didn't you hear or understand when Jerry said it?" Brien blinked a few times as he always does when he imagines Bernadette might swat at him. Not that she's ever done such thing. That didn't stop him from speaking up again.

"The best thing we can do is go get Frank!"

"You're preaching to the choir! To do that we need to know where he is. We're doing our best to track him down," Peter said.

"So are the police in several counties," Kim Reed added. "Normally, I'd be inclined to believe that was a good thing. Under the circumstances, maybe not."

"Exactly my point!" Brien added.

"Hey, I wish we had more to go on when it comes to finding Frank. Rikki sent us the photo they have of a nondescript white paneled van parked on the frontage road early this morning. As you suspected, Jessica, there's no way to know if the van headed north or south on I-215. We examined the footage from the camera located at a truck weigh station a few miles north of the spot where they found Randall Roberts' body. More than one white van passed by this morning, but none of them matched the one in the photo. We're trying to locate other cameras along I-215 in both the north and southbound lanes, but we don't even know for sure that the van used the freeway."

"I've started looking at alternate routes north and south," Kim Reed interjected. She glanced at Brien before continuing. "Brien called me while you were still dealing with the break in at Frank's house. He gave me a quick update and told me there was something dicey about the detour signs you ran into on the frontage road. I can pull up the routes I've traced. One of those routes could also explain how Rikki got past you without any of you seeing her." She paused. "Brien mentioned that, too. It's a shorter, more direct route to Perris, but probably not faster than the freeway unless she had information about a slowdown or accident."

"Before she had hers, you mean?" Laura asked.

"Yes. I could check traffic reports if you think it's worth it. Maybe Rikki took that back route because she went somewhere other than Perris. I can do a little more digging into that possibility. The northbound lane where she wrecked takes her away from Perris, not to it—where was she going? Why do you suppose she left the crime scene where Randall Roberts was murdered after you all pointed out the critical evidence investigators missed?"

"Great questions, Kim. The quickest way to get answers is to ask Rikki. If your friend, Carmel, is right Laura, and Rikki's not scheduled for surgery as George was told, she ought to be able to speak to us soon. I'll try to reach Rikki at the hospital early tomorrow morning."

"That'll be easier to do if she's no longer in the ICU. If you can't get through to Rikki, maybe she'll call you. I can ask Carmel to see if she can pass along a message."

"Good. I have a few other questions for her besides the ones you just asked, Kim. Like what happened to the money and the ledger Frank gave her for safekeeping and what does she know about Sergeant Ellison. If what Carmel heard is more than just another rumor, I'd like to know who took that potshot at her before running her off the road."

"Chica, even if she's in good enough shape to answer your questions, she might not know who caused her accident. She might not remember what happened. She's out of the loop now, too, right?" Bernadette asked. I shrugged in reply.

"I think so, according to George, but maybe it's another rumor. It's another reason to speak to her as soon as she's able to accept a phone call."

"So far, we only have Carmel's word for it that Rikki's accident was no accident. Hospitals are hotbeds of gossip. You'd think if someone shot at her, Rikki would know it even if she's not getting official updates."

"True, but that doesn't mean she'll tell us. She was wigged out when I spoke to her at the murder scene near the railroad tracks. I thought she was ticked at me because we found the gun and note instead of her. Now I'm wondering if she was stressed out because someone threatened her. Why not call for backup?"

"Well, she could have been anxious because she was supposed to be someplace else and would have left already if you hadn't found the new evidence. She sure went somewhere in a hurry," Kim said. "Nothing relevant went out over the police channels, but that doesn't mean Rikki didn't get a call."

"If she did get a call through unofficial channels, maybe it was a ruse to lure her onto the highway to ambush her."

"That's a horrifying possibility, Jessica," Laura added. "It makes sense, though, if it's true somebody shot at her."

"George Hernandez is sending us the accident reports—maybe someone the police interviewed at the scene saw what happened," Jerry suggested.

"That would be great, wouldn't it? Who knows? Maybe Rikki started those rumors about being shot at for some reason that eludes me now." Paranoia was running wild in my poor addled brain.

"If she's a dirty cop, it might be better to appear to be a victim rather than a perp," Brien added excitedly.

"What a crafty move that would be!" Tommy exclaimed, and then paused. "I could totally see her doing that."

"It would have been risky. She had to hit that concrete barrier just right to make it convincing, without killing herself." I'm sure Peter knew what he was talking about. He must have encountered plenty of accidents that weren't really accidents in his black-ops days. Bernadette spoke almost as if she'd read my mind.

"Sometimes an accident is just an accident..." Bernadette shrugged and paused. "Nah..." she added quickly. "It wouldn't surprise me if someone wanted to shoot Rikki." Her eyes bore into me as she said that.

"Hey, I've been tempted to smack her, but I wouldn't shoot at her. We promised George no more guns, remember?" It wasn't funny. I sighed wearily. "This conversation is a good reminder for me to remain skeptical no matter what Rikki has to say tomorrow. It also makes me realize that while I'm sorry we may no longer have her as a source of information, who knows how much we can believe her anyway."

"George is a standup guy. Until we know who's taking her place, we'll have to rely on the information he can get or whatever we can dig up on our own."

"I agree, Jerry. If George hits a roadblock, Don can pitch a fit and demand access to the formal documents related to the investigation. What's going on behind the scenes is puzzling to me, though. I wish we had an insider who could help us understand what's really going on. It's harder than ever to determine if Rikki's a friend or a foe now that these dirtbags have started turning on each other."

"You think?" Laura asked. "I'm sorry. That sounded snippy. I'm stressed out, too. We're not just trying to find somebody we happen to know. This is about Frank who's in the mess of his life! It's been almost twelve hours since he left that little cocktail napkin for you to find—the last evidence we have that he's alive."

My stomach roiled at the words and a flash of terror lashed at me. Anastasia must have sensed the surge of anxiety. She sat up and put her head on my arm as I fought to keep panic at bay.

"We don't have a body. Frank's a clever and resourceful police officer with plenty of tricks up his sleeve—as his dad assured me. Frank will find a way to get another message to us. In the meantime, we keep working. I intend to ask Rikki who's hunting her and why. Killing her isn't the way to get the ledger or money back if someone believes she still has them."

"For all we know, she does."

"I wouldn't put it past her, Peter."

"I'll call Carmel again first thing tomorrow morning and get an update. Armed guards are stationed on Rikki's floor, and one is posted at her door as well. Rumor has it that there are others patrolling the building, but not in uniform."

"That'll keep her safe if this isn't a fox in the hen house situation," Jerry remarked.

"Uh, I doubt they'll let animals in a hospital..." Kim elbowed Brien. "What? Oh, yeah, it's another one of those metaphysical statements, isn't it?"

"Metaphorical," Kim replied instantly. I suppressed a nervous giggle, not wanting to snicker at Brien's attempts to master the English language. Surfer lingo is his native tongue. With Kim's tutelage, he's made amazing gains since he started working to impress Peter. She gave Brien's hand a squeeze which he returned. We all suspect there's more going on between them than tutoring, but we'll let them break it to us.

"Foxes in the hen house is right given all the trouble these malicioso policia are causing. We need treats." Bernadette left muttering to herself in Spanish about stupid, dirty rotten rascals. Despite the pep talk she'd given Tommy, I could tell our St. Bernadette was waging a battle of her own to keep the faith.

"Maybe hospital admins are worried about the fox wearing a nurse's uniform or scrubs. Carmel says those armed guards are watching Rikki around the clock. Only select hospital personnel are allowed in to care for her." Laura shrugged, drumming her fingers nervously on the table in front of her. Several of us sat in leather club chairs around a conference table at one end of Dad's office. I scooted around a little to face her before I spoke.

"They could be right to worry about someone posing as a doctor, nurse, or orderly. Remember what happened to Libby Van Der Woert when she was in the hospital. If Frank and his dad hadn't intervened, the assassin would have killed her."

"Where's Frank when you need him?" Tommy asked, trying hard to be funny despite the worry on his face.

"Hopefully, he's in the van and they're still on the move. We're monitoring the police radio dispatches in case someone spots them. There's nothing very distinctive about the van, but the partial plate number lifted from the photo should help," Peter's chair squeaked a little as he shifted in his seat. "George is running the plate numbers through the DMV database. If he comes up with something about the van's owner, he'll tell us."

"Okay. We can't just sit around and hope that van turns up—with Frank in it. Let's do our best to forge our way through the list of names Frank gave us. We already know something about two of them—Randall Roberts and Jimmy Dunbar."

"I wish I had more on that front, too," Peter said. "Kim has a copy of the information we dug up so far. It's very possible you've run across a couple of the people on that list, Jessica. There's a police sergeant on it—not Ellison, but a guy by the name of Harry Mik. It wouldn't surprise me if you've heard of him because he has a history of complaints lodged against him. That includes charges of excessive force and planting evidence, as well as personal problems involving domestic abuse. For years, he's been the head of a major crimes unit like the one they have here in Indio. The one he honchoes is in a town called Hillsdale, northwest of the spot where Frank and the guys with him switched from the car to the van."

"Isn't he something special? A sergeant no less! He must have pull to be honchoing anything anywhere with that kind of trouble on his record. He just has to be one of the goons who hauled Frank away this morning!" Tommy's face flushed, and he stomped his feet. Anastasia, our furry, four-footed personal therapist, ran to his side. Like magic, one touch of her soft head stopped Tommy's meltdown in its tracks.

"It ought to make you feel better to hear that Mik's on administrative leave," Peter added. "We haven't found any new charges against him in the wake of the French Connection. Obviously, he wasn't picked up during the sweep."

"Neither was Randall Roberts. Banner Falls is northeast of that spot along I-215. Kim, will you check the distance between Banner Falls and Hillsdale? If our dead 'Barney' and the violence-prone Harry Mik were acquainted, you could be right, Tommy."

"With his record, Mik's a hot head. The kind of guy who might lose it, kill a colleague, and leave him lying in a ditch." Tommy sucked in a great gulp of air as Jerry spoke those words. Then he choked. In a flash, Anastasia ran, grabbed a bottle of beer from a side table, and ran back with it. Despite our worry about Frank, Anastasia's astonishing behavior sent up a round of cheers.

"Anastasia the wonder dog to the rescue!" In case there was anyone in the room who still doubted Brien's words, Anastasia returned to the side table, pawed at a bottle opener until it fell to the floor, and then took it to Tommy. I gasped.

"You don't even have to tell her to fetch!" Tommy exclaimed.

"Fetch what? I know you're not talkin' about me, are you, Tommy Fontana?" Bernadette swept into the room with chips, salsa, and a plate of cookies. Treats for the lovely Anastasia, too. The smart girl, already seated at Bernadette's feet, reached up and pawed at Bernadette's pocket. When Bernadette pulled a dog biscuit from her pocket, Anastasia received another round of cheers.

"Anastasia," Tommy said. "Where's Frank? Fetch Frank, okay?" Anastasia cocked her head to one side and then dashed over to me. She pawed at my arm before placing her head on it and whining just a little.

"Aw, she wants you to do it."

"I'm doing my best, Brien. I spoke to Dick Tatum a little while ago. He didn't mention Harry Mik's name, even though I sent him a copy of Frank's list. Hillsdale is in San Bernardino County, right? That's outside the area in which Dick works as a public defender. In fact, the only name on the list he recognized is Kenneth Humboldt—Captain Kenneth Humboldt. Dick reminded me that Captain Humboldt was among those who opposed adding cold case teams to police forces in the county. He objected to using resources to investigate cold cases like Kelly's death. Dick claims he's never heard anything to suggest Humboldt's dirty, just haughty, rigid, and insensitive."

"Wow, I suppose by comparison that makes him a saint," Laura quipped. "Frank must have had some other reason for putting him on a list of cutthroats. I doubt a man of his rank would be crammed into the back seat of a car doing the dirty work, don't you? He's sounds more like a string-puller from behind the scenes." Laura's comments were dead on.

"Humboldt's with the Riverside Police Department, not the County Sheriff's Department, so I'm not sure how much personal contact Frank had with him. I recall Dick mentioning Humboldt, but I'm certain Frank would have chimed in about the man if he'd had contact with him."

"Maybe they met later because of the French Connection," Kim suggested. "According to the organizational chart, Humboldt oversees special operations. That must include coordination with operations the feds organize." She looked up at me. "Another fox in the hen house—that's disturbing, isn't it?"

"You've got that right. Have you seen photos of the men on Frank's list? Are any of the officers six-foot, heavily built, men—black or white?" I asked. "That's how Millie described the two men getting into the back seat with Frank." I'd already shared Millie's story with everyone, but recounted exactly what she'd said about the men she'd seen before going on.

"Harry Mik," Kim responded almost immediately. A picture of a big beefy Caucasian man appeared on a screen projected from Kim's laptop. "Not Kenneth Humboldt," she added as the image of a thin white male with only a fringe of hair and a big grin replaced Harry Mik's photo.

"Okay, so maybe Millie saw Harry Mik getting into the back seat. Let's go through the other men on Frank's list and see if any of them fit the description of the black cop she saw. Randall Roberts was our 'Barney' and one of the occupants in the front seat. We're also still missing our 'bingo cop.' Are any of the names on Frank's list members of a tribal police force or working as a community liaison with tribal police?"

"No tribal cops, but I'm not sure about a community liaison angle. We can check." Kim, Tommy, and Laura all sat in front of computers. I did, too. Their fingers flew over the keyboards as they searched the web for pictures of the men Frank had named. Jerry had his phone out and Brien was pecking away at a tablet lying on the table in front of him with the fingers on one hand. He shoveled cookies into his mouth with the other.

"You know what? Now that we may have identified two occupants of the car, I'm going to search for connections between Harry Mik and Randall Roberts," Laura said.

"I'm doing that, too," Jerry added. "While we're at it, we might as well post Devon James' picture—if Kim can locate one." Kim's fingers flew and before Jerry finished his next sentence, she projected an image for us all to see. "He's the cop being held in connection to the murder of William Hargreaves. A black police officer with the LAPD, but he's not six feet tall and he's still in custody."

"Obviously, he's not one of the police officers Millie Nordstrom says she saw this morning. It's too bad we can't interview him. We've got Millie under surveillance. Send me the pictures of Harry Mik and Randall Roberts and I'll have the man on duty in the morning ask Millie if she recognizes them."

"That's a great idea, Peter. If we keep at it, maybe we can find a candidate for her to I.D. as the other guy in the back seat with Frank. You can send a photo of him along, too."

"If we can't find him using Frank's list, we'll expand our search to see if Mik and Roberts are palling around with other police officers whose names aren't on it. Right now, I think we should concentrate on the shortlist Frank gave us to see if we can identify the four men in the car with him. Finding connections between them is good, too. That might help us figure out where they've gone.

"The Cat Pack's work is never done!" Tommy sighed in mock desperation. "So little time, so many rats to find."

"It's too bad the guys on Frank's list don't wear a special dirty cop club uniform, so you can spot the maleantes," Bernadette snapped.

"That sure would make our job easier. For now, I'm going to assume Frank's given us a head start with the list he left for us. Maybe they're not wearing a uniform, but there must be a common thread or ties between them. Let's find them!"

14 WHO'S WHO?

"The name's a fake. I can't find a police officer named Toby Foster anywhere in the systems I've searched. A creepy fake, maybe. There's an informant by that name—another dead one." Kim Reed didn't take her eyes off the computer screen open in front of her. She hit a button and a printer in a corner of my father's home office came to life.

Without saying a word, Laura dashed over to the printer, pulled the information, and stuck a photo of the informant on a cork inset alongside a large white board that was normally hidden behind gleaming burled wood panels. I fought off a wave of nostalgia. It had been years since my father had used this room to manage his projects from home.

The rogues' gallery of dirty cop photos representing the men named by Frank was pinned in a neat row on Dad's corkboard. They included a couple of men who were tall and black. Neither had popped up in any of the photos Kim had found in her efforts to put Mik and Roberts together. Kim and Laura had succeeded in spotting photos of both men at several official county functions. So far, though, none of the photos captured the two men in the same frame. There was no photo of the two men slapping each other on the back or raising a glass of beer at a bar like the Copper Penny, the place in downtown Riverside where Frank and his pals sometimes dropped by after hours.

"Do you mean he was found dead like Jeff Baker?" I asked.

"Not just like Jeff Baker," Laura said. "This one was beat up, but he died of a drug overdose."

"Did anyone suspect foul play?" Jerry asked.

"Not that I can see," Kim replied. "What I can tell you is that his rap sheet included charges filed in both San Bernardino and Riverside Counties. He moved frequently and used shelters and SROs in both areas. His last known address was at an SRO in a rundown motel in San Bernardino."

"Is that where they found his body?" I asked.

"No. He was killed in Riverside, in an alley not too far from where Chester Davis was murdered when you were investigating Kelly's cold case."

"He got around for a down and out guy. Death put an end to that, didn't it?" Tommy asked in a sad, weary tone.

"Betsy tells me homeless drug addicts are always on the move. Sometimes that's because they're looking for drugs or dealing to support their habit. They make the rounds of soup kitchens, too."

"How do they get around, Peter? I sometimes see them on the street pushing a shopping cart, but they can't get from Riverside to Palm Springs that way," Brien asked.

"They stash their cart somewhere, and hitch rides or catch buses. Some agencies will give them vouchers for travel to a shelter or to another town. Betsy calls them the "new nomads." Peter had a question for Kim.

"How do you know Toby Foster was an informant? Do we have any idea what information he was providing and to whom?"

"Toby Foster's death was mentioned in an online news post. 'Police found the body of a local man Saturday morning in an alley behind a local restaurant. An addict and informant, Toby Foster, is reported to have died of an overdose.' That's it. There's not even any reference to the fact that he was beaten before he died. That came up in another report, although there's no mention of him by name in that one. 'The body of a man was found in an alley behind a local restaurant. Investigators don't believe foul play was involved, even though the man may have been involved in a physical altercation prior to his death from a suspected overdose. His name is being withheld pending notification of next of kin.' So far, I haven't found anything that can answer your questions."

"Cops know who other cops use as informants. Sometimes they even share them."

"That's true. The dirty cops have the edge when it comes to that too, unfortunately." Peter and Jerry paused after that exchange. I could feel a drop in the energy in the room. It had been a long day and we were all tired. I spoke up to try to get things going again.

"I'll check in with Dick again in the morning. He remembered the investigation into Jeff Baker's murder because it went nowhere fast. I'll see if he can tell us anything about Toby Foster. Dick reminded me that dead addicts don't get much attention even when they're beaten to death. Addicts who die from an overdose get noticed even less. As we've already learned, overdoses aren't always accidents."

"It ought to matter that both Jeff Baker and Toby Foster weren't just addicts, but police informants," Jerry interjected.

"Dick didn't say anything about Jeff Baker's role as an informant. Maybe that's what triggered his interest enough to investigate the case further. He's asking an old law school chum of mine, Renee Collins, to make discreet inquiries about Jeff Baker. I haven't seen her in years, but Dick says she works at a clinic offering free legal aid services. That brings her into contact with lots of the local addicts on a regular basis. I'll see if she's willing to add Toby Foster's name to her conversations with her clients."

"Isn't it another odd coincidence that both addicts died in Riverside a few weeks apart and after taking a beating?" Laura asked, her voice raspy with weariness.

"I agree. Given what Dick said, it's possible no one considered it odd or examined the two incidents closely enough to spot a connection between them even if there is one," I added. "I'll ask Dick to pull the police reports and postmortems for both men. If he doesn't have time to review them, I will." I felt exhausted too, but my bigger concern was how much work we'd done without it feeling like we were any closer to finding Frank. Tommy sure had it right when he'd railed against the ruthlessness of the men we were facing. I shuddered as I glanced at the images of police officers hiding their dirty deeds behind the uniforms they wore.

"Thanks for the stepped-up security here, Peter." I'd employed Peter's firm long enough to anticipate that we might be in for trouble by inserting ourselves into Frank's situation. This was the first time, however, that I'd come home to find SUVs blocking my driveway. "The row of tank-like SUVs is a new angle."

"It won't take any effort for members of law enforcement to get in through the front gate. I want to slow them down if they get this far hoping to make a grab for you."

"That wasn't exactly what I had in my mind when we spoke about making it more secure around here. I was more concerned about the kind of problem we've had in the past with bad guys posing as service providers." That spurred my Cat Pack pals to speak up.

"Peter's got the right idea, though. If the dirty cops with Frank can't get him to tell them whatever it is they want to know, why not barge in here and grab a close friend? Especially since we've made it harder for them to get to Frank's parents, his kids, and his ex-wife," Jerry commented.

"Besides, from what you told us, Sergeant Ellison got an earful from Frank's neighbor about how close you are to the family. If he's a member of the dirty cop club, they all know about you by now, even if they hadn't already pegged you as someone close to Frank." That was Laura speaking in a chiding tone as if I'd somehow objected to Peter's reasoning. I was waiting for Bernadette to put in her two cents worth when Brien jumped in and took the conversation in a new direction.

"Unless Ellison's a lone wolf," Brien countered. "A lone wolf who's still out there and probably looking for you."

"Thanks for pointing that out! An armed and dangerous lone wolf on the prowl doesn't sound much better to me than a pack of dirty cops. The organizers of the French Connection operation just did a sweep that was supposed to nab these guys. Why are they still out on the streets? How many more of these creeps are there?"

Anger welled up in me. Unjust authority is a pet peeve that makes my blood boil.

"It's kind of like the *Dawn of the Dead*, isn't it?" I paused, trying to make sense of yet another oddball comment from Brien. Tommy got it instantly.

"Ooh, he's right! It's like a zombie apocalypse of dirty cops."

"The entire force hasn't gone over to the dark side. George told you there's a B.O.L.O. out for Ellison to question him about the break-in at Frank's house. Maybe someone's already onto him if he's dirty," Laura added.

"That must be true, since someone jumped on it when we reported that Ellison was at Frank's house today. George says his presence there wasn't because of any official business. Internal Affairs has had a conversation with him. You'll love this. Guess who one of the people behind the rumors that Frank's on the take is?"

"The crafty police sergeant who wields a mean crowbar when he's on the hunt for other people's money," Kim replied.

"You've got it."

"If Ellison was already under enough suspicion that IA was snooping around, why would anyone take him seriously when he badmouthed Frank?" Laura shook her head.

"No one filed charges against Frank," Jerry said. "If Don's right, Frank's interview with IA wasn't even about him. They asked a bunch of tough questions that worried him. That's not too surprising to me as a P.I. One of the things I've noticed when I'm sneaking around and poking my nose into other people's lies is that it's easy to become paranoid. When you're undercover like Frank and playing a role that requires you to be a liar, it gets harder to judge who's telling you the truth."

"I hear you, Jerry. Maybe that's Rikki's problem—she's paranoid. She didn't say her suspicions about Frank came from any formal investigation, either, but via the cop grapevine. Rumors—like the ones flying around about Rikki at the hospital. Anyway, I'll rest easier once we hear Ellison's been picked up."

"Me too. Until we know who's who in law enforcement and we

get Frank back, the SUVs will stay where they are. I want another layer between you and any bad cop who tries to get to you."

"I'm not balking. How could I do that after telling Don to stay put or insisting that Millie let you keep her under surveillance. She's the person I nominate as most likely to be sought out by the crowbar-wielding sergeant-at-large. Millie is an eyewitness who puts him at the scene close to the time someone broke into Frank's house. She can also testify about where the crowbar and the gloves came from even if the lab can't retrieve physical evidence linking them to Ellison." I paused to give someone else a chance to speak when I remembered the other reason I wanted someone watching over Millie.

"While we're still talking about Millie, I want to mention another situation that puzzles me. Millie was very concerned about the fact that her standoffish neighbor, Michele Bodenheimer, has been in a bad way since her brother moved in with her. Sergeant Ellison didn't worry Millie at all, but Michele's brother, Josh, did."

"Michele Bodenheimer is the neighbor who lives across the street, right?" Bernadette asked.

"Yes. She was helpful enough—to the officers who made the rounds this morning and to me. Her description of the car and the partial plate number she remembered should help corroborate Millie's testimony about Sergeant Ellison's presence at Frank's house. Here's what's puzzling. Michele Bodenheimer told me she lives alone, despite what Millie told me later. I'm sure someone was in the house with Michele, and curious enough about our conversation to stay close. According to Millie, the brother's a nasty guy, but why would Michele lie about his presence? When I asked if there was anyone else in the house who might answer my questions, Michele wasn't just evasive, she shut me down." When I told them more about what Millie meant by nasty, Tommy had a suggestion about Michele's behavior.

"She's probably desperate to believe the brute's moved in temporarily and that's what she means when she says she 'lives alone,'" Tommy said.

"If he's as difficult as Millie makes him sound, the poor woman may be afraid it'll provoke a confrontation if she admits he's there and he's forced to speak to the police," Laura added.

"Or she knows he's had trouble with the police before," Kim suggested. "Do we have a last name? Maybe he's still in trouble."

"Josh is the only name Millie gave me. We've got so much on our plates already; I don't want to make it a big deal. With Peter's guys on duty, it won't be easy for Josh or Sergeant Ellison to get to Millie." I stretched and yawned. "Let's get back to work."

An hour later, I wished we'd made more progress. We did have the names of two of the men in the car with Frank, as I eyed them among the photos arrayed in front of us. The two towns in which Mik and Roberts resided were less than sixty miles apart—not much more than an hour's drive even on backcountry roads. I felt certain there was more going on between them than what we'd dug up showing both men at official county functions.

Peter and I also created and posted a timeline. With input from the others, we'd done our best to document the day's events. Peter and I wrote what amounted to our own version of incident reports about what had gone on at Frank's house and out there on the roadside. Jerry had taken the lead summarizing what we knew about the break-in and vandalism at Frank's house, as well as the names and addresses of neighbors he'd interviewed even though they hadn't given us new information. Laura pulled together the scanty information we had about Rikki's accident and her situation at the hospital. Tommy did the same for the conversation he and Jerry had with Don.

It was boring and tedious, but I didn't want to overlook or lose a single thread in the tangled web of lies and deceit we'd encountered so far. Anastasia, who'd been sleeping in a corner of the room, came to let me know she needed a break.

"Anastasia, do you need to step outside?" I asked. She woofed, making a funny sound as she yawned at the same time. "I need to stretch my legs and get the blood circulating better. Hopefully, some of it will reach my brain."

"What I need is food and a brewski. Anybody else?" Brien asked.

"We have leftover sesame noodles, don't we?" Bernadette had

called the caterers we often use for Cat Pack get-togethers. Peter the giant, ex-black-ops, hard-nosed security specialist can't abide eating "anything with a face or a mom." Despite the last-minute request, the caterers had shown up at six-thirty with something for everyone, including vegan dishes like the sesame noodles.

"I'm sure we do," Laura replied in response to Peter's question. "I don't think we finished anything the caterers brought. Dibs on the roasted vegetables and feta—sorry, Jessica, but I said it first."

"There's plenty for both of you," Bernadette assured me. "Take Anastasia for her walk and I'll save some for you."

"Don't leave the property," Peter added. He didn't have to remind me to stay close with photos of dirty cops staring at me. I felt their eyes on me as I left the room. I know full well, however, that it isn't the paper versions of bad cops who can hurt me—or Frank.

15 AN ERRANT GOLFER

It was one of those deceptively perfect evenings in the California desert. Perfect if you ignored our frenzied efforts to counter the latest episode of murder and mayhem and the fact that Frank wasn't here with me. I breathed deeply, trying to figure out what we ought to do next. The sky was filled with a dazzling array of stars in a cloudless sky. Could Frank see the same starry sky wherever he was tonight? A wave of warmth washed over me, thinking of the way in which Frank had embraced me here, in almost this same spot. Had that only been last night?

A gentle breeze sent a wisp of hair to tickle my cheek. Filled with a potpourri of flowery and herby fragrances, the summer heat would soon purge the desert of the flowers, leaving only the smell of toasty earth and the hardy brush that can handle triple digits. That included the drought-hardy bougainvillea that bore their magenta blooms in defiance of the heat all summer long. A gust set fallen bougainvillea leaves in motion making skittering sounds on the stamped concrete. Anastasia had been a little wary when we stepped out onto the patio, but now she scampered after the leaves.

Where are you, Frank? I wondered, as I walked Anastasia around the perimeter of the expansive patio system that runs along the back of my mother's house. The pool lights cast an almost otherworldly light. Shadows shifted as the breeze rippled along the top of the water. In the distance, I could hear the familiar whir of a golf cart. Diehard golfers often play until the last glimmer of daylight forces them to return to the clubhouse and call it a day. Anastasia cocked one ear and listened.

At both ends of the property, privacy walls amble toward the golf course, stopping before they block the view. Soon, we would have a wrought iron fence to keep Anastasia from wandering onto the course in an unguarded moment. The friendly dog loves to watch the golfers at play. So far, she hasn't bothered them, but why take a chance?

Always delighted to spend time outdoors, Anastasia suddenly quit snapping at the bougainvillea leaves and stepped closer to me. She went on point. I froze.

Why hadn't we installed the fence already? I hollered inwardly. We'd learned the hard way that wily villains can get past the guard gate posing as service providers—a dilemma for well-heeled residents of gated communities everywhere. Peter's point about that also being true for law enforcement struck home in a visceral way as my pulse raced. I could no longer hear the golf cart motor. Had it stopped—nearby? How close?

"Inside, girl!" I whispered. "Let's go!" Anastasia stood her ground and growled as I heard a scuffle on the other side of the wall to my left. Someone took a punch and landed on the ground with an 'oomph.' I winced, knowing all too well how that feels. Suddenly, a man scrambled into view from around the corner. He was hunched over, dazed, and unsteady on his feet as he struggled to regain his footing. Anastasia lunged at the man, barking wildly. That caused him to stumble again.

Blindingly bright security lights shined on him. In his madras shorts and polo shirt, he might have passed as a golfer except that a trickle of blood ran from his bottom lip, and in one hand, he held a gun. Anastasia lunged forward again, and this time clamped her jaws on the hand holding the gun. He yowled. The gun dropped to the ground, and Anastasia released him. Before he could make another move, one of Peter's men knocked the intruder's legs out from under him. He hit the ground harder than the gun. A second member of Peter's competent team quickly retrieved the gun that was lying on the ground.

I heard gasps from behind me. The moment the security lights came on, the patio screen doors flew open. Cat Pack members now streamed out from Dad's office and from the kitchen where Brien had gone with Bernadette to find food. Two of Peter's security associates hauled the man to his feet.

"Welcome, Sergeant Ellison. We've been expecting you," I said in an attempt at bravado. I should have added "sort of" to the "expecting you part," since we hadn't known for certain which members of law enforcement might breach security at the guard gate. Sergeant Ellison gave me a puzzled look as he stared at me standing next to the fluffy poodle sitting calmly beside me. Now that she'd quit snarling and barking, she didn't appear to pose a threat to anyone.

"Where do you want him?" Peter's associates asked.

"Kitchen," Bernadette replied in a gruff tone. "I've got water boiling." That evoked a double-take from Sergeant Ellison and me. My mouth popped open when I saw the grim face on my pint-sized companion's face. She was also wielding an enormous French knife.

"The knife's an improvement over your dad's gun," Laura whispered as we all followed Bernadette and the thug into the house. Ellison's feet weren't even touching the ground as Peter's men carried him indoors. Laura had made a good point. Bernadette had kept her promise to me—and to George Hernandez—no more guns! Peter leaned in and spoke in a low voice.

"Ellison should have been disarmed sooner, but the gun wasn't visible when my men first spotted him out on the golf cart path. We wanted to let him get close enough to make a move. He never would have fired a shot at you, trust me." Peter was more serious than I'd ever seen him. Why not given the range of threats we might be facing from ticked off drug cartel members, dirty cops, and cagey politicos willing to play games while people's lives were on the line.

"Thanks, Peter," was all I could think of to say as we stepped into the house. My anger grew at the nerve of the jerk sitting at a table in the morning room just off the kitchen. Having a gun waived at me was better than being shot at, but it still made bile rise in my throat. Not to mention that this slug had destroyed the wonderful home Frank had made for his children.

"You're in big trouble, aren't you, Sergeant?" I asked as he sat cuffed to a chair. "What brings you to our lovely community on a night when you ought to be half way to Canada or on a plane to some country with no extradition agreement with the U.S.?"

He didn't reply. Standing nearby, Peter stepped behind me, and folded his arms making his enormous biceps bulge. Brien moved next to him and did the same. Keith Ellison stared at them defiantly. Then, Bernadette joined me, holding an even bigger knife. In her small hands, it appeared to be almost as large as a machete.

"Jessica asked you a question, muchacho. Answer her!" Bernadette snapped.

"You ought to give el muchacho a thump on the head just for being caught wearing those horrid plaid shorts after five," Tommy said from where he stood on the other side of the table in the morning room. Jerry elbowed Tommy to get him to shut up.

"What is this?" He asked. "Who are you people?" He was surrounded now. Peter's security associates had returned to their posts outside, but the Cat Pack members had all crowded into the room.

"Oh, come now. You know exactly who I am. Millie Nordstrom told you all about me before you left Frank's house in such a hurry that you forgot your crow bar. She doesn't have it anymore, though. It's been taken into evidence along with the gloves you left behind." I shook my head. "You're not a very good bad cop, are you?"

I tried to use a tough dame tone as I spoke. It probably sounded about as hokey as the voice Kathryn Hepburn used in that *Bringing up Baby* farce. Bernadette must have thought so, too. She stepped in front of me wagging the knife she held almost at eye level with the sergeant.

"We don't have much time. Let's get right to the point," she said using the knife for emphasis. "Where's Frank Fontana?"

"How do I know?"

"You'd better know something. We don't like dumb cops any better than we like dirty ones." That was Brien chiming in. The muscles in his jaw flexed along with those in his biceps as he fixed his gaze on the weasel. Ellison glanced at Brien before his eyes returned to Bernadette who was still holding that knife inches from his lip that was growing fatter by the minute.

"What did you do with the ledger? Where's the money? What the hell were you doing on my patio with a gun?" I asked, hoping to rattle him by pummeling him with questions.

"If I had the ledger or the money, why would I have gone to Frank's house or tracked you down?"

Bingo! I thought. If we had any lingering doubt about who'd ripped Frank's house apart, or why, the man had just cleared that up.

"Is that why you're here?" Kim asked from where she stood near Tommy and Jerry. "You believe Jessica has the money and the ledger?"

"What other reason would I have to risk my neck trying to get through the security around this place? I don't care if Frank's messing around with you or any other…" Bernadette wagged that knife a tad closer to his face.

"You better keep it clean, tipo duro, if you know what's good for you! Just answer her questions—politely." A wave of confusion swept over Keith Ellison's face.

"Tee po do-what?" Peppering him with questions may or may not have put him off balance, but Ma Barker Bernadette was throwing him for a loop. Not that I found his hapless fool routine any more convincing than his errant golfer masquerade was.

"Tough guy—she called you a tough guy. It took a real tough guy to destroy Frank Fontana's house like you did. Was it your idea or did one of your sleazy cop friends put you up to it?" I asked. His demeanor shifted, and a belligerent expression stole over his face.

Now we're getting somewhere, I thought. The angry guy sitting there gritting his teeth was much closer to the man I'd expected Sergeant Ellison to be.

"I don't know about you, but he screwed me!" He kicked a table leg as he spit out those words. Bernadette took a step closer.

"What did I say about keeping it clean?"

"Sorry. You've got me all wrong. I'm not IED. I'm the one who tipped Frank off about those lunatics. You obviously aren't working with them or you'd already know where Frank Fontana has gone. I'd be interested to know that, too. What are you—a group of crazed vigilantes?" His eyes swept the people huddled around the table. He was already surrounded, but we closed in on him as if that would help us get closer to the truth.

"What's IED?" He gazed at me suspiciously before mumbling a reply.

"I'm so dead. IED is a group of crooked cops. They're dirty and proud of it. They call themselves the Inland Empire Desperados—I-E-D."

"Please! If such a thing exists, are we supposed to believe you're not one of them?" Kim asked, almost snarling. Something in her tone set Anastasia on edge and put her back into full-blown attack poodle mode. She growled and bared her teeth. Ellison leaned as far back in his seat as he could and rubbed the hand Anastasia had chomped down on hard. He ought to be grateful Anastasia hadn't used her bared teeth when she gripped his hand like a vice or he'd be bleeding. "Did you kill Randall Roberts?"

"What? Who? No, no, no! I didn't kill Randall Roberts or anyone else. When I first heard rumors about the group, I thought it was a joke. Then one of my informants showed me bruises he claimed he got when they smacked him around. The guy was a big-time druggie, so I told him he was full of it. He told me he could prove they were real because they weren't just a gang of thugs—but on the take." Ellison's voice cracked. "He brought me pages torn from a ledger. I wasn't sure what to do with them. When he turned up dead from an overdose a few days later, I went to Frank."

"When did you do that?" I asked.

"Weeks ago. I showed the pages to Frank and I saw him put them in his safe. I'm not ashamed to say I was scared after Toby died."

"Whoa, wait a second," Brien said. "Toby what?"

"Don't you mean Toby who?"

"¡Claro que sì! Answer the man!"

"Toby Foster."

"Now that's interesting, isn't it?" I muttered. "You must have suspected his death wasn't an accident, especially since someone beat him to within an inch of his life before he overdosed." Ellison's eyes narrowed with suspicion, and then he looked at me as if I was crazy when I continued. "Why didn't you go to the police?"

"I am the police! Frank was the police, too. He told me he'd get me out of the jam I was in, so when they did that sweep and picked up people involved in a big drug ring that included cops, I thought he'd made good on the promise. I figured the feds were going to clean house and it wouldn't be long before they exterminated all the rats. Then last night these guys came looking for me. I recognized one of them—one of the guys Toby told me left those bruises on him."

"Name, please," Laura said in such an abrupt tone, I glanced at her. "I said please." She was speaking to me. Ellison must have figured another mob moll was on his case since Laura appeared as though she might spring across the table and throttle him.

"Mik. His name is Harry Mik. He's a big guy with a nasty temper. You don't want to get on his bad side. He wasn't alone—he had a hulking pal with him. I can't tell you his name because I don't know it. Fortunately, I saw them before they saw me."

"A black man?" Kim asked. Ellison nodded.

"Okay, so what happened today?" I asked.

"I spent the night in a crummy motel trying to make sense out of what was going on. Early this morning, I tried to pay Frank a visit even though I'd heard rumors he was on the take, too and scored big stealing money that should have been turned in as evidence. I didn't believe it. When I got to his house, though, there he was, walking out of his house with Harry Mik and his pal who had made that house call last night! I didn't stop. When I came back later, I was too late. Frank was gone. His safe was empty—no money—no ledger pages. Just idiot boy, Keith, left holding the bag."

"How do you know Mik and his pals weren't at Frank's house to cause him trouble since you're so sure that's what they had in mind for you last night?" He scowled at me in disgust.

"A couple of the guys with Frank were laughing. I don't think that's what would have happened if I'd answered my door, do you?"

"So, is that when you decided to rip Frank's house apart?" I asked.

"At first I was too angry to think straight. I didn't know what to do. I called work to see if anyone had been looking for me. I mean, what if my buddy, Frank, and those goons were waiting to grab me?" I shook my head not sure I believed a word he was saying. Ellison ignored me and went on with his tale of woe.

"I made up an excuse about why I wouldn't be in the office today. Then this call came in that a person had been reported missing—no name, nothing about being a cop, but I immediately recognized the street address. I drove back to Frank's house, parked down the street, and watched. I waited for another dispatch with more information about what was going on—nothing!"

"What did you make of that?" I asked, wondering where he was going with this and wanting him to get to the point.

"That there's a cover up going on or a set up in the works—with yours truly as the fall guy. When I first got to Frank's house, Rikki Havens was talking to Frank's kid. I could tell the girl was upset, but no one had called an ambulance or reported a kidnapping. I heard the B.O.L.O. go out a few minutes later describing the make and model of the car Frank got into with his good buddies. I figured Frank had taken a hike, his kid was hysterical, and Rikki Havens was covering up for him."

"Why would she do that?"

"I don't know—maybe Frank was two-timing you and she's got a thing for him, too. I doubt she's in this alone, though, since it isn't just about Frank. Something's going on or Mik and the rest of the IED would be in a holding tank by now, right? Rikki is up to her eyeballs in all the secrets and lies, hiding the truth, maybe, to cover for lover boy. Why not set me up to save Frank's behind?"

I tried to ignore his insinuations that Rikki and Frank were involved in a relationship that wasn't strictly professional. Doubts nagged at me. Could it be true? Was that why he gave her the money and the ledger? Phrases from Frank's note zipped through my mind. My cheeks warmed as I recalled the sweet, intimate word he'd written. Ellison was a liar. Rikki might be, too. Out of the corner of my eye, I saw Kim slip away. The movement brought me back to my senses.

"If anyone made you look guilty today, it's you, Ellison. You set yourself up."

"Rikki got to the ledger pages before me. She can do whatever she wants to do with them, can't she?"

"What does that mean? Are you saying Rikki's a member of IED?" I asked.

16 DUNBAR'S TIP

"Maybe. No. I don't know, but there's something up with Rikki. I saw her talking to these guys who pulled up in front of Frank's house minutes after she reported trouble. Feds, if I had to guess— FBI or Homeland Security because they wore suits and the car they drove was too snazzy to be DEA or AFT. I took a few pictures on my cellphone. I had the dash cam running, too. If you want to retrieve it, be my guest."

"Where's your car?" Peter asked. "And the phone."

"I've got the phone on me. The car's in a lot where I store my RV. When I heard the B.O.L.O. sent out to find me, I got rid of the car. I borrowed a pickup truck that my friend leaves in the lot. The chatty neighbor fingered me for the break-in at Frank's house, didn't she? She went on and on about how close you are to Frank. That's when I decided maybe I had another way out if he'd given you the goods instead of leaving them in his safe for Rikki to find."

"Wrong again, dude!" Brien added.

"Like I believe you, *dude*. Not that any of you would tell me if those pages were here."

"Whatever," Brien said, shrugging. "As far as I can tell, you're out of options with the good cops and the bad cops." Ellison shut up and eyed us all once more.

"If you're not IED, are you going turn me in?"

"Why shouldn't we?" I asked.

"If you do that, I'm dead. You might as well hand me over to IED." Kim had come back. She'd gone to grab one of the photos pinned to the corkboard in Dad's office.

"Is this the man you saw with Frank and Harry Mik this morning?"

"That's him. If Harry Mik doesn't finish me off, he can do the job, don't you think?"

Peter motioned for me to step away, so we could speak in private. Well, not in private since our entourage followed, but we were out of earshot from Ellison.

"Maybe we ought to hang onto him for a while longer," Peter suggested. "Let see if he's telling us the truth about the suits who paid Rikki a visit before we arrived at Frank's house."

"It could be in our interest, and Frank's, to keep him alive if it's true that IED is after him. That's giving him the benefit of the doubt that there is such a thing. We could turn him over to George Hernandez, but that'll put George in a bad spot, and he won't be able to keep him long without filing charges. Once he does that, both the good cops and the bad cops will know where Ellison is," Jerry added. I nodded as Kim weighed in.

"Hanging onto him will give us a chance to ask him more questions depending on what we learn after we check him out. His phone should tell us where he was when he called his office this morning. Let's see when he last called Frank and who else he's been calling in the past few weeks when he was such a good cop and turned over the ledger pages to Frank. If he only gave Frank a few pages from the ledger, why didn't he act surprised or confused when you accused him of trying to get his hands on the entire record book?" Kim asked.

"Good point. He didn't ask me 'what ledger' once in indignant innocence which appears to be his favorite tone when he's not flat out acting like a jerk," I replied.

"Once we review the pictures on his cellphone, we'll know if we need to retrieve the dash cam from his car or do more digging elsewhere to find out who paid Rikki a visit so soon after Frank went missing."

"Okay, let's keep him overnight. Where should we put him, Bernadette?"

"In Anastasia's doghouse, if we had one. I don't like having this guy in the house. He's a maleante if I ever saw one. Nobody does what he did to Frank's place or comes after you unless he's off his rocker or breaking bad."

"He was plenty loco to think he could get past the security here. He wouldn't have gotten as far as he did if Peter hadn't decided to dangle you like a hunk of cheese in the mousetrap he set up here." Tommy popped a bite of cheese into his mouth. Ellison's arrival had interrupted the food break. Fueled by a post-adrenalin blood sugar crash, the forks were flying. My stomach growled as I eyed the plate of food Tommy held.

"My crud detector's wailing and it's not just because he came after me with a gun. He's dirty. I just can't figure out how," I said. "While we hang onto him, let's do as Kim suggests and figure out what's up with Sergeant Keith Ellison." We still hadn't solved the problem about where to put him. "Bernadette, if Peter's guys make sure he stays there, why don't we put Ellison in the casita?"

"Si, if he gives your guys any trouble, I've got a storage closet in the garage that will hold him."

"What about it Peter?" I asked.

"Sure. Brien can fill in if my guys need help during breaks or shift changes. We're spread thin right now with a team here, one at Don's, and a man in Perris—on top of our other clients."

"Hey, I'm happy to help," Brien said, his voice muffled as he chowed down on a salted caramel brownie.

"It's settled then. We'll revisit the issue of what to do with him again in the morning after I call Rikki. I'm going to put her on the spot about the feds and see what she says. I don't just want to know who they are, but what business she has with them." Laura had picked up a plate of food, too, and handed me one as we returned to reveal Ellison's fate to him.

"That's if you can get through to Rikki at the hospital without any problem," Laura said.

"Hospital? Was Rikki Havens in that accident—today?" The sergeant went on alert.

"Yes. You didn't know that?" I ratcheted up my crud detector to "high" as he replied.

"No—not for certain. When I drove by the wreck after leaving Frank's house, I thought it was her car. I heard the call go out about an accident. They didn't say anything about a cop in that dispatch either." He shrugged as if the subject matter no longer interested him. "By then, I had more important things on my mind like ditching my car and figuring out where to go to get away from the police and the IED."

"And you came here. How clever." I couldn't resist mocking him. Yet another coincidence that rankled. How is it he happened to be so close to Rikki when she had her accident? If he believed Rikki was part of a cover up, I could imagine the raging Sergeant Ellison shooting at her and running her off the road. I'd had enough of this guy for a while.

"Where's the phone?" I asked.

"Left pocket of my shorts." Peter helped Sergeant Ellison stand up and held onto him while I removed the phone. By the way he got out of the chair, I could tell he was paying for his wrestling match with Peter's guys. Ellison must be a desperate man not to have given up after he'd gone the first round with them. Or maybe he didn't know what he was doing after he took the punch they doled out. He'd seemed dazed and confused when he came around the corner—with a gun.

If he was telling us the truth about how those ledger pages ended up in Frank's safe, Ellison must have trusted Frank. Millie had assumed he and Frank were friends, had recognized him, and felt comfortable enough to confront him. Still, what kind of man destroys a friend's house and then goes after a woman he believes is intimately involved with him?

"Bernadette, why don't you get our guest a plate of food he can take with him, so we can call it a night?"

"Sure. Even a condemned man gets a last meal, doesn't he?" Ellison appeared to be knocked off balance once again which was fine with me. I couldn't be sure if it was the offer of food and a place to sleep for the night, or the condemned man comment Bernadette had made. It didn't really matter, but I'd like to keep him that way.

"Brien will you escort the good cop to his accommodations, please? He's had such a rough day, he must be exhausted." Confusion gave way to contempt as he reacted to my sarcasm.

"He'll take his meal on a paper plate with a plastic spoon. CJ's on first watch. Make sure you and CJ search him—and clear the room of sharp objects. We don't want him to get any lame ideas about trying to develop his shiv-making skills before he goes to prison." Suddenly, Peter's phone beeped. He checked the call and went on alert.

"I've got to take this," he said as he dashed from the kitchen to take the call.

When Peter returned moments later, Ellison had a plate of food in his bound hands as Brien led him onto the patio where CJ was waiting. I relaxed as the glass sliders closed behind them. The air in the room felt lighter, as if Keith Ellison's presence had weighed it down or worse—tainted it somehow.

"What's going on?" Tommy asked as Peter returned. He was up on the balls of his feet in his eagerness to hear who'd called.

"George Hernandez said he's been trying to call you for over an hour, Jessica. I told him we've been busy dealing with an uninvited guest and you'd call him about it in the morning. Anyway, guess who he's got in custody?"

"Who?"

"Jimmy Dunbar. George decided not to wait until morning since the guy's name was on Frank's list. Dunbar didn't need much persuading to spill his guts. Frank's disappearance and Rikki's accident have spooked him. He tried to play one round of 'let's make a deal' before George scared the hell out of him."

"How did he do that?" Bernadette asked. "George can be grumpy, but he's a marshmallow."

"Only when you're waving a plate of cookies under his nose," I snapped. "Did he threaten Jimmy Dunbar?"

"Yeah—threatened to keep him for a few hours and then give him a police escort home."

"A perfect way to make him look like a snitch."

"You've got it, Kim." Peter remarked. "Here's the scoop. After an hour or so of playing games, Dunbar admits he was asked to search Don's office for a ledger."

"By whom? Why would he agree to do it?" I asked.

"Dunbar likes to gamble, and he owes 'some people' money. George says the bookie who called Dunbar offered to forgive his debts if he came up with the ledger. He says he not only went through Don's office, but a locker at work, his patrol car, and even his personal car when he drove it to work last week."

"And came up empty," Kim noted.

"Yep. That's another reason he decided to tell his story to George. The offer of incentives turned into threats last week. The bookie took him aside at the casino and suggested he'd better get creative and find the ledger before Internal Affairs caught wind of his problems," Peter said.

"That must have made him a little anxious. Did the bookie say what he meant by 'creative?'" Jerry asked.

"No, but Dunbar told George his bookie was sporting one hell of a shiner, so he took that to mean he ought to do 'whatever it took' to find that ledger."

"Whoa! Don's lucky his house didn't get the crowbar treatment." Brien had hustled back after delivering Ellison to the casita. I'd heard him whisper, "What'd I miss?" to Kim when he bolted back inside where we were talking. Apparently, she caught him up quickly.

"Maybe Ellison was given similar marching orders," I said.

"That's a possibility if dirty cops killed Toby Foster because they found out he'd taken pages from the ledger. It wouldn't have been much of a stretch to tag Ellison as one of the likely recipients of those pages. Other members of the police force must have known the sergeant was one of Toby Foster's contacts."

"Maybe useless information IED gave him to pass along to the police," Kim suggested. "Until he decided to turn them in after they roughed him up."

"I wonder who kept the ledger, don't you? What kind of accountant leaves something like that lying around where low-level dealers and informants can get to it?"

"One who's acquired a drug habit that's getting worse," Laura said. "I'm sure you don't mean accountant in any professional sense. Members of the cartel might use a pro, but we don't know for sure the ledger was being kept by cartel members, do we?"

"Estupenda, Laura!" Bernadette exclaimed. "Maybe the accountant is someone in IED! Why wouldn't this group of maleantes keep records to use against each other?"

"A dirty cop's club with an organization that includes a position as blackmailer-in-waiting," Tommy said. "Makes sense to me." I glanced in the direction of the casita.

"Can I nominate Sergeant Ellison as blackmailer-in-waiting? Somehow, that fits his character much better than the story he's told claiming he was a good cop trying to help an informant. I believe him when he says he hoped Frank could get him out of a jam."

"I could believe that if his IED friends found out what he was doing. He could have torn those pages out and given them to Frank hoping to hang onto the rest of the ledger for more insurance," Brien added.

"That doesn't fit with the explanation Frank gave Don that Jeff Baker had the money and the ledger in a backpack. How did he get it from Ellison?" Kim asked.

"That's a good question. Maybe the bookie can answer it. Did Dunbar give George the bookie's name? If he's scared enough, the bookie might be willing to come clean about who gave him the black eye and put him up to getting Dunbar to search Don's office."

"Dunbar did give George the bookie's name. He's going to pick him up tomorrow. George can ask questions that are more specific about IED tomorrow since Dunbar didn't mention the group. George says he's never heard of them."

"It could be another fabrication by Ellison! Or, since Toby Foster's name was on the list, it's possible not all the names Frank gave us are members of IED. Dunbar could be a hired hand as he claims to be."

"That's entirely possible." Peter glanced at his phone before continuing. "Here's the real news George got from Jimmy Dunbar. Dunbar claims he might know where 'some people' are holding Frank."

"No! Let's go!" I cried.

"What are we waiting for?" Tommy added.

"Hold on. Hold on. I'm working on it. Actually, Betsy's doing the legwork for us." Peter added. Betsy Stark, Peter's hardworking partner, was at a planning session for a charity event and hadn't been able to join us for dinner, a kidnapping, a murder, and mayhem.

A dynamo who grew up the hard way in the Coachella Valley, Betsy's on a mission to give back. Her roots reach way back into the Coachella Valley's history when native people were the only ones who lived here. Through her grandmother, Betsy's ancestry is, in part, Cahuillan. That had to be the reason Peter had asked for her help.

"Are you saying Jimmy Dunbar has identified the 'bingo cop' Rikki thought might be one of the guys who took off with Frank?" I asked.

"Yes, although he's not with the tribal police. He's a member of the Hemet police force, one of Jimmy Dunbar's colleagues before he transferred to Palm Springs late last year. The deal is that Gavin Eckhardt moonlights in security at a tribal casino in the area." I sucked in a gulp of air.

"Eckhardt's on Frank's list!" His photo was among those pinned to the corkboard—one of the black officers.

"And, Ellison I.D. him for us as the big man who got into the car with Frank this morning."

"The place Jimmy Dunbar's talking about is in a neighborhood on reservation land not far from the casino where Eckhardt works."

"How does he happen to know about that?" Kim asked warily.

"George says Dunbar saw Eckhardt chatting with his bookie and followed the two of them as far as he could by car, before a set of gates barred him from entry onto the reservation. Then, he parked, and on foot slipped around the gate arm. He searched the neighborhood until he found Eckhardt's car. That was after his bookie had offered him the debt forgiveness incentive, but before he showed up with the black eye and threatened him. Dunbar says he visited the place several times after that and saw at least a couple of other people he recognized as police officers going in and out of the same house. He mentioned Harry Mik by name."

"That guy is everywhere, isn't he?" Jerry asked.

"Apparently, his reputation precedes him, since Jimmy Dunbar told George that Harry Mik's not a guy you cross and live to tell about it."

"So, why can't we park and walk around the gates like Jimmy Dunbar did?" Tommy asked.

"Since we're not sure who to trust, I thought we should check out Dunbar's claims by asking Betsy to use her ties. I'd rather have someone she trusts check out the place first rather than barge in there. We don't want to get shot or create a situation in which they shoot Frank and take off—if Dunbar's right and they're holed up in there." I sighed.

"I wish I could work around your logic, but one encounter with a gun-happy bad cop's enough. Your point about putting Frank at risk matters even more to me than worrying about my own neck."

"Besides, we don't have any legal authority to ask for access, unless we get George involved," Laura said.

"Betsy claims we might have a better chance than the police to get in there and look around under the circumstances. Our desire to check on the wellbeing of a friend could be more compelling than concerns about criminal activity. If there's been a crime, then the tussling will begin about how to handle the matter given the jurisdictional issues it could raise. In the meantime, George didn't wait to speak to us. He's watching the main entrance and exit to the reservation. If he spots the van or anyone else leaving the area, he'll pull them over once they're on the public roadway."

"That's dangerous for him to do, isn't it?" Kim asked. "If IED exists, the desperado part of their dirty cop club name is real enough."

"He's not alone. George has hand selected two officers to help and recruited several of his retired buddies to set up roadblocks in both directions leading away from the reservation and casino to check passing vehicles, just in case someone slips by."

"How will we know it's safe to go in there?" Laura asked.

"Betsy started at the top, contacting her friend, Rosie, who's the most senior member of the tribal council. She has a nephew who's got old-school skills as a tracker, and Betsy's going to ask Rosie to have him check the place out for us. If there are people in there with weapons, he'll know it."

"Then what?" Tommy asked.

"We'll have to come up with a plan to stage a raid—most likely with the help of the tribal police."

"I didn't know I'd need my camos. Should I go get them?" Tommy asked.

"Dibs on the night vision goggles!" Brien exclaimed.

"No camos. No night vision goggles!" I snapped. Tommy's bottom lip poked out and Brien adopted a forlorn expression. I didn't fall for the whipped puppy tricks they pull on me when they don't get what they want. "What happens if the place is empty?" I asked.

"Betsy will request permission for us to check the place out if it's not occupied. If Dunbar's telling the truth, something's been going on at that location. If Harry Mik's been there, maybe he left evidence of his presence behind that could tell us where they are now."

"That's good thinking, Peter. Maybe we can find clues that Frank was there, too." Bernadette was raring to go despite the fact it had been such a long day and she was almost twice my age. I've never figured out the secret to her vitality. She's told me her perpetual hopefulness stems from her faith. Faith that was put to the test at a young age when the man she loved disappeared.

Peter had given her the location of the neighborhood and Kim peered at the maps on her phone.

"It's not anywhere near the back routes I've been checking that led from the murder scene on I-215 to Perris. I've focused on north and southbound routes, not any headed west. I'll do that and see what route the van might have used if that was their destination."

"Back routes would have been a better bet to avoid detection, especially once the B.O.L.O. went out," Jerry said.

"That's a good point. Did George ask Dunbar if he ever saw a white van parked in the neighborhood?" I asked, looking for more reasons to feel hopeful we'd found Frank.

"I don't know, but Dunbar wasn't anywhere near there today anyway," Peter replied.

"Okay, well, I wish we could tear out of here. The good news is that we may only need to find one more of the four men who left with Frank this morning. Let's get back to work while we wait to hear from George or Betsy."

"I'm at it already," Kim said. "We've not only found our bingo cop and the other back seat passenger in the car, but I've got a picture of him with Barney." She passed around the photo of a middle-aged black man in a red baseball cap. He towered over the smaller man. Randall Roberts also wore a red cap.

"Only one more to go," I said. "Let's see if we can find our fourth man who was driving the car."

17 MIDNIGHT RAID

The call came in an hour later. By then, we'd gone through dozens more photos. Kim's idea was a good one. We used the names of the three officers we'd identified to find pictures of them on social media—personal photos as well as photos of official events, training sessions, meetings, and celebrations involving police business.

We identified several other suspected members of IED using the old "birds of a feather" angle that social media facilitates. In the photos of the known culprits, we often found names for their associates. Some had initials that matched those on the ledger pages Ellison claimed to have given Frank. Even though identifying those other cops wasn't our primary aim, I was grateful Peter had photocopied those pages before we'd turned them over to Rikki. When the phone rang, we were all ready for something that felt like a more active pursuit.

With the dreadful day coming to an end, instead of calling it a night, we hit the road. The reservation wasn't in Hemet but another half hour away. We were all too wired to be sleepy. Our emotions ranged from anxious to excited to a hopefulness that bordered on giddiness.

"Don't get your hopes up," Peter cautioned before we left. "According to Betsy's friend, the place is unoccupied. It's not only empty, but appears to have been cleaned out pretty well according to Rosie's nephew." I felt disappointed, but at least he hadn't found a body.

"We understand. That's why we get to go along, right girl?" Tommy asked Anastasia as we prepared to leave. "It's a midnight raid by the Cat Pack and their wonder dog!"

It was past midnight when we arrived at the reservation. George Hernandez and the officers staking out the entrance to the reservation flashed their headlights as we turned onto the blacktop roadway leading onto reservation land.

Coyotes yipped in the distance as we pulled over and opened the doors of Peter's SUV. We picked up Betsy and her friend, Rosie, after they'd opened the gates that closed again once we drove inside. The lights were still blazing at the casino not far from us. I was surprised by how little traffic we'd encountered even when we drove past the casino. There was no movement at all as we rolled slowly along the streets in the sprawling, quasi-rural residential neighborhood.

Rosie was silent. When we'd caught the two women in our headlights, the tableau was a study in contrasts. Betsy at six-foot-two inches tall towered over her tiny companion. Rosie had to be shorter than Bernadette, who doesn't quite reach the five-foot mark. Betsy wore a professional-looking pantsuit while her companion was dressed in an ankle-length skirt and a short-sleeved blouse. A necklace and bracelet made of large beads clanked as Rosie climbed into the front passenger seat. When Betsy had taken her seat next to me, she introduced Peter, Bernadette, Laura, and me to the woman who'd insisted on coming along as our escort despite the late hour.

"And that's Anastasia," Betsy added, pointing to our canine companion who occupied the third seat in our row.

"It's nice to meet you, Rosie," Bernadette said from the third row of seats behind me. "Thank you for coming out in the middle of the night to help us find out what's happened to our friend."

"I'm happy to help friends of a friend help a friend," she said, chuckling quietly. I doubt I'd be as chipper if someone had asked me for such a favor—even if the request had come from a woman as wonderful as Betsy Stark.

"He must be a good friend for so many of you to be out looking for news about him in the middle of the night." She glanced in the side mirror as it caught the reflected image of an SUV following us. Jerry drove that one, with Tommy riding "shotgun." Brien, who usually claims that seat, hadn't objected when he'd slid in next to Kim.

"He is," several of us replied almost simultaneously.

"We must find him," I said almost in a whisper... not adding "before it's too late."

The road ahead was dark except for the beam of our headlights. The moon cast enough light that I could make out the contours of fences and structures bordering the blacktop road. When Rosie had buckled herself in, she'd leaned over and shut off the air conditioner. She rolled down her window and Peter did the same. Anastasia whined just a little, so I rolled hers down too. She poked her nose out as far as she could while strapped into her harness.

With the windows open, I could hear the crunch of our tires as we rolled over gravel at the edge of the narrow road. A dog barked from a few streets over, and crickets chirped. The cool breeze that swept through the SUV as we moved along carried odors of flowers and soil, mixed with what could have been paint or lacquer.

In the pale moonlight, I caught a glimpse of a swing set in one yard. An empty swing swayed in the breeze as we passed. Across the street, a window was open, and I heard a television announcing some new and improved product. An owl hooted. I hoped we knew what we were doing.

No one spoke when Rosie signaled for Peter to turn right. All the homes on the street were pitch dark, except for the one we intended to visit. As we stopped in front of the house, the street was empty. Peter climbed out of the driver's seat and carefully closed his door, so it latched almost silently.

Suddenly, the door to the house opened and light spilled out enshrouding the figure of a man as he stood in the doorway. Rosie waved. By the time she opened her door, Peter and the young man who came from the house were both there to help. She reached for Peter, who picked her up and placed her on the ground.

"Betsy told me you're even stronger than she is. I had to test you," she chuckled again. "Hello, Nick. These are my friends who have lost one of theirs. This one is lost, too, now without him." Rosie pointed to me when she made that last statement. I'm not sure I felt lost, but I was well aware of the gaping hole Frank's absence had created. Nick gazed at me with the same piercing dark eyes his Auntie Rosie possesses. They were filled with compassion like hers, too.

"Please, come with me, and watch your step—the sidewalk is jagged here and there." Anastasia, who'd been so happy with the window open while we were moving, whimpered not to be left behind. "Go ahead and bring her along." Nick said in a quiet voice, but not a whisper. The houses on either side of the one in front of us were set a good distance apart, and on large lots. Perhaps that's why he didn't find it necessary to whisper.

I freed Anastasia from her car seat and put her on her leash. We had to hurry to catch up with the crowd moving into the rambling stucco and wood structure. A lamp was on in the sparsely furnished living room. The odor of tobacco and booze hit me.

"Several men were in here recently," Nick said. "I saw them, but I wasn't surprised because they visit often."

"Are you saying no one lives here full-time?" I asked.

"I can't say for sure, but I don't think so. If we need to do it, I can ask the landlord. Mostly, they came here on weekends. They had friends with them—laughed a lot—smoked, drank, and ate. There's a fire pit out back where they cooked out. Sometimes they watched movies or played card games." I wondered how he knew so much. Had he peered in at them through the windows? I searched the room around me. Nick's description of the activities that went on here made sense. In the low light, the room screamed "man cave." I can't ever remember seeing another room in which I'd seen two double-recliners. The recliners and a large sofa were all arranged to view a flat screen TV mounted on the wall.

Even in the light of a single lamp, I could see that the coffee table was stained with rings from cups. Dark stains marred the surface, too—I guessed they were cigarette burns. As I strained to inspect the room more carefully, the overhead lights came on.

"You need to make sure you can see if your friend was here,

even though he's not here now." She reached out and patted Anastasia on the head, speaking to her in a language I didn't understand. Anastasia appeared to grasp something in her tone if not her words. She stepped closer to Rosie. "I told her to help you find your man." I blushed under her gaze.

"Nick," Betsy asked. "Have you seen this man when you were around here?" He took the phone she offered him and peered at the photo.

"He could have been here a few times, but he's not a regular."

"A few times," Laura whispered under her breath, putting words to my fear that Frank had insinuated himself into this pack of wolves. I couldn't bring myself to consider the possibility Rikki had raised that he was one of them.

We fanned out at that point rather than stumble all over each other. Teams searched the rooms—kitchen, bathroom, and three bedrooms, as well as the large living room. Peter, Brien, and Nick went outside to check the grounds around the house, including a storage shed and a carport.

The place had been cleaned out well. No clothing, food, or trash remained in the house. The beds had been stripped and the medicine cabinet in the bathroom was empty. If someone had lived here or even visited on a regular basis, that didn't seem to be the plan in the future.

It wasn't spotless, but it had been swept and wiped down—we all wore latex gloves to avoid leaving our prints behind, but someone had put in at least some effort to make finding old prints difficult to do. They'd been in a hurry, though, and had overlooked a few things.

A small bag of drugs was taped to the underside of the toilet tank in the bathroom. A few casino coins were at the back of a drawer in one of the bedrooms. In others, we found a matchbook from a men's club in LA and a few coins. Nothing that gave us anything to go on, although Kim noted the name and phone number for the men's club once the matchbook was stowed in a clear plastic evidence bag.

"Look what we found," Peter exclaimed as he and Nick rushed in from a back door in the kitchen. Brien was a step behind them.

Peter dumped the contents of a black plastic garbage bag onto a counter in the kitchen. It was a bag of cellphones. The batteries had been removed from them—even the newer ones that had to be dismantled to do that. Kim's gloved hands flew as she organized the pile of phones trying to match phones and batteries. My heart skipped a beat.

"That's Frank's phone! He was here—today!" I exclaimed. He had it with him when he was with us at our celebration last night."

"Disabled. Which explains why we couldn't use it to track him once we realized he was gone," Peter offered.

"Some of these are cheap burner phones, but these are personal cellphones—five of them. Let's try this." Kim picked up one of the batteries and popped it into Frank's phone without completely reassembling it. The phone came on immediately.

"Marlowe," I said when the request for a passcode came up. Frank and I love noir films. Raymond Chandler's Phillip Marlowe character is Frank's favorite classic movie detective. Kim typed it in and we had access to all Frank's calls.

"Someone must have been in a hurry. They should have removed the SIM cards and destroyed them," Kim added as she quickly tried to reinsert batteries into phones.

"Or tossed this bag in someone else's garbage can. It was sitting right on top of all the beer bottles," Brien added.

I'd let Anastasia off her leash. She'd stood up with her front paws on the counter—something she never did at home. The curious pooch must have wondered what we were all so excited about. I was astonished when she reached out and pawed at a phone—Frank's phone! I grabbed her quickly before she could knock it onto the floor.

"Uh oh, Anastasia's going to be a suspect if they pick up that pawprint and match it to her," Tommy said. "What a smart girl to know which phone belongs to Cousin Frank." Anastasia basked in the praise.

"This could be a gold mine," Laura exclaimed.

"Or a sink hole given how much time it takes to figure out the passcodes on the other phones," Jerry added.

"Not everyone uses a phone that requires a passcode," Kim snapped as she tried another phone. "Dang!"

"No, some use facial recognition or a fingerprint." Jerry remarked as the request popped up.

"Let's try this older model. Yes! Just as I told you, some phones don't require any passcodes at all—see?" Kim held up a phone and scrolled through the photos on a phone that soon revealed the identity of the owner.

"Well, what do you think about that?" We gasped as she held up the phone with a man's smiling face displayed on it. We had found Randall Roberts' missing cellphone. Betsy turned to Rosie and Nick and explained what this meant.

"This phone belongs to a dead man who was with Frank and some other men earlier today. We need to make sure this phone gets taken into evidence in a proper way to get justice for Randall Roberts."

"I know. I watch all those cop shows on TV—chain of custody, right?" Rosie asked. "Call your friend who's sitting out on the road. He can do it, can't he?" Betsy nodded. Then Rosie spoke to her nephew.

"Nick, go open the gate and show the police officer how to get here." I was so grateful that I hugged Rosie. Peter called George to explain what we needed him to do.

Kim was scrolling through the photos on Randall Roberts' cellphone. She stopped when she got to a photo where Officer Roberts was receiving an award. Roberts and another man stood encircled by men sitting on metal folding chairs. The room in which they sat was nondescript, like a meeting room you could find in most any hotel or community agency. Harry Mik sat behind them and to his right was a man whose photo was already pinned to our wall—another of the men Frank had named. This man was clapping. He wore a signet ring on one hand.

"I bet we just found our driver. It's Walter Jenkins and he's wearing a ring like the one Millie saw as the car passed her. This can't be another coincidence, can it?" I asked.

"Uh, I doubt the ring's a coincidence. Walter Jenkins may not be our driver, though. Look closer." Brien pointed at Harry Mik. He held his hands at a different angle, but it appeared that he wore a ring, too. We all gathered closer to Kim trying to get a better look as she flipped to a second photo of the event. Many of the men in the photo wore those rings! Several other faces were among those on the wall of the situation room.

"What do you know? It's a cloak and dagger meeting of the dirty cop club and they're all wearing their secret decoder rings." Tommy followed that comment with a few bars of what vaguely reminded me of the James Bond theme song.

"Randall Roberts is getting his—see?" Bernadette was right. There on the podium next to the master of ceremonies was an open box with the ring still in it."

"I'm going to send the photos to my email address, so we can take a closer look. In fact, I should pull his contacts and recent phone calls too, shouldn't I?"

"From Frank's phone, too," I added. "Who knows when we'll get the call list Rikki promised to share with us from his provider?"

"If we could take these with us, I bet Peter has a data extraction tool that could lift the information from all the phones, and then we'd know who our driver was in a flash."

"I do, but let's see what we can work out. Most police departments have those tools now, too. Grab the info you want to work on right away from Roberts' phone and whatever Jessica wants you to retrieve from Frank's phone. We need to ask George what he wants to do. The data extraction won't take long. Mining it will take longer—but we ought to be able to confirm the names of this crew right away."

"What about George being able to keep this under wraps since it appears Tommy's zombie apocalypse of dirty cops wasn't a complete exaggeration?" Laura had an anxious, worried expression on her weary face.

"I may have a solution to that, too. The feds could pick these up from George and do the data extraction. I've gotten a little feedback from my initial inquiries about what's going on at the federal level. DEA and Homeland Security are looking deeper into the dirty cop business. My contact assures me it's a local problem—no dirty fed cops. Off the record, they're as interested as we are in getting their hands on this group of men. If they find something that will help us get to Frank, I believe my friend will let me know. Not that he was open with me about why they're so willing to cooperate. The person who spoke to me also admitted they're still tying up loose ends after an operation in this area. I took that to mean the French Connection, but he didn't say that or mention Frank or anyone else by name."

"The dirty cop club with links to a Mexican drug cartel must pose risks to border security, regardless of who's involved. I can't imagine why they wouldn't be concerned about the two dozen men in Randall Roberts' photo who've sold their souls to fatten their wallets. Maybe more than that if they can find the ledger and figure out who's on the take. If they're willing to kill low level drug dealers and fellow officers, why not sell out their country?" That was as close as Jerry had ever come to a tirade. The quiet, level-headed one, he was always at the ready to coax Tommy down from a rant.

"DHS is in this. While we were waiting to find out what's going on here, I called and asked my friend if DHS could have sent someone to meet with Rikki Havens this morning. 'They could have,' was his response. George will be here in a few minutes. We'll work this out. In the meantime, make sure you get what you think we need right away. The feds may be willing to let this play out long enough for all the rats to reveal themselves. We don't have that luxury when it comes to finding Frank."

I thought we'd had all the surprises we were going to get for one night, but Anastasia must have taken Rosie's command to help us find Frank to heart. I sprang into action when I heard her yip from the 'man cave.' I dashed in there concerned she might have hurt herself or spotted a bug we'd disturbed as we searched the area. Anastasia was digging furiously at a couch cushion. I held her by the collar, pulling her back a little and peered at the cushion. Nothing. I was glad we hadn't missed bloodstains or something equally disgusting or disheartening. The moment I released her, she started up again!

"What is that dog doing?" George asked as he entered the house. I almost jumped out of my skin. The detective hadn't bellowed as I know he can, but he'd spoken in a louder voice than the ones we'd been using. My alarm didn't faze Anastasia who was still digging like mad.

"Wonder dog has found something. What is it, Jessica?" Tommy rushed to my side as I lifted the couch cushion.

18 BY THE NUMBERS

I almost missed it. I would have dropped the cushion and moved on except that Anastasia was so insistent, and whining with excitement now. Then I saw it. A wrinkled white cloth was sticking out from the crack where the sofa back and seat meet. When I freed it from the crevice, Anastasia woofed and did a perfect pirouette.

"Geez! Frank sure has faith in our ability to find the messages he leaves behind," I muttered. It was a handkerchief. Frank had pulled it, or one just like it, from a jacket pocket as he sat next to me on the patio last night. He'd dangled it in front of Anastasia and then used it to play tug of war with her before putting it away. She'd begged him to play again using every cute trick in the book. When that hadn't worked, she'd stuck her snout into Frank's pocket, pulled the cloth out, and placed it on his lap.

"I surrender," Frank had said, waving the handkerchief like a flag. Anastasia got her wish for another round of play.

"His faith is well-placed," Rosie said, interrupting my tired brain that had become lost in that happy recollection.

In the bright overhead light, my first glimpse of the ancient wisp of a woman who stood between Betsy and Nick had astonished me. Her face was laced with wrinkles that belied her advanced age and yet didn't diminish the force of her presence. I'm sure that's how she commands such authority as an elder member of the tribal council. The smile that crinkled her face now told me her happy spirit had

A DEAD COUSIN

etched many of the lines there.

"He's alive and still has reason to believe they're not planning to kill him right away," Peter said. I was puzzled at the statement. Nick understood.

"Yes. Otherwise, he would have taken a stand here," Nick said smiling in a way that, like those dark eyes, made it apparent that he was Rosie's kin.

"He left that for you," George said when I apologized for not using gloves to retrieve it. "Keep it!" He added as he saw the way I clutched it in both hands. I don't believe I could have let it go, even if he'd threatened to arrest me.

We returned home before dawn. Several of us had fallen asleep in the car on the drive home. I suggested no one leave the Rancho Mirage estate. I felt safer and less worried with the Cat Pack gathered around me. I argued they'd be safer, too, if I wasn't the only friend the legion of dirty cops might want to grab. We had plenty of room for everyone, even though we'd turned the casita into a jail cell for Ellison.

Bernadette flew into hostess mode, but Laura and I begged her to get some sleep and let us tuck everyone in. There wasn't much to do given that Bernadette always had the cleaning staff she hires keep the place "guest ready." She relented once we agreed to let her get up and fix breakfast. Before she said goodnight—which by now, in fact, was good morning—she spotted the handkerchief I still clutched in one hand.

"Do you want me to put it in the laundry for you?"

"It probably should be washed, but I'm going to hang it up like a flag in the situation room to help us keep on fighting."

"You need to sleep a little, too, querida mía. We'll all be better able to help Frank if we're alert." I knew she was right, but I was wired.

"I'll try," I promised. I kissed her soft cheek and hugged her tight.

"We're getting close now. I can feel it!" She said as she brushed my hair back, gave me a hug, and finally shuffled down the hall to her

151

en suite.

Jerry almost had to carry Tommy into the house. They'd collapsed in the room we assigned to them. Kim and Brien offered to share a room, surprise, surprise. Laura smirked as they sauntered down the hall, hand in hand; their poorly kept secret no longer a secret.

Betsy had driven her own car home from the reservation. Since Nick had taken his auntie home, Betsy arrived soon after we did. She and Peter were staying here, too. After the close call with Ellison, Peter wasn't worried for himself—or Betsy. After Sergeant Ellison's treachery, Peter preferred to stay close to the rest of us.

That left Laura and me. A nervous ninny like me, Laura was as strung-out as I was despite the lack of sleep. She'd sleep in a suite she'd used many times near mine—if she could sleep.

"I'm going to make us some chamomile tea," she announced, pulling little single cup teapots from a shelf in the kitchen. She'd spent enough time here to know where Bernadette kept the tea, too. "You go hang that flag in the situation room, and I'll bring our little teapots in there to steep."

"Thanks, Laura. I'll get to work documenting all the new information we've discovered. That'll give us a better chance of figuring out where to start tomorrow... later today... you know what I mean."

"I do, indeed," she sighed, as she filled the first little pot from a hot water dispenser.

In the situation room, I was face to face once again with the dirty cops Frank had named. I felt almost certain that Walter Jenkins was the driver, but I couldn't tell you why. Maybe his name would be found on one of the other phones we'd found, or we'd find another connection between him and Randall Roberts. Did the other dirty cops' phones contain such blatant photos of their club membership? "Dirty and proud of it," Ellison had said.

"Maybe you and your pals were a little too smug before the feds started exterminating the rats," I mumbled. "What are you up to?" I asked, speaking to them aloud as if they could reply. Anastasia, who'd followed me in here, didn't budge at the sound of my voice. She'd fallen asleep on her doggie bed that I'd dragged in here earlier. When Laura walked into the room, Anastasia opened her eyes, but didn't even raise her head.

"Did you say something?" Laura asked as she set the tea down near the chairs we'd occupied earlier.

"I was just talking to the men on our wall of shame." I reached up and quickly rearranged the photos, putting pictures together of the men who'd left with Frank—including Walter Jenkins for now. "What do you think they're doing at this point?"

"On the run, by the way they ditched their phones," Laura said, slumping into her chair as her tea steeped.

"Where to? Why go back to that house before taking off?"

"Maybe they weren't planning to run for it until one of them killed Randall Roberts. Even if they were in trouble because there's a ledger that nails them for taking bribes, there might have been a road back before murdering a fellow officer."

"I hear you, but Harry Mik already had a couple of dead informants to his despicable credit. I don't see any road that wouldn't have led straight to prison, do you?" I asked.

"No, but prison—even for an ex-cop—might have seemed better than death by lethal injection for murdering Roberts. That murder was going to get Mik, or whoever in their crew did it, plenty of attention even if no one bothered to take another look at the death of a couple of drug addicts."

"Why didn't Mik kill Frank while he was it? I agree with Peter that Frank wouldn't still be leaving breadcrumbs for us to follow if he was about to end up like Randall Roberts."

"If the killer was anyone besides Harry Mik, I'd say Roberts was executed for a serious misdeed. But Mik's a man who'd kill you if you looked at him the wrong way. Poor Barney might not have liked being mocked that way and Mik shot him for not being a good sport about the name-calling." Laura shrugged and sipped her tea.

"Mik's a sicko. I'm sure Toby Foster told Ellison the truth that Mik beat him not long before he died. If Mik got wind that Foster was tattling on him, it wouldn't surprise me to learn Mik killed Foster and staged his overdose to make it look like an accident. Killing a colleague is another matter. That would put him on the outs with the good cops. Maybe you're right and Randall Roberts had betrayed IED and he was the designated executioner."

"If I were him, I'd be scared of my dirty cop buddies after killing a member of IED unless they ordered the hit," Laura suggested.

"Even then, why not do it in a less obvious way, or just have Roberts disappear?" I shook my head as I sat down next to Laura, staring at Frank's handkerchief still held in one hand. I hadn't decided how to hang it yet, so I spread it out on the table next to me. The scent of chamomile tea calmed me as I sipped it.

"What if they were sending a message to other members of IED now that the pressures on from the feds? It could have been a warning to keep their mouths shut if Barney's loose lips caused IED trouble. We don't know what happened to the money. I suppose Roberts could have ended up with it," Laura said. "That would make Mik angry enough to shoot him."

"Maybe Barney got greedy. A few hundred thousand dollars would sure go a lot farther if you didn't have to share it. If Roberts told them he hid the money at the house, it would explain why they went there," I suggested.

"Who gets how much doesn't really matter if the stolen money was cartel money. The cartel could be calling the shots now."

"That's true, but given the disruption created by the French Connection and whatever loose ends are still being tied up, who knows where Mik would have to go to return the money?"

"I'm sure if they were making a delivery like that, their contact would have insisted they dump their phones. Since it was Frank's informant who stole the money, that could explain why he was 'recruited'—willingly or not—as one of the couriers." I wrote the number "one" on the notepad in front of me.

"Let's do this by the numbers. We've got to get a focus somehow and we need to narrow the possibilities down to a handful of scenarios. One, being that this is all about the stolen money." I wrote, "stolen money" next to the number one.

"Okay," Laura said. "Let's keep it open right now: a) that they have it and are returning it to the cartel, or b) they have it and they're headed to a safe haven."

"Like Rio?" I asked, wondering if Frank was the only one with a fake passport and open airline ticket to Brazil. Laura nodded before making another point.

"For now, you probably need to add c) they're still looking for it."

"Argh! I want to narrow this down, don't you, Laura?"

"Sure, but we can't afford to overlook something."

"Okay. Scenario number two. It's all about the ledger. That's what Dunbar says he was instructed to search for in Don's office. Ellison claims that's at least one of the reasons he was willing to destroy Frank's house. Not that he wouldn't have taken the money and run if he'd found a few hundred thousand dollars in Frank's safe. Stupid, but then Ellison's an idiot—coming here proves that."

"So far, no one seems to have a clue about where the ledger is, and the pages torn from it are in the county crime lab or evidence lockers at the Sheriff's Department where they stash contraband like money and drugs." I made a couple of notes, including "ledger pages in police custody" and then added a big question mark.

"I don't have the log sheet to confirm where the pages are. Supposedly, the only people alive who knew about the existence of those pages were Keith Ellison, Frank, and Rikki."

"Now you have to add the crime lab investigators, the keeper of the evidence log, and anyone who has regular access to the evidence locker to those in the know."

"You're right, of course. Investigations are too porous, aren't they?" I asked as I added the people Laura mentioned. "We should also include the person or persons who gave Frank assurances that this mess was going to be over for him soon. Now that we have Frank's phone info, I want to see if we can figure out who that is. Frank wouldn't have taken the ledger back from Rikki unless he planned to turn it over to someone in authority. I'm going to assume he did that when he thought this nightmare was over."

"So that makes me want to propose a third scenario. Call it broken promises or a wider conspiracy—I don't know. Is it possible that whoever made the promises to Frank started to act—or was about to act and Mik and his crew got wind of it? Ellison said he thought Frank had tipped off Mik and Eckhardt and that's why they paid him a visit. We know Frank didn't do it, but what if someone else did?"

"A double-crossing insider like Rikki, you mean?" I asked, as I added a note to the ledger scenario that Mik and Eckhardt had some sort of inside information that led them to Ellison. I wrote Rikki Havens' name under scenario number three I titled: Double-Crossing Conspirators.

"You really don't trust her, do you? If it's true that someone tried to kill her, I'd say that puts her on the 'to be executed' list."

"If someone will let me speak to her, I'll ask her in a few hours."

"What if members of IED think she's double-crossed them? Or maybe she's a double, double-crosser! She pretends to give inside information to IED while she's really gathering evidence against them."

"If she was supposed to be an insider running interference for IED, they would have expected her to return the ledger pages to them rather than place them in evidence. She would have had a difficult time doing that with us breathing down her neck," I said.

"Exactly! That's why an IED member shot at her and ran her off the road!"

"Oh, okay. Maybe." I didn't want to do it, but I noted the possibility that Rikki was posing as a double agent. "If you're right, it might explain the timing of her unfortunate accident."

"This is all so convoluted it makes my head hurt," Laura said rubbing her temples. "How can we ever know for sure who's who or who's on which side of the law? Maybe they don't know either. What if they pegged Randall Roberts for betraying them to the feds when it was somebody else?" I gulped.

"Like Frank, you mean?" I asked.

"Yes. Frank was playing a kind of double, double-crosser role given the way he went undercover."

"I hear you. Maybe Randall Roberts did betray IED. He doesn't strike me as the double, double-crosser type, but as a newbie, he might not have understood how secretive he needed to be. A chatty, small town cop with loose lips could have caused lots of trouble for himself and others." I added a note about "accidental double-cross" under scenario three.

"If he was that naïve, it might explain why he was carrying around photos of a secret induction ceremony on his un-password protected phone. Would his paranoid pal, Mik, really allow that?" Laura asked.

"No, unless he didn't know about it until he discovered them on Roberts' phone and that's what got him killed."

"If the feds got hold of those pictures, and knew what they were looking at, Barney could have taken down almost the entire membership! That's a reason to leave him on the side of the road with a bullet in his head."

"Frank would have tried to get those photos to someone who could make good use of them, and probably could have pulled it off without revealing that he'd done it."

"So why aren't all the IED members in those photos cooling their heels in jail cells all over the Inland Empire and surrounding counties?"

"I can't answer that since I've drifted into speculation rather than sticking with what we know," I said.

"That's understandable since there's so little that falls into that category. You're also right that this process is hard on the head. I have a headache now, too. Maybe it's lack of sleep." Laura drained her cup of tea and stood.

"I'm going to try to sleep for a few hours. Hopefully, I'll wake up and it will all be crystal clear." Laura opened her arms wide as she made that crystal-clear comment and then wrapped her arms around me. "You should do the same."

"I will. I'm going to read through the copies of the police reports George emailed me and then I'll take a nap." Laura arched an eyebrow as she peered at me. "A quick read, promise?"

"Scout's honor!" I gave her a lame version of the Boy Scout salute since I was too dopey from lack of sleep to remember the real deal. Laura staggered in an exaggerated way as she left the room, making me smile.

Suppose Frank wasn't forced to go with that gang of thugs? What if he hadn't extricated himself from his double, double-crosser undercover role? That would explain why he hadn't put up resistance and everything seemed so friendly when Ellison was spying on them. On the other hand, he had issued that warning to Evie.

I picked up Frank's handkerchief, hoping I'd suddenly develop the ability to discern something about his situation by holding it. Brien would know what kind of psychic ability that required—and he'd sure try to tell me. I smiled, recalling Brien's frequent malapropisms. One of his superpowers is definitely his ability to entertain us with his earnest mangling of the English language.

I opened the reports and started reading them. Boring! The next thing I knew, someone was calling my name.

"No, go away," I said. I'd picked up something from Frank's handkerchief, all right. My dreams were full of Frank. Frank laughing. Frank whispering to me. Frank with his arms around me—his hands in my hair—and his lips crushing mine. I swatted at whoever was trying to make me let go of Frank. Laughter was followed by the tantalizing aroma of coffee. I sat up, disoriented.

"Good morning, Jessica."

"What are you doing here?" I gasped.

"I should ask you the same question. Bernadette says you promised you'd sleep."

"I did." I replied and then put my head down again, resting it on my arms. In one hand, I still clutched Frank's handkerchief. Up close, I could see what looked like smudges. Then, I bolted from my seat.

"Holy sh... uh, cow!" I shouted taming my language with a priest staring at me. Father Martin jumped backward, startled by my shouting and sudden movement. Fortunately, he was no longer holding the enormous cup of coffee he'd brought me.

"Will you look at this?" I asked. Numbers were written in very small print on the hemmed edge of the handkerchief.

"What do they mean?" Father Martin asked as he took the handkerchief from me.

"I wish I knew," I said as I picked up the coffee cup. When I determined it wasn't too hot, I guzzled it.

"They don't look like Bible verses," he joked after peering at them. I was still too groggy to come up with a witty retort.

19 THE CAPTAIN'S LIAISON

Father Martin spoke again as he placed the handkerchief back on the table in front of me. "Maybe they're account numbers, passwords, or the digital location of information, although it's not an IP address."

"Why didn't Frank just tell us?"

"He must have been in a hurry. Perhaps, copying them down as he read or heard them without getting caught." That made sense. I drank more of the coffee, wondering what Father Martin wanted. Under other circumstances, I wouldn't have found his presence so irritating. That's not completely true. My "spiritual advisor" and I often go at it. Not very spiritual, I know.

"Sorry I'm so out of it. What can I do for you?"

"Bernadette called and told me what's going on. I said I'd come by and offer you my consolation and support."

"You're a little quick on the draw, Father. Frank's not dead yet." He smiled—amused not condescending. "Sorry, again. I'm on edge as you can imagine."

"A sharp edge can help you, but so can a yielding spirit." Father Martin had drifted into Catholic Zen mode. I often enjoy that since when he goes "off script"—steering away from a pedantic catechesis—I find what he has to say more intriguing. Enlightening even.

Right now, I had no time to ponder his words and search for the guidance in them. As he stood there patiently waiting for me to respond, his eyes drifted to the photos of the men on our corkboard at the front of the room.

"Are those Frank's friends?" He asked.

"I wish," I sighed. "Some of them could be. Why do you ask?"

"No reason, really. I ran into him with one of those men a couple of times—once on the street and again at the deli downtown."

"Recently?" I asked.

"Yes." Father Martin appeared a little troubled.

"What is it?" I asked.

"At the time, I didn't think much about it, but under the circumstances maybe it meant something. The first time I saw them together, they were out on the street. I waved, and Frank didn't even acknowledge me. I thought he must not have seen me. Then, last week I ran into them again. Frank and the gentleman were sitting in a booth having lunch. Frank's usually so at ease, but even at a distance I could tell he was uncomfortable. He kept glancing around, even looking over his shoulder. I was almost certain he'd spotted me, but he didn't smile or nod, so I went to the table to say hello."

"And?" I asked as he paused, his eyes idly glancing at the items on the conference table we were using in the situation room.

"I sometimes expect to make people nervous—priests are like cops—they evoke existential guilt." I nodded hoping he'd get to the point. "Frank introduced me politely, but I felt he was anxious for me to leave. I also couldn't help noticing that just as I joined them, he passed something to the man with him."

"Did you see what it was?"

"Yes—he'd covered it with his menu—but I knew what it was. I'm old enough to have used one just like it. It was a ledger. One that might have pages in it like those," Father Martin said, pointing to the pages spread out on the table.

"Will you point the man out for me—or do you remember his name?"

"William Mackintosh," he said, walking up and poking at the picture of a man standing just behind Captain Kenneth Humboldt. Mackintosh wasn't one of the names on Frank's list. Nor had we found anyone with his initials in the ledger pages in our possession. Was there a connection between Mackintosh and Humboldt? Had Mackintosh passed the ledger along to one of the men on Frank's list? I felt sick and it had nothing to do with the fact that I'd downed twenty ounces of coffee on an empty stomach in less than ten minutes.

"Jessica," Laura said excitedly as she dashed into the situation room. "Hello, Father Martin. I'm sorry to barge in. Am I interrupting something?"

"Father Martin just showed me the man to whom Frank may have given the ledger we're missing." Father Martin turned his head in a quizzical way. "I wish I could say more, but I don't want to risk bearing false witness against anyone or allowing conjecture to pass as fact. Once Frank is back, we'll have a celebration and we'll fill you in on all we know then. Please pray for us, will you?" I said quite suddenly with an ardor that appeared to take Father Martin by surprise. Me, too.

"Night and day," he replied as he reached out and embraced me awkwardly. Then he said a lovely blessing, made the sign of the cross, and left the room.

As soon as he stepped out, members of the Cat Pack filed in. Bernadette carried a tray of food and beverages, took one look at me, and stopped.

"Chica, you're a strange color. Did something happen or are you upset about Rikki?" She asked.

"What about Rikki?" I asked

"I haven't told her yet," Laura said. "Rikki's gone. Carmel called me as soon as she reported for duty at eight. No guards. No Rikki. No information about where she went—just that she was whisked out of there by an ambulance around the time we got home." I was shaking from too much stress and coffee and too little sleep.

"That's just great! Now what?" I asked.

"To begin with, you need to eat something. No more coffee, but I'll pour you a glass of water." Bernadette set the tray down on a side table in Dad's office.

"What was that about Frank giving someone the ledger?" Laura asked.

"I don't know it for a fact, but the timing's right, so it's possible we've found the person who assured Frank everything was going to be all right." I explained what Father Martin had said about bumping into Frank less than a week ago, nervous as a cat and handing the ledger to William Mackintosh." Kim slipped into her seat and began typing.

"Why was Frank so nervous if he was handing the ledger over to someone with the authority to fix things and clear his name?" Laura asked.

"Maybe he had to turn it over before he got those assurances. That would have made me crazy nervous," Kim remarked.

"If Mackintosh had to get those assurances from someone else, let's hope it wasn't Humboldt," I said. "Frank wasn't the least bit nervous by the time he joined us Friday night. Whatever went wrong happened after that—maybe he didn't even realize it until Mik and the others showed up at his house bright and early on a Saturday morning."

"It ought to ease your mind to hear that Mackintosh and Humboldt are in different units. Mackintosh is a community liaison." Kim projected a picture of the organizational chart. Then she printed out a photo of Mackintosh that Jerry picked up to post on the corkboard.

"Angel or devil?" Bernadette asked as she peered at the photo. She was holding an empty glass in one hand and a pitcher of water in the other.

"I can't answer that. I don't think it's a good idea to call Mackintosh and ask him to answer that question, do you? Rikki might be able to tell us if we could be certain she's not in league with the devil. Oh yeah, and if she hadn't disappeared from the hospital in the middle of the night after being shot at and driven off the road. That's what the accident report says, by the way. One of the witnesses claimed a car banged into her and then took off."

"Did the police get any information about the car?" Jerry asked.

"Yes, it was reported stolen and found a short time later in flames!"

"What about what Carmel told us—someone shooting at Rikki? Did that really happen?" Laura was chewing on her bottom lip as she waited for me to reply.

"There's no witness account, but George says a friend told him that when they examined Rikki's car, they found a bullet hole in the passenger side door."

"What are we going to do?" Tommy wailed. "Now there are two people missing."

"We do have the numbers Frank left for us," I replied.

"Numbers? What numbers?" Several Cat Pack members called out.

"That was going to be my big news before Father Martin arrived and made his revelation about William Mackintosh. See for yourself," I suggested as I passed Frank's handkerchief to Laura. She examined the handkerchief and then passed it on.

"Could it be the secret code for their decoder rings?" Tommy quipped. I stared at him. When he made a face at me in return, I put my head down and pounded the table with both fists. "She needs sugar. I'm sure she'd prefer that came in the form of a hunk of Frank, but St. Bernadette's divine pancakes and syrup will have to do."

In mock maître d mode, Tommy went to the sidebar, picked up a plate, and set in front of me. He whipped the silver cover from it, and then bowed. The aroma was intoxicating. Tommy did an about face, took the glass of water Bernadette held out for him, turned again, and set it down next to my plate.

"Bernadette has undone herself," Brien said.

"Outdone," Kim whispered like Nancy Reagan coaching Ronnie.

"Oh, okay," he said. "These white chocolate macadamia nut pancakes are the best. Ellison agrees with me. Peter's out there negotiating with him."

"Negotiating about what?" I asked as I stuffed a bite of the pancakes into my mouth. Topped with chopped roasted macadamia nuts and whipped cream, they were dripping with butter and maple syrup. That first bite was filled with white chocolate chips that melted in my mouth. I should have swallowed quickly, but I was trying to savor the moment when Brien spoke again.

"He suddenly remembers the name of the person his informant stole those pages from, or so he says."

I inhaled bits of half-chewed macadamia nuts instead of swallowing them. I choked. Nurse Laura flew into action.

"Speak to me! Can you speak to me?" She asked. I nodded. "Nodding is not speaking." She chided. "Say something!"

"Who is he?" I asked, in a raspy voice. I slugged back almost an entire glass of water before I spoke again. "Where is he?"

"That's what Peter's trying to find out."

"He might be making it up to stay in his cushy accommodations. Now that he's had Bernadette's pancakes, he's never going to want to leave." Kim didn't smile—she was serious.

"Yeah, he could be lying. Stalling, to keep us from turning him over to the police," Jerry added.

"Who could blame him for that?" I shoved more food into my mouth as my eyes wandered back to the photo of William Macintosh. "Trust no one." Those words bounced around in my mind as I looked at the picture in which Macintosh stood behind Kenneth Humboldt. Had one or both betrayed Frank?

"I'm going to call George, thank him for the help last night, and see if he has any updates for us. I need to break it to him that we're holding Ellison and let him figure out what we should do about it."

I heard voices in the hallway outside Dad's office. Betsy and Peter stood in the doorway.

"I wish I could stay, but I have a breakfast meeting. Not that I'm going to eat a thing since I had the good fortune of starting my day with breakfast a la Bernadette. Jessica, I've told Peter this already, but

Nick messaged me that he wants you to call him. He has a friend who needs to speak to you. He says it's urgent. I've got to go. Peter can tell you more," she said as she scanned the table lined with laptops, piles of paper, and other items.

"We would have been out of luck without you last night," I said as I stood up and ran to give her a hug. I can't believe, now, how insanely jealous I was of Betsy when we were both teens and I imagined she was a rival for my beloved Bernadette's affection. "Thank you."

"I'll drop by this evening for an update about Frank's situation, but don't wait that long if you need me before then," Betsy said, as she hugged me back. Then she bent down. "Stay strong little sister," she whispered in my ear before she let go.

As she stepped out of the room, Peter swept her into his arms. He gave her a kiss that sent up a round of applause. I felt a twinge of jealousy—not of Betsy per se, but of the comfortable intimacy she shared with Peter. I yearned for Frank to be close enough to cover his face in kisses. I might not even scold him.

"What's this I hear about numbers?" Peter asked as he squeezed his enormous bulk into a chair at the table.

"How'd you hear about that?"

"I ran into Father Martin before he left. He couldn't resist sampling Bernadette's pancakes. Anyway, he was still pondering a message Frank left you—wondering if it could be a code of some kind."

"What'd I tell you?" Tommy said. "If we only had one of those rings." Laura jumped in and interpreted Tommy's babel for Peter. In the meantime, I passed the handkerchief to him.

"Father Martin said it isn't an IP address. He's right."

"Maybe it's a bank account number where Frank stashed the missing money and he wants us to get it for him. Or, what if Frank uncovered an offshore account where a dirty cop or the whole club is hiding money?"

"Father Martin suggested it might be an account number, too. I suppose they could also be coordinates of some kind. To make sense of them, though, I need to figure out what format to use." Peter used his fingers to partition the numbers. "Not DMS—degrees, minutes, seconds doesn't work. Maybe they're UTM coordinates. Can you give me a typewritten copy, Kim? I'll have my team look at them while we see if we can speak to someone who can help us determine if they're account numbers."

"As in the accountant whose name Ellison remembers right before we turn him over to the police?" I asked.

"Yes, the accountant. Not just because Ellison gave us the name. A more trustworthy source has come forward to identify the accountant."

"Who?"

"The accountant."

20 THE ACCOUNTANT

"What does that mean?" I asked. "Are you telling me you found the guy Ellison named and he's willing to come forward?"

"Not exactly. He's not being completely truthful, either. I'm sure he would gladly have sent us on a wild goose chase to delay turning him over to the police. He's in much better shape after a good night's sleep, but he's still comes across as jumpy and scheming at the same time."

"He's doing as well as we are, then—better than we are when it comes to sleep," Laura said, thumping on the table like a cat's tail switching in irritation.

"Sad, but true. I've agreed that he can stay here while we locate Scott Bender and have a conversation about his accounting practices." My eyes instantly scanned the photos and names posted.

"We don't have anyone up there by that name."

"No, we don't. He's not a cop, but a dealer. Not a street-level drug peddler like Toby Foster or Jeff Baker, but he's not a big player, either. He was Foster's supplier and it's his records Foster stole. According to Ellison, Bender started keeping records when cops he recognized kept showing up at the stash house where he picked up drugs and dropped off money. He saw them taking handouts and started taking names and keeping tabs on the amount of money paid out."

"How did that happen? Was he hiding in a closet or something? Those stash houses must have decent security," Kim asked.

"I asked Ellison a question like that, and he says he wondered the same thing when Foster told him about Bender. Foster claimed Scott Bender told him dope distribution at those stash houses was carried out in a party like atmosphere. Music and a big cookout—booze flowing. Ellison claims that's one reason he didn't believe what Foster said even after he showed up with those ledger pages."

"With cops among the guests I guess you didn't have to worry about getting busted for making too much noise," Jerry commented.

"Foxes in the hen house." Brien nodded his head up and down slowly in his knowing way.

"A hen house tucked away in a nice, upscale community with guards and gates to keep the riff-raff like Toby Foster out. Foster told Ellison that Scott Bender went on and on about the parties and the dirty cops flashing money around while they were there. Foster said it made Bender sick."

"I can understand that. The whole thing sounds like a nightmare to me," I said. "If it had been me, I wouldn't have gone back if it made me sick. Why did Bender decide to keep records?"

"Anger, maybe. Or fear. That's why Toby Foster stole those pages from his friend. He was scared and wanted Ellison or someone on the up and up in the police force to stop them from roughing him up. I'd be surprised if they weren't threatening Bender, too."

"Toby Foster sure made the wrong move when he decided to trust Ellison," Laura said.

"Well, Ellison did go to Frank," I offered.

"Who put the pages in his safe and left them there. What was that about?" She asked.

"Frank must have been working undercover by then. Maybe he wasn't sure what to do with them—especially if he was already having trouble knowing who to trust." I shook my head since I couldn't make sense of it either. "I'm surprised Frank wasn't more inclined to believe Jeff Baker's story if Ellison had told him about the trouble Toby Foster was having before he died."

"That could be why Frank was so upset later," Tommy suggested. "Don said Frank blamed himself when Jeff Baker was killed."

"I've been thinking about all of this, too," Peter added. "Scott Bender must have been Jeff Baker's supplier, too, since that had to be Bender's backpack he stole. Even when Ellison passed on the ledger pages to Frank, Toby Foster's death was being treated as an accidental overdose. I don't see anything in the stories we've heard from Frank or Ellison, or anyone else that connected the dots—not until it was too late, and Jeff Baker was killed."

"That could be it, Peter," Bernadette said. "Frank probably thought he should have seen it, Tommy, but no one did. He didn't get his hands on the ledger until after Jeff Baker was dead."

"Once he had the entire ledger, Frank didn't really need the few pages Ellison passed along from Toby Foster, did he? Maybe that's why they were still in his safe when we opened it yesterday. The bigger issue was who to trust with the ledger when it came time to turn it over. The information in the ledger has more far-reaching consequences than connecting the deaths of Toby Foster and Jeff Baker," Peter asserted.

"True. Let's see what Dick Tatum and Renee Collins come up with. It could be tough, even now, to find a link between the two deaths. It would help if Scott Bender can name names to connect the dots—especially if he can also link the killer to IED. That could be enough to get the authorities to review what evidence they have related to the deaths of Foster and Baker and identify the guilty party."

"Like Harry Mik, you mean?" Kim asked. I nodded, as Peter jumped in.

"Cornering Harry Mik is the key. Bullies like Mik are tough when they're the leader of a pack preying on weak members of the herd. Take them out of that role, isolate them, and they often cower. My guess is Mik will throw everyone under the bus to save his own neck. If we can put him in a compromising position, he'll give up every member of IED—with or without the ledger."

"So how did you find this Scott Bender character?" I asked. "If he's not locked up somewhere, how did he avoid getting arrested when they busted members of the drug ring?"

"Apparently, he was arrested. I checked. The feds rounded him up during their sweep. He was taken to the jail in Hemet. While he was waiting for the officers to book him, he got away."

"No!" Tommy shrieked. I flinched at Tommy's wailing even though I found it as impossible to believe as he did.

"There's a warrant out for him. What else is there to say?" Peter shrugged.

"A fugitive from justice, huh?" Tommy said. "Is he armed and dangerous?"

"Only if you believe the pen is mightier than the sword and he's got enough damaging evidence to hurt lots of people. Maybe not just the cops in his ledger books if they decide to turn on those higher up in the food chain who must be protecting them," Peter replied.

"He had to have had help becoming a fugitive," Kim suggested.

"If that's the case, he's got good cops and bad cops after him. I can't see any reason the bad cops would help him get out jail except to get to him before the feds did. Why isn't he dead?" Jerry asked.

"Ellison didn't say, but I'm guessing Bender somehow slipped away from IED. I asked the devious sergeant if Mik and Eckhardt paid him a visit hoping to get information about where Bender might have gone. He did that indignant denial bit—claimed he didn't stick around long enough to have that conversation."

"Scott Bender must be long gone by now."

"Ellison believes he's still in the area, Jerry. He says Scott Bender's got a sick mom and several younger siblings he supports. In fact, he got into the drug business trying to keep his mom supplied with dope."

"Oh, good grief! I've heard it all now. A drug dealer with a heart of gold. Ellison's got a future as a fiction writer to keep him busy in prison!" This would be unbelievable except that I was staring at copies of pages torn from a ledger. "Why wouldn't the bad cops have drawn him out by making a big scene dragging Mom or one of the sibs away?"

"Because the feds got to them first and put them into protective custody. Someone must have tipped them off that Bender's not just another supplier—they're after him, too."

"He's a popular guy," Bernadette snapped. "I'm guessing he'd be even more popular dead. How do we get him before los zorros do?"

"The foxes..." I said, translating before Brien could ask the question on his lips. I'm sure Zorro held an entirely different meaning for him. At any other time, it would have been interesting to hear what he had to say. Not now. He did an "aha" version of his bobble-head nod.

"Scott Bender's looking for a way out of his situation and we're on the inside track when it comes to helping him out."

"We are?" I asked. "How?"

"Betsy—and her networks. Scott Bender's mom is Native American. She's not a member of the same tribe we visited last night, but word travels fast among members of the tribal communities in this area. Rosie saw to it that word reached the accountant last night. We're about as trustworthy as anyone Bender could turn to for help."

"Are you saying Scott Bender is the friend Betsy was talking about? I don't believe I can handle another coincidence like that." Peter fixed me with his gaze.

"Yes, it's Bender. It's not a coincidence—it's Betsy. Weren't you a little surprised about how quick and easy it was to get into that community last night? Harry Mik and Gavin Eckhardt didn't just pop into Rosie Goldenthorn's life when Betsy approached her about Frank's trouble. Those men have been creating problems for some time."

"Listen to Peter," Bernadette said. "He's been living with Betsy for a while now. Besides, if this mess is such a puzzle for us— imagine how difficult it is for Scott Bender out there on his own, with no one to trust."

"To be completely honest, I had a hand in this, too. Before we left, Rosie asked Betsy a couple of odd questions—did we know anything about a book of numbers? When Nick messaged Betsy today about a friend in trouble and mentioned Scott Bender's name, I decided to have another talk with our houseguest. I brought up the accountant—not him. One thing led to another and soon the two paths converged."

"The two paths converged—ooh, I like that. This is like a movie! *The Spy Who Came in from the Cold*—or wants to anyway. Although you can hardly say it's cold."

"It is in a metaphorical sense," Brien piped up interrupting Tommy's babbling. I held up a hand, hoping to get back on topic.

"How do we get our hands on the accountant?" I asked. All eyes in the room were on Peter. Even the beady ones peering down from the wall of shame.

21 A FULL HOUSE

"If we can get Scott Bender here, we can keep him safe," I said.

"It'll be a full house if Ellison's stays where he is, too."

"True, Kim, but I can move into Jessica's room if we need a room for him. It'll be like old times when we used to have sleepovers. Except for the kidnapping, murder, creepy guy in the casita—you know what I mean?"

"Kitty-cats, I'm not worried about where to put him if we can get him this far," I said interrupting Laura. Tommy meowed. Anastasia woofed.

"I don't know how much planning we can do until you speak to Nick's friend."

"Me?" I asked Peter.

"Yes. Nick was very clear about that in his text. I suspect that's more of Rosie's handiwork behind the scenes. She took a liking to you. You can ask a few questions to determine that our mystery man is the accountant if you feel that's necessary. Then, you need to find out where he is and confirm he's ready to come in out of the cold, as Tommy so aptly put it." Tommy beamed.

"Okay, let me finish my breakfast, throw some water on my face, and then I'll call Nick and ask about his friend."

"We'll keep working on the other loose ends," Kim said. "It

would be great if we can verify that Walter Jenkins is the fourth man in the car with Frank. I also want to see what else I can find out about Mackintosh. His latest liaison assignments, for example, and see if I can find out more about his relationship with Captain Humboldt." I gave Kim a thumbs up as I shoveled food into my mouth.

"I'm not done investigating our houseguest in the casita," Tommy said.

"Great! I know we still don't have the full story on him. Peter may be getting closer to the truth with his question to Ellison about the reason for Mik and Eckhardt's visit to Ellison's home. We still don't know how he came to the attention of Mik and Eckhardt."

"I didn't see Ellison in Randall Roberts' pictures of his initiation into the dirty cop club, but I only took a quick look. I'm going over them again. I'm also going to check him out as if he's IED and search for a photo of him with the men in the car with Frank."

"That's a great idea, Tommy. I wonder how Frank chose Mackintosh to be the recipient of such a valuable piece of evidence."

"Maybe he was Frank's handler, Jerry," Laura suggested. "I'll help. I can check Frank's phone and see if there were calls made between them using the published numbers for Mackintosh. If not, maybe there's some mention on Frank's calendar about regular lunch meetings at the deli out here in the desert." Laura turned to me before speaking again.

"At least you know Rikki wasn't holding out on us by hanging on to that ledger in secret since Frank handed it over to Mackintosh."

"I know. I feel a little guilty about my suspicions—about that— not about her. I still don't believe she was in the dark about the ledger. Even if Frank didn't tell her, I can't believe she didn't peek at the contents of the package he gave her. Wherever she is, she knows more about what's going on than she shared with us and maybe could have helped us find Frank sooner. If she held out on us because she was afraid we'd let leak information, I've got news for her. This conspiracy is so full of holes—it's amazing it didn't collapse from within long ago!"

"That's exactly what's happened. Bullying, over-reaching cops, 'dirty and proud of it'—they went too far," Peter said. "In fact, it occurs to me that the cartel members who were so hospitable while hosting IED members at all those parties didn't get their money's worth out of their investment, did they?"

"True. Are you saying IED members might be in trouble with the cartel?"

"That's exactly my point. Two dead informants, missing money, rumors of a ledger—the cartel wouldn't have missed any of it. One of the hallmarks of their organization in the U.S. is that they prefer to keep it clean—run it like a business in contrast to the murderous rampages that go on in Mexico. The execution-style murder of one police officer by another won't go over well, either. If someone put out a hit on Roberts, it wasn't the cartel.

"They can't be happy about the disruption created by the sweep, although I'm sure the feds didn't bust up the ring entirely. They're probably unhappy with anyone who helped the feds do that..." I stopped before I paralyzed myself with fear not even able to utter Frank's name.

"They're also among the people who'd be happy to see Bender dead. I'm not sure how intent they are on finding him, though, since my guess is they already have the ledger—or they'll have it soon." A round of gasps went up.

"I take that to mean Mackintosh passed the ledger to someone who's making sure it gets to the cartel?"

"Yes. I doubt it would be enough to simply destroy it. Besides, if anyone's going to use it as a tool for blackmail, my money is on the cartel. To be honest, without Scott Bender's testimony, it's not that great a resource. Still, it could be useful as a way to keep shifty guys like Mik in line." Peter shrugged.

"Let's hear what the accountant has to say." I was ready to go make that call when Peter spoke again.

"Here's another bit of news—unrelated to Frank's disappearance. My associate, who's keeping an eye on Millie, took a couple of photos that were good enough to I.D. Michele Bodenheimer's 'brother.' He isn't her brother at all, but a distant cousin. The cousin from hell, given his rap sheet, although Millie's upstanding neighbor wasn't always shy about getting mixed up with him. She's got a record, too. Anyway, to cut to the chase, he's a fugitive, and we passed his name and location on to the FBI. When they went to pick him up this morning, he backed out of the garage before the door was completely open and almost knocked his own head off."

"Thanks for some good news, even if it's not related to Frank's disappearance," I said. "We've put one mystery to rest."

"And a desperado behind bars," Bernadette added.

"True. I'm going to call Nick and see if we can't move another mystery along." Peter wrote Nick's phone number down for me. I grabbed my phone and ran to the bathroom—too much coffee. When I called Nick, he picked up after the first ring.

"Nick, it's Jessica Huntington. How can we help your friend?" I asked, getting straight to the point.

"Thank you, Jessica. I wanted to ask for your help last night, but I needed to speak to Scott first." That settled a few questions buzzing around in my mind. "He's hiding, scared, and still recovering from a beating. Harry Mik and Gavin Eckhardt helped Scott get away from the Hemet jail, and then they beat him. They wanted the ledger, but he didn't have it. When he pretended to pass out, they started drinking. He waited until they were drunk and crawled out behind them. Scott couldn't run very fast, so he hid for hours before they quit looking for him, and then went to my house. He was in bad shape."

"I understand. From what I've heard about those two men, your friend is lucky to be alive. He must have you to thank for that."

"Aunt Rosie more than me. She's a kind woman and a healer." When Nick didn't speak again, I did.

"I have a kind woman here with me, too. If we can get your friend to my house in Rancho Mirage, we can keep him safe and comfortable until we sort out his problem. Peter and the men who work for him can come get him."

"I have an idea about how to get him to you. Peter will draw attention even if he comes here in the dark."

"Okay. I'll need to leave a name at the guard gate."

"Tell them it's Happy Tails Grooming Service. Anastasia will enjoy a trim, won't she?"

"That's true. She loves to be pampered!" I laughed, caught off guard by his clever strategy.

"We'll be there as soon as we can. Thank you, Jessica." I rushed back to deliver the news about how Nick planned to deliver our newest houseguest. As soon as I got the words out, I could tell something was up.

"What is it? Nick's plan's a good one, don't you think?"

"It's not that. I found a link between Humboldt and Mackintosh. They're cousins—Facebook photos." In the first photo Kim projected onto the screen in Dad's office, the two men appeared to be at a backyard barbeque. Kim switched to another photo of both men at a wedding reception.

"Not more cousins? They can't be in trouble with the law like Michele Bodenheimer and Cousin Josh—not yet anyway." I scowled at the image of Kenneth Humboldt beaming at the happy bride.

"William Mackintosh isn't in trouble with anyone. He's dead." I sat down and almost missed my seat.

"How?" I asked.

"A car accident. On a back road, there," Kim said as she pointed to a spot on the map that now filled the screen in front of us. "It's one of the routes Rikki might have taken back toward Perris." I nodded, trying to digest Kim's news.

"If Rikki got a call that a member of law enforcement was killed in an accident not far from Perris, that could explain why she left so soon after we did. Two car accidents on the same day should raise a few eyebrows."

"His accident didn't occur on the same day. He didn't have a concrete barrier to stop him and drove off the road into a stand of trees. No one found the car for several days even though his wife told the police he was missing. His accident has to arouse suspicion, though, since he was shot before he ran off the road."

"This didn't happen on the same day Father Martin ran into Frank having lunch with William Mackintosh," Bernadette added. "I called him and asked."

"It couldn't have been long after that, though, right?" I asked.

"Two days later—leaving him with plenty of time to pass that ledger to someone else," Kim responded. My phone rang. I grabbed it, hoping it wasn't Nick calling to tell us Scott Bender had a change of heart.

"It's George Hernandez. Should I come clean about the sergeant and the accountant?" I asked.

"You want to stay on his good side, don't you?" Bernadette followed the question with a directive. "Try telling him the truth!"

"Hello, George, I was just about to call you." That was true—at least I'd intended for it to be true.

"I have news for you. It appears we're now missing two detectives from the Riverside County Sheriff's Department."

"You mean Rikki Havens, right?"

"Yes, I do. You heard about it already?"

"If what you mean is that Rikki was whisked out of the Riverside Community Hospital and moved by ambulance in the middle of the night, yes. Is there more?"

"Yes. The ambulance to nowhere as far as I can tell. Did your source tell you more than that?"

"According to Laura's friend who works as a nurse at RCH, that's all the rumor mill is talking about. Since you confirmed someone shot at Rikki, I figured the feds took her to a more secure location. Peter hasn't been able to confirm that yet. We only heard it a short time ago, and we've had a few other issues to deal with in the interim."

"In addition to the uninvited houseguest Peter mentioned last night?"

"Yes. The most recent jolt is news about a roadside accident that killed a man to whom Frank may have given the ledger he told his dad about."

"No kidding? Not around here or I would have heard about it."

"No, but not more than twenty miles from Frank's house. The dead man's in law enforcement and has interesting kinship ties to a man on the list that had Jimmy Dunbar's name on it." I filled George in about Captain Kenneth Humboldt who now had a dead cousin in the family. "That's not the big news I have for you. Are you sitting down?"

"I am now. Should I warn my colleagues that I'm about to bellow at you?"

"You don't have to do that—bellow I mean—but if that'll do something for you, go for it! Here's the deal—Sergeant Keith Ellison's the man who invited himself over last night. He used a gun as an invitation to which Peter's associates responded in a most inhospitable way."

"What?" He asked. It wasn't a bellow, but close. "Did they shoot him?"

"No. I said inhospitable, not homicidal. What's more important than chewing me out is figuring out what to do about him. Plus, by the time you get here, we'll have a full house if the delivery we're expecting arrives as intended."

"Spill it," George said, in a quiet tone. I did my best to summarize all we'd learned since we saw him last night—including Ellison's story about IED and his heroic effort to help his informant who doesn't need anyone's help now because he's dead. I was almost out of breath by the time I finished updating him about the imminent arrival of the accountant.

"You've earned your calamity magnet title once again. You do have a knack for attracting trouble."

"You're in this too, now, Detective. Maybe more trouble than you realize until the feds sort the wheat from the chaff. Let's see what happens to the guest you've already got in lockup. If I were you, I'd be very careful about who knows Jimmy Dunbar's there and to whom you release him."

"I don't believe any of the officers here in Cathedral City are mixed up in this, but what do I know? I figured Don was overly suspicious after Frank disappeared. That was before I heard what Dunbar had to say. I'm still holding him, but I haven't filed any charges yet. He's not in any real hurry to get out of here, either. He could use a trustworthy lawyer—if there is such a thing."

"Hahaha. Take a jab at lawyers while we're in the middle of the worst dirty cop scandal that I could have ever imagined. Jimmy Dunbar can't afford Paul Worthington or his firm, although I still may be able to help him. My next call is to Dick Tatum."

"Why didn't I think of that? Dick's a great suggestion. He was a big help to you and Frank. Unless he objects, I'll pass his name and phone number on to Jimmy Dunbar."

"Okay, give me a few minutes, and then I'll call you back. What do you want to do with Ellison?"

"Keep him locked up for now. It sounds like he prefers that to being turned over to me or other members of the constabulary. If he remains willing to stay put, there's no reason to charge you with false imprisonment. You're a lawyer—maybe you should get him to sign a lease agreement as a temporary tenant at Cat Pack Manor."

"Hmm. That's not a half bad idea. I doubt anything Ellison signs would be worth a darn if he tries to sue me later. Right now, I'm the least of his worries. If he even hints at something like a lawsuit, you're coming to pick him up and if IED members kill him, so be it." As soon as I hung up, I realized I had two more calls to make.

"Don, it's Jessica. How's everyone holding up?" He said fine, but it didn't sound like he meant it. "I've got lots of news for you. Have you got a few minutes?" A few minutes turned into half an hour. Somehow, all the news about Jimmy Dunbar, Sergeant Ellison, and the other new creeps we'd come across raised Don's spirits. Or maybe it was finding another message from Frank.

"You're doing a great job, Jessica. Please don't take any chances you don't have to take. You had a close call with the lowlife who's living the good life in your casita. I wouldn't trust a word he says and make sure no one turns their back on him for a second."

"My sentiments exactly. Meanwhile, we'll keep at it. I'll call you again later today after we've spoken to our amateur accountant and fellow calamity magnet. If we learn anything else important—like what those numbers mean that Frank left for us to find—I'll call you even sooner."

"Thanks. The kids wanted me to tell you thanks again for getting their dad back. They've got all the confidence in the world in you and send their love. I'm going to sit here for a few minutes and figure out what sort of update to pass along to them. Evelyn and I love you, too—please be careful."

"I'll do my best. Love you all, too. I'll be back with more, soon." I hope.

22 THE DELIVERY

Scott Bender was wary as he climbed out of the van. When Nick pulled up in front of the house, I feared he'd come alone. There was no one in the passenger seat. As the SUVs moved out of the way to allow him to pull into the circular drive in front of my house, it dawned on me that there was probably plenty of room to hide Scott in the back of the van. Maybe even a place to hide him well enough if a cop had pulled him over.

I opened one of the garage doors and Nick quickly maneuvered so that he could back in—not all the way, because this bay is used for storage. Far enough, though, that he could open the back of the van without being observed by anyone who might drive by.

Scott Bender was waiting, ready to spring out of the van. He relaxed a little when he saw Nick standing next to me. Still, he searched the area around him as he stepped from the van. He was as tense as anyone I've ever seen—poised to run at the slightest provocation. When the lovely Anastasia woofed and then pirouetted, I could see the relief flow through him.

"Welcome, Scott. I'm Jessica and this is Anastasia."

"What a beautiful dog," he said and then broke into a smile. Anastasia made her move and the accountant was ours! She led him inside and I followed. Bernadette met us at the door and the aroma of bread baking enveloped us.

"Don't eat it all," I heard Nick say as he returned to the van and climbed in it. As we went into the kitchen, Nick pulled out, and I shut the garage door behind him. Bernadette ushered Scott to the morning room and placed a loaf of fresh-baked bread on the table in front of our guest.

"Help yourself, Scott. I'm Bernadette. Don't listen to Nick. You can eat as much as you want. There's more cooling in the kitchen and more in the oven." She smiled in the peaceful angelic way she often does. Scott smiled as he reached for the small plate Bernadette offered him, and then took a slice of bread. He must have been hungry—it was gone in a flash. "Do you want coffee or milk or something else to drink?"

"Milk, please." He took time to put butter and jam on the second piece of bread. "Did you find your friend, Frank?"

"Not yet. We're still looking."

"I think I might know where he is." Bernadette set a tall glass of milk in front of him just as he said that. He picked it up in hands that shook as he drained it dry. "Down Mexico way." He said as he set the glass down.

"Que?" Bernadette asked. "What did you say?"

"Mexico," Nick answered. He and Peter had come in through the front door and stepped into the kitchen just as Scott spoke those words. I pulled a chair out and motioned for Nick to sit down. Bernadette reached around to the granite breakfast bar and picked up a plate for Nick. "Tell them, Scott."

"Gavin Eckhardt and Harry Mik were drunk—even drunker than when they were at the stash house parties. They were singing a south of the border song and laughing."

"Was this the same night they helped you escape from the Hemet jail?" I asked. He nodded.

"I bet they figured the jig was up after the raid." Kim and Brien swept into the kitchen with Laura trailing after them. One of them had gasped at what they heard Scott say. He jumped at the sound and was halfway out of his seat by the time Kim finished her sentence.

"It's okay," Nick said, reaching out and placing a hand on Scott's shoulder to keep him from bolting.

"Sorry to startle you. I'm Kim, you must be Scott." Scott eyed them all and then nodded slowly. "This is Brien." Brien nodded at Nick and gave Scott a thumbs up. He couldn't speak because he'd shoved an entire slice of the inch-thick bread into his mouth.

"Hi, I'm Jessica's friend, Laura."

"We're all Jessica's friends," Tommy announced from down the hallway where he and Jerry had just emerged from Dad's office. "What's going on?"

"Scott, meet Tommy and Jerry." Laura said, making the introductions.

"Jessica has lots of friends helping her find Frank." Nick asked. "I do, too, but Scott doesn't have many. It hit him hard when Harry Mik killed Toby Foster." More gasps. From me, too, this time.

"Would you mind telling me how you know that's what happened?" I watched as Scott Bender fought for control of his emotions.

"I knew it was going to happen. Toby showed me how Harry Mik beat him. He didn't even take his ring off, and Toby had the marks from it. I told Toby to leave town, and he did, but he was using drugs, you know? When he needed more, he came back to Riverside to find me. I gave him the drugs he needed and told him to go back to San Bernardino because when I was at the stash house, Harry Mik was asking where he could find Toby. He was mad." Scott quit speaking.

"Why?" I asked.

"Because Toby told another cop what Mik did to him. These guys stick together, you know? I saw Mik talking to this other cop, and that's when he asked him 'Where's Foster?' Toby talked to the other sergeant all the time. When Toby stole those pages from my book, I didn't say anything. I hoped that if he gave them to someone, it would keep him alive. I was wrong. I was so upset, I didn't even care when Jeff stole the book later. It was hard to lose the money, though. It took a long time to save it. Then he died, too." Scott shook his head. My teeth were clamped together so hard my jaw was sending shooting pains up both sides of my head. Tommy stared at me.

"She's going to blow," he whispered to Jerry. I don't believe I've ever been any angrier. Peter spoke, choosing his words very carefully. My first impulse had been to drag Ellison's sorry behind in here and make him stand in front of Scott, but that would hurt Scott Bender far more than it would faze the liar in our casita.

"I'm sorry about what happened to your friend, Scott. We'll fix the sergeant, I promise. If we can find Harry Mik and Gavin Eckhardt, we'll make sure they pay, too." Scott peered at Peter as if trying to decide whether to believe him or not.

"You must have tons of willpower to save up more than a quarter of a million dollars."

"Huh?" Both Scott and Nick looked at Brien like he was crazy. "Where did you get that idea? I had thousands of dollars in there—close to ten—not hundreds of thousands." My mind, blown once again, wandered back to the stack of bills we'd found in Frank's safe. The money Rikki had regarded as part of Frank's "go bag" seemed more likely to be the amount of money Scott had saved. Why did Frank have it?

"Help us out here. We heard Jeff Baker stole your backpack and that there was several hundred thousand dollars in it along with your ledger. Where do you suppose he would have come up with that amount of money?" I asked.

"Oh, no!" Scott slapped his head. "He was even dumber than I figured. I never should have taken him with me to the stash house. Money was just lying around in boxes—some of them wrapped up like gifts. No wonder he's dead."

"Nothing is ever clear about any of this, is it?" Bernadette asked, making eye contact with me. "You want more milk, Scott?"

"Yes, please." Then Scott turned to us and spoke again. "I don't understand it. Harry Mik didn't ask me about the money—just the ledger. Maybe he already found the money Jeff stole. He had bags of it."

"Why am I not surprised?" I wondered, even though I was

stunned by the confusing new twist on the money angle. "Where did you see the money?"

"When I sneaked past Mik and Eckhardt to get away from them, it was on the floor all around them in different bags. They were putting it into boxes that were wrapped like presents. Just like at the stash house. It could have been hundreds of thousands of dollars— more even."

"Scott, did Harry Mik and Gavin Eckhardt say anything about where in Mexico they were going or when?"

"Soon—they said soon. They mentioned a town in Baja I never heard of before—Palma Dorado." Bernadette's head whipped around in my direction. We'd heard of it. It's not a town in Baja, but a resort. A pricey one, too, and one that Mom adored. It was even more spectacular once they rebuilt it after a hurricane tore through the area.

"Cabo," I said. Peter was on his phone immediately.

"They couldn't get that far if they're driving. The police are waiting for them at the border—los federales," Brien said, as his head moved up and down slowly.

"Oh, no. They're taking a plane from San Diego." Peter's head snapped up. He stopped before completing the call he was making.

"Scott, when you say plane, what do you mean? Like with one of the airlines?"

"No. It's a plane that belongs to a friend—the captain."

"As in Captain Kenneth Humboldt?" I asked.

"I never heard that name. Mik and the other policemen talked about the plane while they were at the stash house. They were going to Vegas. It made them happy, but the people in charge at the stash house didn't care for the idea."

"Why do you say that?"

"One of them joked about paying them too much. It might not have been a joke, so I didn't hear them bring it up again there. When I heard them talking about it, it was at the house when they were good and drunk. Happy about leaving town—soon.

"Thanks, Scott." Peter was on his phone again. He hit a single button. "Try treating those numbers I sent you as UTM coordinates for a landing strip in or around Cabo."

"I'm grateful, too. This is such helpful information. I have a friend I want you to meet later. He's a one hundred percent good cop."

"You must be talking about George," Nick said.

"Yes."

"I told you about him, Scott. Aunt Rosie and I met him last night. He's another reason she wanted me to bring you to Jessica. My aunt says you have good taste in men."

"I wish I could say that's always been the case, but I'm working on it. Trust is a tricky thing, isn't it? How about a break? We've got a suite ready for you if you want to take a shower or a nap—let me show you where it is." I had them follow me. Anastasia led the way, bounding down the hall, and then returned to Scott as if encouraging him to follow. Scott limped a little as he walked. Nick kept an eye on him. "I hope you'll wait here with your friend, Nick."

As I showed them into the suite that was in the same wing, not far from mine, it suddenly hit me how "girly" it was with all the poufy pillows and the billowy drapes. That didn't appear to matter to the two young men whose eyes were popping out of their heads. What they noticed was the flat screen TV mounted on the wall. The steam shower in the gleaming bathroom was an instant hit, too.

"If you want to take a swim, there are trunks and bathrobes in the closet." Scott sat on the foot of the bed. He suddenly appeared to be exhausted. One side of his face was still swollen near where he'd been cut by a blow—maybe by that ring Harry Mik wore. A dark color remained under one eye, and there were horrible bruises on his arms. When he sat down on the foot of the bed, he winced as though he might still be in pain elsewhere.

"I'm glad Rosie has taken such good care of you," I said. "There's aspirin in the medicine cabinet if you need it. The shower might help if you're still sore."

"I promised Rosie no more of this drug business. All I want is to get out of this alive and get my family back."

"At least they're safe for now. Peter has friends who will find out where the federal authorities have taken your mom and other family members for safekeeping. I spoke to a lawyer friend who says he believes you can exchange what you know about the drug business and the bad cops to get the charges against you reduced—even without the ledger."

"That's good. I can tell them plenty. The ledger's in here." Scott pointed to his head as he said that. "They didn't know it, or they would have beaten me harder." I was curious about what he meant, but I could tell he was worn out.

"If you need anything else, let me know. I'll be working in an office down the hall where my friends came from. On the other side of the kitchen, okay?" Both young men nodded. It's amazing to me how two kids like them—good friends—could have gone in such different directions. My eyes flitted around the room, and I suddenly remembered how often Tommy's sister, Kelly, had stayed in this room. At nineteen, she was about the same age as these two when her stupid choices ended her life for good.

"Don't worry. I won't let him get lost," Nick said, smiling.

"I'll come get you for lunch in a little while. Don't wait that long if you're still hungry. There are drinks and snacks in here." I opened a cupboard that concealed a small refrigerator.

"M&M's. My sister loves those. I wish she could see this."

"You'll have to come back again and bring her with you." I headed to the door and was about to leave when an image of the sergeant rose up in front of me. "There's one more thing I should tell you. We're holding a man here—under guard. He's a dirtbag—a dirtbag you already know. We're holding onto him until we can figure out how to turn him over to someone who will hold him accountable for the wrong he's done. I don't want you to misunderstand what's going on if you happen to see him when someone comes to pick him up."

"It must be the sergeant. Harry Mik and Gavin Eckhardt are gone by now."

Where? I wondered. *How fast could they get from San Diego to Cabo in a small plane or private jet? Was Frank with them, alive and uninjured?*

"Yes, it's the sergeant. We'll find Mik and Eckhardt, too. They took my friend and I intend to bring him back in the same way Nick has done that for you."

23 DOWN MEXICO WAY

When I returned to the situation room with more coffee, the others were hard at work. Kim had another update for me.

"The friend your dad contacted got back to us. He says the spot where Randall Roberts was killed is a place railways park trains for short periods when there's a traffic back up because of a delay offloading cargo or some other problem on the rails. Peter had it right when he said illegal activity went on there before Frank and the others went through there yesterday. The train stops, and the magic happens. A car, van, or delivery truck shows up. Cargo comes off or is loaded onto the train. It's all over in minutes. Several employees of the railways were arrested during the sweep, so at least some of what was being moved must have been drugs."

"Did they get pictures of Frank's companions in any of those photos?" I asked. "One of them must have been familiar with that location to have chosen the place to make the switch to the van."

"I don't know. I can try to get the photos if you want them."

"Let me think about it, Kim. I'm not sure it's worth the time and trouble, even if it means we might spot another dirty cop we don't already know about." Besides, we may need to move if we can figure out where Frank is.

"This will make you happy. Someone has started to make more arrests. Peter's guys have been monitoring the police channels with Frank's list nearby. Two down and about a zillion to go, see?" There was a big red "X" over the smiling face of two men.

"I wonder what it means. Has Peter heard anything new from his contacts at DEA or DHS?"

"I believe you can ask him yourself," Laura said.

"We've got them!" Peter shouted as he dashed into the room. Bernadette followed close behind. "Their flight destination, anyway. The coordinates designate a landing strip between Cabo San Lucas and San Jose del Cabo. Only two planes have landed there in the past twenty-four hours. One of them piloted by a man named Walter Jenkins."

"I almost can't believe it! The two cities are close—twenty miles apart. San Jose del Cabo is much older, but nothing like Cabo San Lucas. Lots of golf and galleries in the older city, but most of the shopping and nightlife is in Cabo San Lucas. That's where the Palma Dorado resort is located. What do we do?"

"What do you mean what do we do? We go get Frank!" Tommy's mouth hung open as if he couldn't grasp my question.

"I'm with Tommy," Brien said. "What other choice is there? The Mexican police aren't going to be any more trustworthy, are they? Why would they want to help us find dirty cops mixed up with one of their cartels? They have their own version of IED to worry about—if they're not dirty themselves!"

"They must be settled in somewhere by now. If Scott's right, that must mean Palma Dorado."

"Perfect! Let's get down there, start snooping around, and find Frank!" Tommy was bouncing and clapping his hands. Anastasia was doing her best to keep up with him—in step, even, as best she could.

"What do you say, Peter? Can we do it?"

"Commercial flights are booked until tomorrow morning, at the earliest. I found four seats on a flight leaving LAX at 6 a.m. which ought to get us in before 9 a.m."

"No! We've all got to go so when we find Frank he knows we all love him." Tommy was beginning to flush and his eyes filled with tears. "Do something, Jessica!"

"I can check on a charter, but that usually requires a little notice. Let me call Dad, first. Maybe he can arrange for us to use the corporate jet."

"Paul might be able to help, too," Jerry suggested. "I'm not sure how happy he'll be to rescue his rival for your affections, but he won't let that stop him from doing the right thing."

"I don't want to ask that of him. It puts him in an awkward situation with the firm, too. If he does a favor for one associate, he can't very well refuse others. I'll call Dad. He can help me figure this out."

"Do you think they'll have room for us at Palma Dorado?" Tommy asked, vibrating with anxiety and excitement. "Please tell me they'll let you bring your service dog along. You know what, Jerry? Dave and Timmy are in Cabo—they do shows in a nightclub down there. Maybe they have room for us and won't mind a dog."

"I don't believe it's the dog they'll mind," Jerry said, and then caught himself when Tommy put both hands on his hips. "We're going there on business—maybe dangerous business—even if we take precautions. We don't want to get friends in trouble, do we?" Before the debate could continue, I spoke up.

"We stick together. We keep our mouths shut about why we're in Cabo even if we run into people we know. Palma Dorado will accommodate pets—in their villas—not at the resort hotel."

"A villa would be good, right? You can probably squeeze most of us in there, so we might only need one or two." He didn't wait for an answer but turned to Anastasia.

"Did you hear that? Your momma's going to get us a villa." Then he started to sing that old Frank Sinatra or Bing Crosby song, *South of the Border,* Scott had mentioned. Holding out one hand for Anastasia, she hopped up onto her hind legs, and stepped along beside Tommy as he danced.

"Thomas, this isn't a vacation. You need to settle down," Bernadette didn't have a knife in her hand, but she was wagging a big wooden spoon she'd brought with her from the kitchen when she heard the excitement going on in the situation room.

"He won't be like this all the way to Cabo, will he?" Laura asked.

"Not if he knows what's good for him. Bernadette will toss him out of the jet somewhere over the Sea of Cortez and let him swim the rest of the way."

"Go home and pack while Jessica makes the arrangements," Bernadette chided.

"Pack? Why? At a place like Palma Dorado, they'll have everything we need. We know this isn't a vacation, but we don't want to create suspicion. We'll blow our cover if we don't go shopping, to the spa, the nightclubs, and..."

"That's enough, Tommy!" Tommy's eyes and mouth flew open at the tone in Jerry's voice. I was shocked, too. That was the first time I'd ever heard Jerry speak to Tommy in that way. I held my breath, waiting for a tantrum or a crying jag. Instead, Tommy suddenly settled down.

"You're right. I'll sleep in a tent on the beach. Can we please just bring Frank home before they kill him—his fellow cops—not the frigging drug lords."

"I'm going to see what kind of arrangements I can make for support. If Mik and his pals believe taking off for Mexico is their get out of jail free card, they're wrong, Tommy. There's plenty of corruption among the Mexican police, but they don't want our fugitives from justice any more than we want theirs. They've got all the dirty cops they need. When it comes to tracking fugitives from the U.S., they've been very cooperative in the past few years. Trust me on that. I'll check to see if the feds have issued warrants for the arrest of Mik and Eckhardt—for Jenkins, too, now that we know he was the fourth man in the crew that picked up Frank Saturday morning. Heck, let them arrest Frank, too, if that's what it takes to extricate him from Baja."

"Even if they haven't issued arrest warrants, they ought to be willing to subpoena all of them as witnesses to crimes committed during the operation of the drug ring. We could get Frank out of there that way, too." Peter nodded, enthusiastically.

"Okay, I'll bring that up if I need to."

"If that doesn't work, maybe I can get Dick Tatum to help us. He just texted me that the post mortems for both Toby Foster and Jeff Baker identified marks as being left by Mik's ring. In an earlier complaint filed by Toby Foster, hospital staff took photos documenting the same bruises which Foster told them Mik had caused. No arrest warrant was ever issued since Foster died not long after that and his death was ruled an accidental overdose. Dick can ask for that to be done now on behalf of both dead men. At least Harry Mik won't go free."

"Why not get Dick moving on it? It can't hurt to have another warrant out for a man like Mik. Do you want everyone to go home and pack? We won't need much since if we can't find Frank in a day or two, we ought to come home and put together another plan. If, and when we do find Frank, he's going to want to get out of there ASAP."

"I'll book the villas for three nights. If we want to leave before then, we'll do it. Will you want to bring a team with you?"

"Let me worry about that after I speak with the feds and see what they're willing to do," Peter responded. "You've got your hands full finding accommodations for us."

"Do you think this resets our seventy-two-hour clock?" I wondered if bumping up against that limit was behind Peter's concern about keeping our visit short.

"Maybe, but we're only halfway through that clock anyway. I don't want to tell too many people about this, but Don, Dick Tatum, and George Hernandez need to know. Someone's going to have to babysit while we're gone."

"Unless the feds are willing to come and pick up our houseguests. Is there any way they can reunite Scott with his family members? Federal protective custody is a good idea for him if it can be arranged."

"That's a great solution for Scott, Jessica. I'll raise the subject in a 'what if' kind of way. Who knows how long that might take to arrange, though." I suddenly realized how silent it had become in the situation room as Peter and I hashed things out.

"So?" Laura asked.

"I don't believe anyone should leave." As soon as the words were out of my mouth, I realized that wouldn't work. "Shoot! Do you all have passports? Are they up-to-date?" I heard a chorus of "yeses."

"You've got to go get them. How should we handle this, Peter? The last thing we need right now is to have one of our cats get nabbed by a fleeing rat. We haven't changed our clothes or showered or anything like that. Maybe everyone needs to go home."

"We've got a laundry room to wash and dry clothes. There are bathrobes in all the closets and plenty of toiletries. I don't see any reason we can't all be cleaned up and ready to go in a couple of hours. Do you?" Bernadette looked around the room. That summoned a resounding round of "nos."

"I'll go shower right now," Laura said. "Can I borrow a t-shirt and sweats?"

"Sure. You can, too, Kim. Tommy's right, though. We can shop when we get to the resort if it's not too late."

"Yes!" Tommy said. "If you guys strip down, I'll wash and dry our clothes. Sorry, I don't iron, as Jerry already knows."

"Wrinkles don't bother him for some reason."

"There's an iron and ironing board in the laundry room if the 'wrinkle free' cycle on the dryer doesn't do it for you," I suggested.

"Once I'm cleaned up, why don't you all give me your keys, tell me where your passports are, and one of Peter's guys can escort me to collect them. Are they easy to find?" Jerry, one of the most well-organized among us, piped up immediately. Kim and Brien took a little longer. Heck, I needed a minute to remember where I'd stashed mine.

"That'll take a while, but at least it'll keep everyone from scattering in different directions," I mumbled, trying to figure out if there was a better way to do this. "I can't come up with a better idea. Brien could escort you if he didn't have to wait for Tommy to wash his clothes. I have swim trunks, but other than that, there's nothing in the house that'll fit him." Brien took that as a cue to strike a bodybuilder pose. I shook my head. "Peter, if you can spare someone, let's go for it!"

"I like the idea, although Laura doesn't need to leave. All my associates are bonded and licensed by the state. You can trust them to go through your stuff. Keys, please. Write down where the documents are supposed to be—add your phone number in case there's a problem."

"Post-it note time!" Tommy sprang into action, leaping down the hall as if he were Nureyev. Anastasia bounded after him. We all stared for a good thirty seconds before Bernadette took charge.

"That's a yes, Peter. I'm already cleaned up, so I'm fixing lunch. Jessica, get busy with the flight and the hotel! I know where our passports are."

"Aye-aye!" I said, saluting Bernadette as she bustled off and I called Dad. I'd hardly finished explaining what we needed before he put me on hold.

"Wheels up in less than an hour. The plane will be at the Jackie Cochran by two at the latest. They'll file a flight plan if you tell me when you want to leave. It's not a very long fight. If you leave by four or five, you should arrive at the resort in time for a late dinner. Someone at Palma Dorado should be able to tell you if Frank's there. You have a recent picture of him, right?"

"I do. Thanks so much, Dad. I hope you're right that someone recognizes Frank, tells us which suite he's in, and we can take him along to dinner. A piece of cake, right?" I started to fidget. Soon, I'd be bouncing like Tommy. Anastasia was on the job, though, putting her head in my lap and looking up at me with her soulful eyes to calm me down.

"Let's hope so. Don't do anything stupid. Let Peter and the people he enlists do the heavy-lifting on this one. No guns! The Mexican police won't be as lenient as George Hernandez on Bernadette or anyone else in your party who brandishes a gun—even if they don't fire it wildly!"

"Bernadette's learned her lesson. I don't want anyone to do anything that might get Frank shot. George is in the loop. Don will be soon, and Peter's on the phone to los federales and whoever else they suggest we speak to—maybe even someone with the Mexican

197

police who specializes in finding U.S. fugitives. It'll be hard to make a move without advice from a member of law enforcement. Hopefully, not an untrustworthy swine like the guys with Frank."

"I hope that also means if Peter's contacts tell you stay put in Rancho Mirage, you'll do it." I didn't even want to suggest that option to Tommy.

"Don't worry. We'll do as we're told." I crossed my fingers.

"Sure, you will. If anything goes wrong, your mother will never let me forget it. Please don't break my heart, Jinx." My eyes teared up when he used that silly nickname derived from Jessica Alexis. It was a holdover from a childish demand I'd made when I learned Dad's real name was Henry even though everyone always called him Hank. I hoped my current idea to take the entire Cat Pack to find Frank wasn't as ridiculous as that one.

"I'll be careful, and I do listen to Peter." I hadn't made a reservation anywhere in Cabo yet. Arriving on a Sunday night, we'd be able to find rooms somewhere—even if the resort was booked. "Please ask the crew to plan for a four o'clock departure. We'll be there by three-thirty at the latest."

"Will do. Love you!"

"Me, too. Thanks, Dad—especially for making this happen at the last minute."

"I'd appreciate more notice when you invite me to the wedding."

"Wedding? What wedding?" I heard him laugh as he hung up. My face burned as I recalled Frank's declaration of love, written with passion and determination in the note he'd left with his dad. No doubt, in a moment when he was profoundly disturbed at the prospect of losing everything, including his life. I hesitated to take his words seriously, even as my heart pounded furiously.

"Earth to Jessica. This is Tommy calling!" Tommy stood in front of me in a bathrobe with a towel wrapped around his head. He undid the towel and drooped it over his shoulders, leaving his red hair standing up on end. "Did you say we're leaving at four?"

"That's the plan." He leaned in and kissed me all over my face. Anastasia loved it and wanted in on the lovefest. "Stop it, Tommy.

You're wet!"

"You should be too—go! We've got a schedule to keep. We're going to get Cousin Frank back, aren't we, wonder dog?" Tommy did a little kick and then stepped around in a circle. Anastasia did the same—perfectly in sync.

I stared in amazement as I called Palma Dorado. "Reservations, please."

24 A FAMILIAR FIGURE

"Please say it's true. I can't believe my eyes." After lunch, when I went to tell Scott and Nick what was going on, I had a visitor with me. Scott's fifteen-year-old sister, Tina, was at my side. The federal authorities holding Scott's family in protective custody in Riverside took no time at all arranging to pick up Scott once Dick Tatum called them. Two officers were waiting in the great room to escort them to the safe house. Their unmarked car was parked in the driveway next to Nick's Happy Trails van.

Dick Tatum said it had been his idea to bring Scott's sister along. He wanted to reassure him that a star witness against IED wasn't going to sit in a jail cell or be alone. Holding Scott in jail wasn't safe. They couldn't afford to take any chances given the information in his head, even though a new round of arrests was already underway. This round had already snared a judge, a prosecutor with a District Attorney's office, and several other ranking members of law enforcement. The details weren't available yet because the operation wasn't over. I hoped Captain Kenneth Humboldt was among them.

More arrests would come. Peter had informed them of Scott's incredible ability to recall the information written in his ledger. He'd tested him using the pages torn from his missing journal. To our amazement, Scott Bender appeared to be one of those people with an eidetic memory—like the actress Marilu Henner. His testimony alone ought to root out more culprits. Peter's words about cowering bullies came back to me moments later.

When we walked through the great room toward the front door, two uniformed officers from Cathedral City were waiting alongside George Hernandez. Not for Scott Bender but for our other houseguest who stood in between the two officers in handcuffs. When he saw Scott Bender, he blanched and then swayed as if he might faint. Whether Peter was right about Harry Mik or not, I had no doubt this liar was ready to rollover on his fellow desperados.

"Hello, Sergeant. Did you tell them what Harry Mik did to Toby Foster? I saw you talking to him. Did you think he killed me, too?"

"That's not why he's under arrest, Scott, but I'm sure the questions authorities have for Sergeant Ellison have only just begun." If looks could kill, I would have dropped to the floor. I'd be lying, though, if I said no one had ever thrown imaginary daggers at me like that before. Besides, it's the real ones—bullets too—that worry me.

"Good luck finding the money or the ledger without my help," Ellison growled through gritted teeth. I rolled my eyes, figuring he was yanking my chain or trying to stall again.

"We no longer need the ledger; we've got a copy— or will soon!" I winked at Scott as I said that.

"I saw the bag of money. Mik has it," Scott said.

"That's nothing. Chump change lifted from evidence rooms they're taking to el abogado. They're using it to get out of trouble with the cartel. The big money's in the Grand Cayman Bank."

"Bzzz! Wrong answer. Say goodbye, Ellison." My mouth fell open at Peter's antics. I'd never seen him act that way before. Sergeant Ellison appeared to be at a loss for words as Peter waved goodbye. George ushered Ellison out the front door, carrying a loaf of Bernadette's homemade bread with him.

"I expect you to keep me posted, Jessica."

"Thanks, George. Will do!" I hollered after him. Peter was on his phone again.

"Grand Cayman Bank," he said.

"What is it?" I asked while he waited for a response on the other end.

"Once we figured out the landing strip coordinates, we found a string of extra numbers on the handkerchief Frank left us. We were certain they went with an account somewhere. We have what we believe is a passcode, too. What we hadn't figured out yet was which bank the account was in. I'm hoping..." Peter quit speaking for a moment.

"Bingo! How much? IED is a greedy bunch, aren't they?" He hung up and turned to me.

"Ellison wasn't lying when he called the money Jeff Baker stole chump change. They'd better hope the cartel doesn't have an accountant as good as our friend here or it's going to be payback time. It might be the last straw if they discover twenty million dollars is missing."

"Greedy and overconfident. What if el abogado knows that already and the delivery they're about to make is a set up? Frank could be walking right into a trap bigger than the one he's already in!" Scott had been quiet as events swirled around him. Dick Tatum had told him and his sister to stay put as he followed George. Perhaps wanting to make sure George and the sergeant were gone before leaving with the young people in his charge.

"El abogado means 'the lawyer.' He speaks Spanish, but he's an American. I don't know his real name, but he's tall, with sandy hair and blue eyes. He wears little round glasses and suits that fit him perfectly. Everything about him is like that—perfect. Sometimes he almost glows he's so polished." Scott smiled.

"Can I take him with me for a minute?" I asked the officers waiting with him. "I'm just going into another room where I can show him something."

"Hurry, please. We need to get a move on."

"Mom will worry if we don't get back soon," Tina added. "Go, this must be important."

Scott and I hustled to the situation room. Nervous Cat Pack members were on our heels. Anastasia was, too.

"Do you see him in any of the photos?"

"There sure are a lot of them. I've seen him before—and him.

That one, too. Not el abogado." Then he stepped closer to the pictures we'd posted from Randall Roberts' phone. Scott pointed to a man seated near William Mackintosh. "That's him."

"Thank you, Scott! You've been wonderful." I gave him a hug. He winced a little, but also smiled broadly. I ripped that photo from the wall and took it with me as we headed back to the great room. Scott and his sister were gone in no time after that, and so were we an hour later.

When we piled onto the jet bound for Cabo, all the arrangements for our accommodations had been made. The resort had gone out of their way to handle my request for last minute reservations. For years, my mother had been a regular visitor at Palma Dorado. I made sure to drop her name right away, and even though we hadn't been there in over a year, the resort still had her account on file. Reviewing Mom's account added a lilt to the softly accented voice on the other end of the phone. Cha-ching!

When I asked Cecilia to reserve two villas and gave her the names of all the people in our party, I could hear more cha-chinging. Cecilia was also delighted to help me when I asked how late the resort shops were open and if we could have a chef prepare a late dinner for us in one of the villa kitchens for ten o'clock.

The flight went off without a hitch, and the pilots were on standby if we needed to leave before Wednesday afternoon. Someone Peter had spoken to earlier in the day, left a note with customs at the airport to expedite our arrival. That went smoothly; although I couldn't shake the uneasy feeling that we were being watched.

As I waited to climb into the van that would take us to the resort, I glimpsed a figure out of the corner of my eye. Gone, in the fraction of a second, I couldn't even be sure if the person was male or female. There was something familiar in the way the person moved, though.

When we arrived at the resort, the driver took us directly to our villas which were located side-by-side. Cecilia was there to greet us. Anastasia went to work on her immediately as our escort showed us around our stunning accommodations. The view from the foyer, over the infinity pool to the sea beyond was breathtaking.

Romantic, too. I missed Frank. He loves the ocean. Was he on a balcony or veranda nearby taking in the view, or did they have him locked up in one of the lovely suites at the resort? Was he well? Or had Mik hurt him the way he'd hurt Toby Foster, Scott Bender, or Jeff Baker?

Stop it! Suddenly aware of the buzz around me. Oohs and aahs came from Cat Pack members as they churned about. Not Peter. He stood still, staring at the sea framed by the open doors leading out to the veranda.

"We'll come back again when Betsy and Frank can join us," I whispered as our guide moved to the right. She led us through the enormous open great room into an expansive, well-equipped kitchen with views of a sprawling veranda, lit by torches. Brien went straight to the refrigerator.

"Whoa! This is even bigger than the one at your house, Jessica. He opened the freezer, found a box of ice cream bars, and helped himself. "Anyone hungry? It's going to be a few hours before dinner."

"We have shopping to do," Tommy said to Cecilia. "Where's the nearest mall?" Jerry rolled his eyes at Tommy's pushiness about shopping. I'm used to it, and I can afford it, but it embarrasses Jerry. It makes me happy to indulge my impish friend and the love of his life.

"The Palma Dorado shops are attached to the resort hotel. It's a short walk through the palm gardens or you can ask the driver assigned to your villa to take you there." Laura ran her hand over the polished marble tiles next to the fridge, offset by gorgeous hand painted tiles in the backsplash.

"I want to see the rest of the villa first. Then you can lead the way, Tommy." As she turned to exit the kitchen, she bumped into a handsome man with jet-black hair and eyes to match. His face was even more alluring when he broke into an enormous smile.

"Excuse me, encantadora dama!" He bowed and with a flourish of his arm that embraced everyone in the room, he introduced himself to us. "I'm Chef Eduardo Muñoz. At your service for the evening. I heard you tell the charming Cecilia that you're going to shop. What would you like me to prepare for you while you're gone?"

"They haven't had a chance to review the items you suggested yet," Cecilia said, perhaps intending to chide him. She couldn't help smiling at the man whose grin was infectious.

"Our friend is vegan, but this close to the ocean I hope fresh seafood is on the menu."

"Perfect! It would be my pleasure," he said as he took Laura's hand, raised it to his lips, and kissed it. He never took his eyes from her. She smiled shyly, which surprised me since Laura's usually wary of smooth operators like Eduardo Muñoz.

"Which one of you is the vegan?" He asked suddenly as he turned to search our entourage. Peter raised his hand. Before Eduardo or Peter could say a word, Tommy had to make his preferences known.

"Not me. I'm a hardcore carnivore. I don't mind seafood as long as it comes with a side of beef—surf and turf would be excellent."

"That sounds awesome—I love steak and lobster. You do, too, don't you Kim?" Brien asked.

"Sounds great to me, although I'd like something with a little local flare!"

"That I can do!" Eduardo replied with another snappy bow.

"If you blood-thirsty carnivores will let me speak, I believe Chef Muñoz has a question for me—the vegan."

"You look like a man who enjoys adventure—does that include spicy food?"

"Within reason—more jalapenos than habaneros. It depends on how they're handled, I suppose."

"For you, I suggest vegan chipotle queso, jackfruit fajitas, and Spanish rice—you'll love it, I promise." Then he turned toward Laura again.

"For you, Senorita—a medley of fresh seafood: sea bass, scallops, and coconut encrusted prawns. How about your beautiful women friends we haven't heard from yet?"

"The seafood medley sounds wonderful," I replied. "I'm with Kim, though, about a touch of local flavor."

"¿Puedes cocinarme una salsa molé poblano?" Bernadette asked sweetly.

Uh-oh, I thought. This charmer's being put to the test. Bernadette makes a fantastic molé—several of them in fact.

"Para ti, cualquier cosa!" Bernadette smirked at his reply. "For you, anything" was easier said than done, as he accepted the challenge Bernadette had set out for him. He'd be hard-pressed to come up with a suitable molé in such a short time frame. Bernadette's works of culinary genius were all day affairs.

"I can tell your entire group has come here with a spirit of adventure. You must allow me to show you around after dinner," Eduardo said. He was speaking to all of us, but gazing at Laura again.

"It'll be so late," Laura said. I agreed. We'd all taken naps during the flight, but that hadn't made up for the sleep debt I'd acquired. On the other hand, I wouldn't sleep much anyway.

"In Cabo San Lucas, the party rarely starts before midnight."

"Have you heard of Chiquita's Bananas?" Tommy asked.

"Of course, it's one of the hottest spots in town. Very retro with an extravagant floorshow. Dancing, too. It's like the nightclubs you might see in old Hollywood movies or in old Havana. Would you like me to take you there?"

"Yes, Eduardo. Jerry and I have good friends who produce and perform in the show."

"You must introduce them to me, so I can tell them how fabulous their shows are. Do you enjoy dancing, Laura?" He spoke her name as if he were marveling at its beauty. Bernadette glanced at me and then rolled her eyes.

"Yes, I do, Chef Muñoz."

"Eduardo. I insist you call your future dance partner by his first name."

"I love to dance, Eduardo."

Oh, no. Now what? I thought as Laura spoke his name in almost the same enchanted way he'd used hers. When I'd considered the range of problems we might face in Cabo, a smooth-talking, fast-working Lothario had not been among them.

"Let's do it!" I said. One rule we'd made was that no one would go off on their own. We'd stick together or venture out in twos and threes. This could be a chance to have a look around undercover, so to speak. No way was I going to allow Laura to go off in a twosome with this guy. Just when I was concerned that I might have to wave my hand to break the spell on them, Eduardo shifted gears.

"Then it is settled. You go shopping and buy clothes to wear to the most entertaining supper club in town. I'll prepare your dinner. You'll devour my delicious food, and then we'll go to Chiquita's Bananas and make new friends."

"Supper club," Brien muttered. "I like the sound of that."

25 CHIQUITA'S BANANAS

We swept into the beautiful nightclub. In our slinky new dresses and accompanied by the men in silk shirts and linen slacks, we fit right in. Eduardo had captured the ambiance well when he'd described the place as a throwback to the era of supper clubs—like the Copacabana during its heyday in New York.

Cigarette girls walked the floor selling tobacco products including hand-rolled cigars from Havana. In a corner a few tables away, a figure stood, hunched over. The person was wearing black pants and a black shirt—maybe a uniform of some kind, although I couldn't see anyone else dressed the same way. I had that experience once again that I was being watched even though the figure in black wasn't even turned this way. A woman carrying a basket of flowers stepped toward us, and when I peered around her, there was no one standing in that corner.

"An orchid?" The woman asked. "For the lovely ladies."

"I'll take one." Brien held out a U.S. ten-dollar bill. The woman, who I judged to be in her seventies or eighties, snatched it and the money vanished! Then she handed Brien a large, white orchid which she instructed him to put on Kim's wrist. As she began to leave, Eduardo spoke.

"Una mas, por favor." He handed her money and the crone gave him another orchid which he placed on Laura's wrist as the woman had shown Brien to do. I suddenly felt as if I was doing the watching—observing something that ought to be more private.

"Where's the restroom?" I asked. Bernadette leaned in. She spoke so I could hear her easily above the noisy nightclub, but without revealing our conversation to others at the table.

"It's toward the back of the bar we passed when we came in. You'll see the signs. Chef Muñoz has found his new favorite dish, hasn't he?"

"Don't let Laura out of your sight. I haven't seen her this gaga over a man since…" I paused, trying to remember when she'd been so apparently smitten. "Never! Not even in high school. Except for her one lapse in judgement right before Roger was murdered, she's always been so level-headed." I stood up and felt a little woozy. How could that be? I'd only had one glass of wine. No sleep and too much stress must have amplified its effect. Maybe something like that was happening to Laura.

"Are you okay?" Peter asked. "Where are you going?"

"Restroom," I replied.

"Do you want an escort?"

"No. Bernadette found her way there and back without any trouble. I think I can manage."

"Hurry, though, so you don't miss the show! It's going to start any minute now." That was Jerry, who must have caught a tiny bit of the pushy bug from Tommy. He was unusually insistent—for him. The pressure must be taking its toll on all of us. I hadn't seen Tommy, who'd ridden in the limousine assigned to the villa he and Jerry were sharing with Kim and Brien, since we arrived at the club. Brien couldn't wait to get to a supper club, so he and Kim had ridden with us. According to Jerry, Tommy had gone to say hello to his friends before the show started.

"Tommy's the one who's going to be upset if he misses his friends' opening number. Is he still backstage?" Jerry nodded.

"Don't worry. He can see plenty from where he is. Go! Hurry!" I nodded as I hustled away. I followed the route Bernadette had pointed out. The restroom was at the back of a large, gleaming bar that was retro and outlandish at the same time.

The place was jumping! It was even noisier here as a crowd of people tried to speak to each other over music that was louder here. Then the canned music stopped, and the lights blinked.

"The show will start in ten minutes." I shook my head. The voice over the PA system sounded like Tommy—an over-the-top excited version of him.

I sped up and hurried toward the restroom. Just as I turned the door handle, someone bumped into me from behind. Then I was shoved into the restroom door, forcing the door open and me inside. I blinked a couple of times in the bright light. The light wasn't why I blinked, though. I was trying to make sense of the sight in front of me.

"It was you at the airport," I said to the woman dressed in a black shirt and slacks. Her hair and eyebrows were dyed black, too. Her hair was pulled into a tight bun.

"What are you doing here?" She hissed.

"You know what I'm doing. We came to get Frank and take him home. I should ask you the same question. You're supposed to be in a hospital with armed guards and nurses watching over you."

"Ask any question you want—it won't matter—unless you mess this up for me! If you tell anyone you've seen me, I'll know it!" I didn't buy that for one minute.

"What is your game, Rikki?"

"Don't call me that! See your show and then go back to your villa. Stay there if you know what's good for you." Then she checked her image in the mirror. She was still recognizable as the devious detective, but something else was different about her besides the new hair color and style. She couldn't have been in the hospital long enough to have undergone plastic surgery. Rikki Havens, or whoever she called herself now, turned back to me as she reached for the door handle.

"Jessica, I don't play games." Then she took off, leaving me standing there so bumfuzzled it took me a few seconds to remember why I was in a restroom. I was still wary as I left the restroom a few minutes later and returned to my seat. I wanted to tell Peter what I'd discovered, but as the lights went down and the drums began to beat, I saw Rikki again. She pressed her fingers to her lips as if shushing me before she disappeared into the deepening shadows of the dim light.

I slipped a pen from the purse I held in my lap. Then, I placed it on the table and slid the cocktail napkin out from under my wine glass. In my absence, it had been refilled. I jotted a few words to Peter. As nonchalantly as I could, I asked Bernadette to hand it to Peter.

Don't look around. Rikki's here in disguise. Wearing black. She's not happy to see us.

Bernadette did as I asked without even glancing at the note. She was enthralled. When the music started, a staircase appeared on stage. Women in elaborate costumes descended the winding staircase. It was like one of those 1930s revues—an homage to Busby Berkeley, perhaps.

The women began to sing as they stepped in time to the strains of one of Tommy's favorite songs—Barry Manilow's *Copacabana* hit. As the women reached the bottom of the staircase, they fanned out in both directions.

Peter gave nothing away as he glanced at the note I'd sent him and then slid it into a pants pocket. He waited another couple of minutes before he stood up, stretched out his back, and sauntered away, toward the restrooms. Everyone was so engrossed in the spectacle on stage that they didn't appear to notice his departure. I continued to search, surreptitiously, for Rikki.

Bernadette gasped. I jumped at the sound.

"What is it?" I asked, looking around me once again. Had she seen Rikki and recognized her?

"No creo in mis ojos! It's Tommy." Bernadette pointed at the stage as the last woman descended the staircase.

"No way!" I said, adding Bernadette to the list of Cat Pack members who'd lost their senses, including me. I hadn't caught another glimpse of Rikki since I sat down. Had I imagined the entire episode while in a waking dream state from stress and sleep deprivation?

"How can you tell?" Laura asked.

"I've seen him in tights before. Lots of times when he's teaching Anastasia to dance with him."

"He and Anastasia had a pretty good ballerina thing going on," Brien added. "You've got to admit her bunny hop is pretty good, too, huh, Jessica?" I was too stunned to reply. "That's him, all right, with a big bunch of bananas on his head."

Tommy wore an enormous ruffled skirt split up the middle, a la Carmen Miranda. When he took center stage, the women on the other side stepped back, swishing and swaying, as they started singing a reprise of Copacabana. Then, gasps went up around the room.

Anastasia entered from offstage—on her hind legs, wearing a frilly skirt and a little bunch of bananas on her head. Tommy spun, took a couple of steps toward her in time to the music, and then stepped around in a circle. Anastasia matched his moves, perfectly in sync. They repeated the series until he and Anastasia met.

As Tommy moved back to center stage, Anastasia hopped after him. Tommy must have signaled because the poodle dropped down on all fours. The two went through a difficult series of dance steps, with Tommy leading and Anastasia following, as he traced a complex pattern in which Anastasia stepped around him, under a raised leg, and even jumped through his looped arms at one point. That had the audience clapping and whistling. When Tommy stood center stage and waved goodbye. Anastasia did, too. As he turned to leave the stage, Tommy peeked over his shoulder and Anastasia hopped up and put her front paws on his shoulders as he headed offstage.

Tommy had almost reached the curtain on the opposite side of the stage where Anastasia had entered. Tommy came to a sudden halt. When he did that, the enormous headdress he wore tilted. It must have been heavy and pinned on. He tilted backwards, but Anastasia pushed back, and he righted himself. When he glanced at the curtains again, he tried to turn and go the other way—too fast, apparently. Now completely off balance, he staggered toward the edge of the stage. When he tried to right himself this time, he overcompensated, staggered the other way, and whacked one of the dancers in line. She wobbled and set off a chain reaction of sorts as dancers who were still in motion, struggled to stay in rhythm with the music. A few, also wearing extravagant headdresses, lost their footing. After a round of "ohs" and "nos," audience members must have concluded it was part of the show because they jumped to their feet cheering wildly.

We all stood, too, so we could see what would happen next. As Tommy floundered, the headdresses' forward movement took him back toward the curtains. Movement from backstage caused him to react. His headdress leaned, taking him perilously close to the edge of the stage. An arm reached out as if making a grab for Tommy. That's when pandemonium broke out.

Maybe it would be more correct to say "poodlemonium." Anastasia had tried to keep up with Tommy as he careened one way and then another. She came to a halt when she saw the person behind the curtain grab Tommy's arm and yank him toward the curtain. Her head tilted to one side and then she wagged her poodle pompom tail as if she was happy to see the person.

I wasn't happy when I caught a glimpse of a black shirt sleeve as Tommy tried to wrestle free of the handhold. I almost ran for the steps that led up onto the stage near Tommy. I moved as fast as I could without mowing down revelers and servers. I kept my eyes on Tommy. He must have said something that convinced Anastasia he was in trouble. She grabbed that shirt sleeve and pulled at it. Then she shook it fiercely and yanked so hard Rikki fell to her knees onto the stage, no longer concealed by the curtains. As she hit the floor, a gun fell out of her shirt or from somewhere else.

"GUN!" One of the women on stage hollered in a booming male voice. Rikki scrambled to her feet and retrieved the gun just as I reached the stairs. She turned to dodge back behind the curtains, changed her mind, and plunged from the stage into the shrieking crowd. Rikki turned tables and chairs over as she fled. I thought she was running to get away from me until Peter flew out from behind those curtains, leaped into the crowd after her, and tried to navigate the obstacle course she'd created.

I ran up onto the stage to check on Tommy and Anastasia. The chaos unfolding below was beginning to get scary. I grabbed Tommy by the hand, pulled him to his feet, and hung on to him firmly as we took center stage. "Anastasia, come!" I bowed, forcing Tommy to do the same. Bless her heart, Anastasia bowed, too. Terror gave way to cheers—along with a few boos, I should add. Apparently, not everyone was impressed with a floorshow that included an attempted abduction at gunpoint.

26 PERRO BAILANDO

When the curtain finally fell on the first act, members of the chorus line ran over to Tommy. I was afraid they'd be mortified or angry at the disaster onstage and the near-riot that had ensued. I felt better as dancers embraced Tommy.

"That was fun, but a little warning next time would be better," one of them said.

"That was soooo Lucy Ricardo," another said.

"Riiickyyy!" A third called out laughing in a high-pitched voice. "That was perfect!" I couldn't remember Tommy yelling her name, but he must have.

"Bizarro World Rikki, in this case." Tommy griped. "I didn't even recognize her at first. She was just standing behind the curtains, staring. I thought she might be a crazed fan, but then I realized I couldn't have any of those. Not before tonight, anyway. Then, I thought she was looking for someone in the crowd. That's before she reached out to grab me! What was that?"

"I'm not sure. Let's get back to our villa and we'll talk about it." Dave and Timmy motioned for us to follow them down a hallway lined with dressing rooms. They stopped at one with a post-it-note on the door that read "Tommy & his Wonder Dog." They weren't at all disturbed about events. In fact, it was just the opposite.

"That was spectacular! We're going to be on every blog from

here to Istanbul. The phones were flashing like mad from the moment Anastasia stepped onto the stage. I bet you're going to be on the front page of tomorrow morning's paper. I hope they got a photo of the woman in black, too!" Dave was almost breathless as he spoke.

"The total black getup was *the* best. We're going to have to work something like it into the show. A lacy black widow costume maybe."

"The gun might have been just a teeny-weenie bit over the top. Let's nix it next time. We'll have her sling a banana across the stage, instead," Dave suggested. "Can you do it again next weekend?"

"We may have blown the element of surprise," Tommy offered.

"That's true. The banana instead of a gun might not be enough of a twist either. Can Anastasia tango?" Timmy asked.

"Jerry and I are just here for a couple of days—on business, I'm afraid. Then it's back to God's waiting room for us."

"Oh, we do miss how peaceful it is in Palm Springs. Almost nothing this exciting ever happens there, does it?" Tommy and I exchanged glances but said nothing.

"Feel free to use my act any way you want. Thanks for the chance to surprise my friends." Tommy embraced his friends and exchanged "air kisses" before opening the door to his dressing room. "It was a surprise, wasn't it?"

"Oh, yes!" I replied, giving Tommy a real smooch on the cheek.

"Can we keep the dog?" Dave asked. I knew he was kidding, but I gripped Anastasia's collar and pulled her a little closer to me. She leaned in against me, as if she appreciated the gesture. It had been a zany couple of days for her, too. I patted her head and that set her tail wagging.

"Sorry, guys. She's Jessica's service dog. I couldn't take her anywhere if she didn't have that dog close by." A commotion ended the discussion.

"Hey, Jerry, come give the star a big kiss! Wasn't that the opening night to end all opening nights?" Dave asked.

"Something like that," Jerry replied as he rushed to embrace Tommy. He must have seen through Peter's efforts to reassure everyone that it was okay to finish watching the show. The performers on stage now sure had a tough act to follow. "Well done. Do you need help getting out of that outfit?" Tommy nodded, almost whacking Jerry with the headdress. Jerry immediately went to work removing it. Not more than a few feet behind Jerry, the rest of the Cat Pack came down the hall toward us. The Cat Pack plus one.

"I promised to introduce you to everyone. Do you mind doing that while I change?" Tommy asked me as he stepped into the dressing room. Jerry followed, carrying the bananas. I handed him Anastasia's costume that I'd removed but still held.

"Hello," Dave called out when Eduardo dashed ahead of everyone, with his hand outstretched, and smiling ear-to-ear.

"Meet Chef Eduardo Muñoz," said. "This is Dave Toomey and that's Timmy Simmons." Bernadette stepped in and took over as I sidled over to Peter. The two men were already acquainted with St. Bernadette, I assume, by the hugs and kisses. The others waved when she pointed them out to Tommy's friends. Peter, who stood behind the others, stepped back to stand next to me.

"Is she gone?" I asked Peter as soon as the others were engaged in conversation.

"Yep. She must have jumped into a cab or ducked into a nearby shop. By the time I made it through the nightclub and out the front door to the street she was gone."

"What is her deal?" I asked, speaking mostly to myself.

"Did she say anything to you that hinted she intended to abduct Tommy?"

"No. In fact, she told me to keep my mouth shut about the fact that she's here in Cabo. Ten minutes later, she's making a spectacle of herself." I went over events with him since I wasn't sure when he'd returned to the melee after checking out the restroom area where I'd had that creepy encounter with Rikki. "Tommy thought she was a stage-struck fan or watching someone in the crowd from backstage."

"Could she have seen you from there?"

"Maybe, but why? As far as she knew, I'd done as she asked. I hadn't spoken to anyone or used my phone. I wasn't going anywhere!"

"You know, Tommy did almost take a nosedive off the stage. If she hadn't grabbed him when she did, he could have fallen."

"Are you saying the lady in black who hissed at me like a snake was hiding in the wings watching over Tommy? Why would she have a gun?"

"For protection—or she could have been gunning for someone else."

"Like me, you mean?"

"No. She had a shot at you already. Why not pop you one in the head and leave you in the ladies' room?"

"True. The lady in black wouldn't be front page news if she'd done the deed that way." Peter looked askance. "Not what she had in mind, I'm sure. If this evening is any indication, the pace has picked up, and we have no time left to lose when it comes to finding Frank. It's late. I'm exhausted. Let's go back to the villas and try to sleep. At daylight, which is only a few hours from now, we're going to search every nook and cranny of this place until we find Frank. Rikki's not here for nothing. I wish I knew how she found out Frank was here. Or what she plans to do with him if she finds him before we do."

"Or knew enough about our itinerary to be waiting for us at the airport," Peter said.

"We didn't bring much with us—do you have a way to sweep the villas and our belongings in case Rikki's eavesdropping on us?"

"I can make that happen. We're all still using our cellphones— we've had a problem with eavesdroppers on them before as you know. Let's switch to burner phones. We'll take a page from IED's playbook and pull the batteries and SIM cards from our personal phones. We can leave them in the villa's safe until we're ready to return home. Why make it easier for Rikki or anyone else to track us or eavesdrop?"

"Good idea—the lady in black will have to go back to using old fashioned methods if she wants to tail us. Maybe she's watching me in case Frank finds us or sends another message telling us where he is."

"Maybe he will," Peter said shrugging. "Let's not count on it. Who knows what Rikki's up to? Her old-school surveillance skills must be rusty. So far, she hasn't been very good at concealing her presence."

"We haven't been good at keeping a low profile either. Rikki may not be our only stalker if the members of the paparazzi are now intent on finding Tommy and his wonder dog."

"At this point, they'll be looking for a woman wearing an enormous bunch of bananas on her head." Tommy came wandering toward us.

"Speak of the devil," I muttered.

"Can we go back to the villa now, please? I've had all the show business and funny business I can stand for one day."

"By all means," I replied. "Peter's already called his guys and told them to meet us out front." Peter glanced at me, his brow furrowed. "Oh, come on. I'm not a fool—well not a total fool. I've seen one of our drivers before. I also caught them sending each other hand signals I've seen your guys use before. Not that I know what they mean."

"Thank goodness we still have some secrets," Peter said, as I left to herd the cats. Eduardo was nowhere to be seen.

"Chef had to leave," Laura said before I could ask about him. "I told him we shouldn't see each other again. This was scary tonight and I don't want him to get hurt hanging out with me."

"That's a good idea. You don't have to say goodbye forever. Let's find Frank and put this mess behind us, so it'll be safe to date you!" I put an arm around Laura's shoulders and walked to the nightclub's exit where we could see the limos waiting for us. Peter kept watch as we dashed to the cars.

Tommy may still have been incognito, but Anastasia was not! In the nightclub and on the street, I could hear oohs and aahs as she passed, along with cries of "perro bailando!" We jumped into the limos as a television news team rushed toward us with their cameras running trying to get a close up of the dancing dog.

I searched the crowd as we pulled away from the curb. My heart raced when I caught a glimpse of Rikki. Still dressed in black from head-to-toe, her presence didn't appear to draw any attention. The person speaking to her sure got mine.

27 EL ABOGADO

"Okay, people. Old phones in here." As we ate breakfast—a DIY affair—we organized the day. While the hilarity of the previous evening's events hadn't fled entirely, Rikki's sudden appearance had a sobering effect on us all. As day three began, the seventy-two-hour clock was ticking loudly. "Let's do our best to keep a low profile today, even though the media has the film clip of us getting into limos with el perro bailando."

"Should we wear disguises?" Tommy asked. Peter ignored the suggestion.

"Please use the burner phones to stay in contact today. Check in every couple of hours, so we know you're okay. Just say "I'm OK" and hang up to keep the line open."

"Unless we're not okay," Tommy added.

"Yes—if you're not okay, we want to know that. Please don't forget to call and check in, though, because I'll assume you're in trouble and we'll start looking for you. We can't afford to waste time or resources given how little of both we have."

"I'm going to contact housekeeping," Bernadette said. "I've got a cousin who works for the resort. If I show her a picture, she can tell me if she or any of her friends have seen Frank."

"Make sure you give her your burner phone number. No calls or messages on the landlines installed in our villas, okay?"

"Why don't I try to find out what's going on with room service?" Laura asked.

"No!" Several of us responded. "You're putty in Eduardo's hands. If you go anywhere near anyplace that has to do with food, he could show up."

"I'd love to fix his wagon now that Jessica's told us he's black-widow Rikki's spy. You could be right—there's something about him." Laura paused getting dreamy-eyed. "Oh, all right. I'll go ask to see a doctor about an upset stomach. I'll find out where they send you if you get sick or injured at the resort."

"I'll go with you, Laura. I hurt, and I'm bruised all over. I won't have to make anything up if we speak to a doctor or nurse. I could easily direct the conversation to the subject of what they do when resort guests come in with black eyes or stuff like that. And ask how often that happens—how recently—not that I'm saying Frank's been beaten up." Tommy stopped abruptly. "We're all taking Frank's picture with us?"

"Yes, that should help us find him if he's here somewhere. Be discreet if you can—don't just confront people out in the open."

"Will do, Peter. Laura raised a good point. Maybe room service has taken food to Frank. I don't mind being around food," Brien offered. "Eduardo can't manipulate me, even though he does have a great smile. He's fun to have around, and he can cook, too!" Good grief! All we needed was a budding bromance to cloud the issues.

"And he was standing next to Rikki when we left the nightclub last night! Doesn't that make you a little suspicious of Eduardo's charm and friendliness?"

"I'll go with Brien," Kim offered. "I won't let him get stuck trying every hamburger in the place—even if Eduardo shows up and bats his eyes at him."

"I hope he does show up. I'd like to confront the bro with a few tricky questions."

"No, Brien. If we see him before he sees us, we'll do nothing of the sort. We'll follow him and hope he leads us to black-widow Rikki's web or to Frank." Peter cleared his throat. "Don't worry, we'll be careful, and we'll call you if we find them."

"Good idea. We should also talk to the pool guys," Brien added. "I need to keep using my pool maintenance expertise or I'll lose it."

"I doubt Frank's been out for a swim, but let's check. We'll talk to the cabana boys, too," Kim added.

"Peter, if you haven't done it already, why don't we pay a visit to resort security and chat with them about how it's going?" Jerry suggested.

"That could turn out to be interesting. I'm not sure how much they'll tell us, but maybe we can get them to tell us if there's any unusual activity going on. I've had our drivers out scouting the grounds since dawn—on foot and by car. They noticed several limos pulling up in front of The Palm Towers Club, last night and this morning. Some coming and going in hot little sports cars, too. It looks like they're private residences—high-rise condos that are available for purchase."

"They aren't exactly private residences. They're high-end timeshares, usually sold in quarter-year increments. That doesn't mean you can't buy a bigger chunk of time than that. Conceivably, someone could buy up all the weeks and use it as if it's a private residence. Lots of services and amenities—which is what the 'club' part means, but it's usually referred to as just 'The Towers.' It would be just like our clubby dirty cops to set themselves up there, wouldn't it? Why don't I see if I can get a resort realtor to take me on a tour?"

"I'll go with you," Bernadette offered. "I'll put a little salt on your tail in case you get carried away now that you're wielding the black AMEX card again."

"It's for a good cause," I said. "As concerned as he is about Frank, even Father Martin will have to let me off the hook."

"Yeah, well, it won't hurt to take me along in case you're tempted to go off the deep since your shopping mojo's in high gear. Plus, I'm good at getting people to gossip. If we don't see what's going on over there, I'll work on the realtor to tell us."

"We should continue to appear to be guests, shouldn't we? What if Laura and I stop at the spa for a pedicure or a massage or go for a swim in the resort's lagoon pool?" Tommy was a little down about the debacle last night. It was good to see him perk up.

"Why not?" I asked. "No all-day spa package, though, okay? We should all report back in here and regroup by lunchtime."

"Let's do it!" Peter announced. "We'll meet here for lunch no later than one o'clock."

"Excellent!" Brien exclaimed. "Eduardo left us plenty of leftovers."

Anastasia, who'd been watching us quietly, must have figured we were going to take a break. She jumped up and carried a stuffed giraffe, dropping it at my feet. She bowed and stretched, wanting to play.

"What are we going to do with wonder dog?" Tommy asked.

"Bernadette and I aren't going anywhere yet, so she'll have company. If I can get an appointment to tour The Towers, I'll take her with me. I've got no place to hide now that the incident last night has been paired up with my telenovela-worthy past."

That's what had bummed Tommy out the most about last night. Some sleuthing news reporter had made a connection between the clip of me hustling into the limo with Anastasia and the mess churning up again in LA. Paul had emailed to give me a heads up about it. Cassie was making shocking allegations that she was the victim of a conspiracy of dirty cops in cahoots with her husband's lawyer. They were intent on ruining her reputation, her career, and her life!

Somehow, in her twisted logic, I was part of the conspiracy, too. Working in the same firm as her husband's lawyer, I was having a lurid affair with Paul Worthington. As a result, I've had "undue influence" on him in my efforts to seek revenge for the fact that she'd followed her heart and become involved with James Harper before we'd divorced.

"The only way I'm going to dodge the double whammy of video clips from el perro bailando and diva diablo is if I remain secluded in the villa for the rest of our visit."

"That's another option," Peter suggested.

"If there's a chance something's going on in The Towers, we need to have a look just in case the activity's related to Mik and the gang. The resort realtor will check the guest portfolio on file to make sure I'm no looky-loo. Once the realtor sees Mom and I have a track record of visits, my request will be taken seriously."

"They must have more than your past visits on file," Laura added. "They've probably already calculated your net worth and put that in your guest portfolio. You'll get your appointment."

Laura was right, of course. Kay Sarginson was one happy realtor and would have picked us up in fifteen minutes if we'd agreed. Peter and I had come up with another option before he and Jerry took off to chat with resort security. As we'd planned, I insisted my driver and a bodyguard be allowed to accompany me to avoid problems with the paparazzi. Kay Sarginson didn't challenge my request and agreed to meet us at the gate in an hour to give us access to the enclave.

I called Peter, who returned half an hour later without Jerry, who had joined Kim and Brien. Security had suggested they speak to separate crews in charge of security at the villas and The Towers. Peter was going with me to speak to security personnel at The Towers. Jerry was going to do the same back here at the villas once Kim and Brien finished their other tasks.

Bernadette and I put on one of the classy resort-wear outfits we'd bought during our shopping spree, which as Bernadette claimed, had indeed turned into a spree. A time-limited one, given we'd promised to be back at the villas for the dinner created by Eduardo. Despite whatever dubious game he was playing, Eduardo's skills in the kitchen weren't phony. The meal—even the molé—had been as amazing as he'd promised.

"We sure fit the bill as vacation-happy real estate shoppers, don't we?" I asked.

"Yes, we do, especially with Anastasia high-stepping it like a royal pony."

The Palm Towers Club was adjacent to the resort complex. With a dozen floors featuring large condo units, there were only forty units in the entire club. The first floor was devoted to communal space—a private pool, spa, fitness center, a lobby, and bar. Rooftop dining was only one of the amenities that made The Towers stand out. Our realtor met us at the gated entrance to the parking structure set aside for The Towers' guests.

"There doesn't seem to be much happening," I said as we followed Kay Sarginson to a small area designated as parking for "visitors." From what Peter had said, I expected it to be a hive of activity.

"I'm going to have a look around while you're with the realtor. If I'm not back when you're done, just leave without me. I'd like to see who belongs to the snazzy Porsche, if I can." I wasn't sure which one he meant, because I saw two of them as we pulled into our parking space near Kay Sarginson who had slipped into a spot tagged with a "resort realtor" label.

"You need to be careful like the rest of us. You don't exactly blend in—here or anywhere else," Bernadette said in a chiding tone.

"Bernadette's right. Besides, we haven't had a chance to get our realtor in a chatty mood yet. Maybe we can find if some unusual activity is underway."

"I'll resort to stealth only if I have to do it. My first effort is to see how much I can learn from security. Speaking to them is on my 'to do' list, remember?" Peter asked. At least he'd traded in his black t-shirt and black chinos for casual resort wear. Nothing flashy—a silk shirt in an olive color, khaki shorts, and a pair of topsiders without socks. That might reduce his profile a bit if he decided to poke around on his own. Peter remained in the car as our driver opened the car doors for us. Our realtor bustled toward us with an outstretched hand and a friendly smile.

Within minutes, Kay had taken us through the stunning lobby area and shown us around the first floor. There were several people milling about in addition to the staff. Despite the early hour, there were also two men sitting in the bar with what appeared to be mimosas or some morning starter drink like that. No one I'd seen before. I was relieved and disappointed they weren't faces we'd seen in the photos of IED members.

"Do you want to start with one of the larger units that has weeks available for sale?" I nodded as we stepped into the elevator and Kay used a key to expedite access to the floor where the condo was located. An "express option" she said and gave us a wink.

Before the doors closed, I caught a glimpse of a man who must have disembarked from another elevator. Dressed in a silk aloha shirt and swim trunks, he was accompanied by a tall woman with a model-perfect body. She carried a large, expensive beach bag and wore a sheer, gauzy cover-up over a bikini.

I felt my skin ripple as the sandy-haired man glanced our way. He wore dark glasses, not the round spectacles Scott had described. The glasses hid the color of his eyes from me, too. Before I could point him out to Bernadette, the elevator doors shut, and we zipped up to the fifth floor.

Kay gave us a "ta-da" as she opened the double doors leading into the foyer. The twenty-foot-high barrel ceilings were stunning and appeared to float above gleaming limestone walls and floors. The decor and furnishings were marvels to behold as well. Another sight drew me forward through the beautifully appointed room toward an ocean vista.

A wall of pocket doors was wide open. There was nothing between us and a spacious balcony that promised spectacular views. Anastasia and I made a beeline for the veranda. My eyes dropped immediately to the beach below. The man with sandy hair was about to step into a cabana. He held a newspaper in one hand. As I watched, he took off the dark glasses and replaced them with another pair. Before he ducked into the cabana I caught a side view of the round wire-rimmed glasses he'd put on.

"El abogado," I murmured. Kay Sarginson and Bernadette had joined me. I nudged Bernadette, who seemed puzzled by what I was saying and my apparent interest in the beach that was now devoid of people. I'm pretty sure she got it when the realtor spoke.

"Oh, yes. Is Mr. Abogado a friend? I'm not surprised. He's a lawyer like you. I'll bet he's told you how wonderful it is to come here where everything's taken care of for you. A great escape from the hectic pace in LA and the killer business schedule he keeps."

Kay Sarginson had no idea how correct she was about the killer part of his business. At least we'd found "the lawyer." He was a man with a sardonic streak to call himself Mr. Abogado. I'm certain it wasn't his real name, but a smug, even foolhardy, act given his role in the drug ring the French Connection operation aimed to destroy.

28 STILL IN THE GAME

I scanned Kay Sarginson's face for any hint of irony or innuendo in her choice of words. Nothing but realtor bliss as far as I could tell. A gorgeous, multi-million-dollar property, a fish on the line who could afford the price tag, and who, as it turned out, had a friend who was already a property owner. I wouldn't be surprised if she was already trying to decide how to spend the commission she'd earn.

As far as I was concerned, I was ready to go. Given that we'd set up the tour, however, it only made sense to continue our charade. I felt a little guilty about how disappointed our companion would be when she didn't make the sale. Such is the life of a realtor. I sighed as we moved through the rest of the condo with three exquisite master suites. Even if I'd checked out after finding el abogado, Bernadette was still in the game.

"Three suites won't give us as much room as we need, will they, Jessica?"

"We can always arrange reservations at a villa, too, I suppose."

"That's true, but I thought your friend, Mr. Abogado, told you he had more room when he offered to let you stay at his place." Kay took the bait.

"That's because he owns one of the two penthouse suites. When I say he owns it, I mean it! I can't offer you weeks in that condo because he owns them all. Well, not him, but his corporation. I guess you can't completely get away from business even in a paradise like this, can you?"

"Not a man like Mr. Abogado who juggles many corporate interests in addition to Inland Empire Investments." It was a test for Kay. I used the name on the account Peter had uncovered at the Grand Cayman Bank.

Peter had passed along the information about the account to his fed contact. His friend agreed to check it out further, but not to take any action until we found Frank. I wasn't sure what might happen if the account was suddenly frozen or the assets seized while the IED members were still at large and had Frank with them. I dreaded the thought of what Harry Mik might do in anger or panic if the account was his and he discovered a problem with it. Now, there was el abogado to consider as well.

"I don't know him as well as you do. Nor do I handle the finance side of sales. I'm not sure what else keeps Mr. Abogado on the go besides IED. Here's another option!" Anastasia, who'd been remarkably quiet, reacted when Kay snapped her fingers. She loves spirited people and followed Kay as she retraced her steps to the foyer. Kay's enthusiasm had waned when she had to give me the bad news that there weren't any units available that were as large as el abogado's home away from home.

"I was going to show you a unit on a floor below us. The square footage is a little smaller, but it still has three master suites like this one. Here's the exciting possibility, though. There's a unit next door that has weeks available, too. That condo only has two master suites, but together you'd have five. Let me show them to you."

"Kay, you're so clever!" Bernadette exclaimed. "That could solve your problem, Jessica." I nodded as we followed Kay, who kicked her realtor mojo into high gear again.

As soon as we reached the three-bedroom unit on the fourth floor, Bernadette pulled her next stunt. We were in the kitchen when she reached over and pulled the leather portfolio I carried in one hand away from me. Anastasia's leash was in the other.

"You need a free hand to feel the wonderful texture of this upholstery." As she grabbed the portfolio, she turned away from

Kay, and opened it. With a crafty move, Bernadette helped a couple items flutter to the ground. One was a receipt; the other was one of the 4x6 photos of Frank Fontana Kim had prepared for us. Bernadette hesitated before picking it up to make sure Kay saw it.

"Another handsome friend," Kay said as Bernadette picked up the photo.

"Yes," I replied. "Except that Frank Fontana beat me to the punch and accepted the offer to stay in the penthouse." Kay nodded.

"I saw his name on the guest list. It's a full house for the next few days, as I recall. Meetings of some kind—or maybe a reunion since some of the visitors have been Mr. Abogado's guests before. We had to hustle to process the requests for guest passes when your friend arrived yesterday." A thrill coursed through me as Bernadette tucked Frank's photo back into the portfolio. We were only yards away from him at this point. "I hope he's feeling better. I heard he and another guest weren't doing so well after they hit rough weather during the flight." My heart sank. Rough weather by the name of Harry Mik was more like it.

"I hope so. I'm planning to join him for dinner." Kay knew more than I did since I was making it up as I went along.

"That ought to be scrumptious. Eduardo Muñoz has turned out to be an amazing addition to our staff. You'll love how they set up the al fresco rooftop dining area as the sun goes down. All the twinkling lights come on and the stars shine—it's very romantic. Would you like to see the condo next door? I have one more that's on the second floor. The views aren't as great, but it's quicker getting to the beach from there! It's considerably less expensive to purchase weeks, too. Then again, you wouldn't have the opportunity for all the extra room you have on this floor. An opportunity that won't be around for long, I can assure you." I heard what she was saying, but my mind was in tumult. We'd found Frank. How could we get him out of there—fast?

"Please show us the rest of this condo," Bernadette asked. "As you can see, Jessica's deep in thought considering the wonderful suggestion you've made. We talked about lots of options, but it didn't occur to us that there might be two next to each other. I bet there's no way to put in a door that would make them adjoining units, is there?"

"Wow, that's a great idea. I've never had anyone ask, but I suppose as long as you were willing to put it back the way it was if you wanted to sell it, why not?" Their conversation continued, but I couldn't hear what they were saying. It wasn't just my addled brain that got in the way—my phone was ringing, too.

"You're not going to believe who we saw at the spa—living it up like they're here on vacation—Harry Mik and his buddy Eckhardt!" Tommy exclaimed. "We're tailing them, but we may have to give up soon. I don't golf, although Laura says she does."

"Please, make sure they can't see you."

"Too late! They've seen plenty of me already. I was in the men's steam bath when they walked in."

"Call Peter and Jerry—now!"

"We did, but I couldn't wait to tell you about it. Jerry's on his way here. Brien and Kim, too. Peter didn't answer, but Jerry said he's with you, condo hunting!"

"Peter drove Bernadette and me here, to The Towers, but he's gone off to speak to security and have a look around." I paused, wondering how much more I should tell him about el abogado and Frank.

"Tommy, call me if you find out where they're going. I'll call Peter, okay? Be careful!" I said once again as I ended the call and immediately called Peter.

"Jessica," Bernadette called out. "You've got to see the view of the beach from the master suite." While I waited for Peter to answer his phone, I dashed to the master suite.

When Anastasia and I joined Bernadette and Kay on the balcony, Bernadette grabbed my arm as if to restrain me from leaping from it. The woman coming out of the cabana in which el abogado had gone wasn't dressed in black. Rikki wore white—kitchen whites like a culinary helper might wear. I heard a quiet growl come from Anastasia, who was peering through the wrought iron bars as Rikki walked toward us. I wondered how Anastasia recognized Rikki from this distance. Surely, she couldn't catch her scent from here.

Rikki was moving rapidly toward us. Anastasia growled again. I backed up a step, and then stopped. Eduardo emerged from the cabana, waved at the people inside, and then took off after Rikki. When he caught up, they began to speak about something in earnest.

"That's Eduardo!" Kay exclaimed. "You must meet him."

"We've met," Bernadette replied. "He fixed us a wonderful dinner last night."

"He did?" Kay asked. "That's odd. He's not on the culinary staff assigned to the villas." She shrugged.

"He must have been filling in for someone," Bernadette offered.

"I'm sure you're right. That's something he'd do for a friend in a heartbeat." Anastasia growled again. This time she barked, too. I grabbed Bernadette by the arm as both Rikki and Eduardo's heads jerked up. They could search for us all they wanted. We were back inside, and I'd bent down to quiet Anastasia.

"I'm sorry. Anastasia hasn't adjusted to the new setting. Maybe I should have given her another day to settle in before taking her to see the sights."

"Aw, she's just tired, Jessica. We all stayed out too late last night." Kay's eyes suddenly widened.

"Oh, my goodness, she's el perro bailando, isn't she?" Kay bent down, showing a real interest in Anastasia for the first time. Anastasia had calmed down, but I hadn't. I gave Bernadette a pleading look. We needed to leave.

"You've shown us enough to get an idea of what it would be like to have a place here. Why don't you give us an estimate for what it would cost to buy the condo upstairs, or the two on this floor? We need to know which weeks are available to purchase, too, right?"

"Yes. Bernadette's right. I must be tired, too, not to have asked you which weeks were available in each unit. It would be better to have the information in writing given how much I suddenly feel at loose ends."

"It is almost lunchtime. We could have lunch…" Anastasia, who was back in good-girl mode, nuzzled the hand of her latest conquest. "You need to go feed her, don't you? I bet her schedule's off even

233

though you didn't change time zones."

"Mine is, that's for sure! Thanks so much for arranging to show us around on such short notice." When we stepped into the hallway, a housekeeping cart was sitting nearby. I'm not sure why the place needed to be cleaned—it was spotless as far as I could tell. A laundry bin farther down the hall was filled to overflowing with bedclothes. The other condo on this floor must have been in use recently. On the way down to the lobby in the elevator, Kay took a phone call. I used the opportunity to try calling Peter again. His phone rang and rang.

"What is it?" Bernadette whispered. Kay was chatting away on her phone. A soundtrack of jangling bracelets and jingling keys accompanied her as she spoke. As she grew more animated, the sounds got louder.

"Peter's not answering his phone. Tommy called him a while ago with no luck either."

"Is Tommy the one who called you upstairs?" I glanced at Kay before I spoke. When she met my gaze, she mouthed the word "sorry."

"Please don't apologize," I said, pointing to my phone as I put it to my ear to make a call of my own. I called Peter again. Kay nodded. Jingle, jangle, and a peel of laughter provided cover for my hushed conversation with Bernadette.

"Yes. He and Laura ran into Mik and Eckhardt."

"Ay yi yi! No wonder you were upset. I thought it was about Rikki."

"Her, too!" I added. Peter still didn't answer. I gave up.

"Maybe he's in the car, and the parking lot's blocking his signal," Bernadette offered. "He'd better have a good explanation after telling us all to check in!"

Kay was still on the phone when the elevator came to a halt. As we stepped into the lobby, I saw Peter, but only for a second as the doors closed on an elevator across from us. An express elevator heading straight to the penthouse. He wasn't alone. Two members of resort security were with him. Maybe the trip to the penthouse was his idea—part of his inquiry into security at The Towers. I didn't think so. Bernadette's worried expression told me she didn't think so, either.

"Come with me, will you?" Kay hung up the phone as she stepped from the elevator and motioned for us to follow her. She went to a reception area against the far wall of the lobby and set her phone down on the counter. Her bag, too. When she did that, I could see several key rings, including the one she'd used for our tour. I elbowed Bernadette and nodded at them. Brien was right that Bernadette has ESP. Not only did she get my message to help herself to a set of those keys, but she must have understood why I wanted them. A front desk receptionist walked up to Kay.

"I want to give these two guests a couple of the gift bags you have back there. Will you grab them for me please?"

"You're going to love these!" Kay remarked as she turned toward us for a second. As soon as Kay turned around to get the tote bags from the front desk receptionist, Bernadette reached out and palmed the keys to The Towers. She stepped closer to me as we accepted the bags from Kay. A heavenly fragrance came from the one she handed me. "Consider it a small bribe. I'll have the information you want delivered to your villa first thing in the morning. It was a pleasure meeting you."

"Thanks so much," I said as I held out my hand and Kay shook it. Anastasia raised a paw.

"A pleasure meeting you, too, Anastasia." As soon as we returned to the lot, Kay got into her car, and we hurried to our limo.

"What's going on with Peter?" I asked as I opened the door.

"Get in. We're all supposed to go back to the villa and wait." That's all the driver said as he left the parking garage and wound his way through the resort to our villa.

29 A DESPERATE SCHEME

"Wait for what?" I asked before exiting the limo.

"Peter didn't say. He just said I should go back to the villa and wait, and so should all the others."

"That's rather cryptic, isn't it?" The driver shrugged. I was about to leave when another question came to mind. "Was he alone when he gave you those instructions?" I asked.

"No. He was still with members of The Towers security force." My crud detector went into the red! I strolled into the villa, taking my time, and trying to figure out what to do. No Frank. No Peter. No connection with the feds. Double-crossers and double, double-crossers at every turn. An infestation of dirty rats, too, and time was running out. I fed Anastasia, and then sat down on the veranda, stunned and hoping for inspiration. Bernadette joined me.

"I wish we really were having dinner with Frank tonight—under the stars—or in the condo. I wouldn't care which, would you?" As I asked the question, I got an image of an empty condo with el abogado, his model girlfriend, and desperado pals all dining, drinking, and smoking big, fat cigars rooftop. Not a completely empty condo—I don't think Frank and Peter were going to the party. It wouldn't surprise me if in between puffs on their cigars Mr. Abogado chatted with his guests about how to kill Peter and Frank without sullying the wretched lawyer's penthouse. My heart raced, and desperation took over as a scheme formed in my mind—a desperate scheme.

"Call me off the charts nuts, but I have an idea. What if we follow the suggestion Tommy made this morning? Would your cousin in housekeeping loan us a couple of maid's uniforms?"

"Uh-oh, you're not going Lucy Ricardo on me, are you? Did you catch that from Tommy, too?"

"Heck, I'll buy them from her if that makes it any easier."

"Then what? We knock on the door and holler 'housekeeping' before barging into the penthouse with a toilet brush and a roll of paper towels from our villa?"

"You're firing on all cylinders now, Ethel! We need a housekeeping cart and one of the big laundry carts, too, don't we?"

"Ay yi yi, estoy loco, también!" Bernadette said and then pulled Kay's keyring from a pants pocket. "This looks like a passkey to me. It might unlock the housekeeping storage area and laundry—if we can get that far. I didn't see any of the help walking through the lobby, did you? There must be a service entrance."

"Call your cousin and ask. I'm sure you're right that the cooks and housekeepers don't waltz in through the front entrance. That explains why we didn't come face-to-face with Eduardo and his culinary helper, Rikki. They were headed toward the front entrance from the beach. I was a little worried about bumping into them before I saw Peter in the express elevator to el abogado's penthouse lair."

"Okay, here's another question. We've been told to stay put. How are we going to get to The Towers, so we can sneak in through an employee entrance, use what we hope is a passkey to the laundry room, before going upstairs to haul Frank out of the penthouse in a laundry basket. Peter's driver doesn't seem to be in any mood to negotiate."

"We need wheels, don't we?" Tommy popped into my mind again. "Tommy, where are you?"

"The 19th Hole, keeping an eye on Mik and Eckhardt. We're all here, hiding in a booth, and having a cold drink."

"How did you end up there?"

"We signed up for a round of golf and rented a couple of golf carts. I don't play, but Kim, Laura, and Jerry do. Brien and I were going along as designated drivers. Before we could rent clubs and tee off, Mik and Eckhardt bypassed the course and headed here. We followed them."

"In the golf carts?" I asked.

"Yes. How else were we going to keep up with them?" Tommy seemed puzzled.

"Get in the golf carts, now. Don't return them—come straight here."

"Won't we get into trouble for driving a stolen golf cart?"

"No. You must have seen people riding around in them while you were roaming around the resort. It's just like it is at the resort courses in the desert. There aren't any cart police. Come back, now!" Before he hung up, I added another point. "Don't call your driver. I'll explain when you arrive. We'll have lunch ready."

"That'll get Brien moving. He's been talking about Eduardo's salted caramel brownies for the past half hour." As soon as I hung up, Bernadette had information from her cousin.

"There's an entrance the help uses that's just off The Towers' main kitchen. You need a keycard to get in, though, unless you have someone already inside who can let you in. She says the help can also get in using the guest entrance from the parking garage, so long as they use the service elevator once they're inside. You need a keycard to enter that way, too."

"I didn't see Kay swipe a keycard, did you?"

"No. I saw her punch in numbers on a keypad when we followed her into the parking garage. When we went in through the guest entrance, she used a key to open the door." Bernadette examined the keys she'd lifted from Kay.

"This one's definitely the elevator key. She used this one to let us into both condos—a passkey. Maybe it works on the side entrance, too, but there are a couple others."

"It won't take long to try them all. If none of them work, I'll go inside and ask to be seated in the Tapas Bar. That venue is open to the public. Mom took us there for happy hour once." Bernadette nodded. "I'll sit down, order a drink, and then scoot off to the restroom. I can sneak around and let the rest of you in through the side entrance. We don't have the code to get into the parking garage, so we'll have to park the carts and slip in on foot around the parking gate. We could just knock the arm off, but that might set off an alert to security."

"I hope the keys work, so we don't set off any alarms on the doors either. We gotta look natural, too, so they don't get suspicious if they have cameras on the side doors. Let's hope the service elevator takes staff all the way to the penthouse. The only option might be the express elevator we saw Peter and the security guys using—who knows if we have the right key for it. Anyway, my cousin, Anna, says there ought to be clean uniforms in the laundry room. You get fired if you're caught with goop on your uniform at The Towers."

"Did she wonder why you were asking all these odd questions?"

"Yes. I told her we're trying to plan a surprise party for someone. That's true, isn't it?"

"Let's hope it's a surprise."

By the time the Cat Pack members pulled up in front of the villa, Bernadette and I'd hatched the scheme. It included a couple ideas about what to do if the condo wasn't empty of villains. If we didn't hear from Peter by dusk, we'd put the plan into motion.

We tried to nap after lunch—hoping to be as fresh as we could for our plan. It was fraught with holes. There were plenty of chances to get caught. If that happened, I hoped I'd have a chance to call Peter's men and scream bloody murder to get them to come running. I'm sure Peter must have worked out contingency plans in case one or more of us got into the sort of trouble that could be awaiting us.

At dusk, we all dressed in the resort wear we'd bought. If we were presentable, and appeared to be ready for an evening out, we might be able to wiggle out of any trouble we encountered early on. I hoped we could be convincing as confused tourists, looking for food and entertainment, if we got caught wandering around in The Towers where we didn't belong.

Everything started off fine. In fact, we got an unexpected break when we reached The Towers parking area. The gate arm rose as we approached it in our golf carts. The golf carts must have had transponders on them. One of the keys worked on the side entrance. It took a bit of fumbling to find it, but it didn't take long. Once inside, we were stuck. I couldn't see any indication of where to go except toward the main lobby. There was no "employees only" sign or service elevator in sight.

"Lets' get onto the elevator and see if there's an option to get to a service area that way." I was anxious as we called the elevator Kay had used. We tried to chat amiably, but I worried that our group was big enough to draw attention—even without Peter-the-giant in our midst. When the elevator arrived, it was obvious Jerry was feeling exposed, too.

"Go, go, go!" He prodded in a low voice pushing us onto the elevator. As soon as the door closed, I saw an option to head to the basement. I used Kay's key, gave it a turn, and held my breath until the button lit up and the elevator descended.

"What was that about, Jerry?" Tommy asked.

"I didn't want anyone else to get on the elevator with us— especially not Rikki. I thought I saw her."

"In the lobby?" I asked.

"Yes, but I'm so wired at this point, I could be hallucinating." He shut up as the elevator door popped open. "Laundry" was painted on the wall in front of us. "Maintenance," "Storage," and "Supplies," too. Big arrows pointed to the right. All good news. What spooked me was the word "Security." The big arrow pointed left.

"Don't let the doors close, okay? Bernadette and I will check to see if the coast is clear." Bernadette and I ran to the door marked laundry. It was already unlocked. Linens were stacked on shelves, and parked on racks, that shielded the cleaning equipment from our view. No uniforms were in sight. I didn't see any employees moving around, but it was steamy and humid in there. The smell of laundry products hung in the air. Equipment was running—was someone doing laundry?

"There!" Bernadette whispered loudly. I almost had a heart

attack. I hugged her anyway. She'd spotted a rack loaded with uniforms. We made a quick check of the area around the alcove in which those uniforms hung. I peeked around the racks in our way and saw a bank of commercial laundry equipment with no one attending to them.

"Get dressed. I'll get the others." In less than a minute, I was back with my wary Cat Pack friends. Bernadette had already slipped into a housekeeping outfit that resembled hospital scrubs. She pointed out how the items on the racks were organized by size—sort of.

Tommy and Jerry had no trouble finding similar outfits worn by maintenance or janitorial staff. Brien was another matter. In the end, the only thing we found big enough for him was a Chef's shirt—like the one Rikki was wearing. He put that on and with his black slacks, I figured he could pass as a chef. That's if no one looked at his shoes. None of us would pass the test if there were footwear requirements. That was another reason to get this done quickly!

"I see empty laundry baskets. I'll get one," Laura whispered. "You need to find a housekeeping cart loaded with all those tiny bottles of pricy shampoo and stuff."

"We could pose better as lookouts if we had a broom or something," Tommy said.

"See what you can find in here," I said, pulling the keys from a pocket in the smock I'd put on. "Bernadette and I will check out what's in the storage or supply rooms—if we can find them." We'd no sooner stepped out into the hallway when I heard the pinging of the elevator. I almost knocked Bernadette down when I shoved her back into the laundry room.

"Hide!" I whispered. I didn't have to tell anyone twice. Bernadette and I dashed behind the rack of uniforms and pressed into the curve of the wall that made the space an alcove. I saw Tommy grab a comforter and dive into a laundry basket—he motioned for Jerry to join him—then pulled the comforter over them both. Brien ushered Kim and Laura into a nearby closet and shut the door.

As the door to the laundry room swung open, whatever

equipment had been running stopped. It suddenly became so quiet that I could hear Bernadette breathing! I squelched a yelp when the employee suddenly belted out a few bars of a song about bad, bad news. I prayed it wasn't a portent of things to come. It seemed like we were stuck in there for an eternity, as the laundry worker did whatever he needed to do. The roar of the machines started again, and I breathed a sigh of relief when our musically inclined visitor sang his way to the door, did a spin that Anastasia would have adored, and left. No one moved for two or three more minutes. Then, I dashed to the door, peeked out, and motioned for Bernadette to follow.

In the storage room, we found the cart we needed already loaded with supplies. One of those small broom and dustpan combos was in a corner. We grabbed the goods and left them in the corridor as we rallied the troops. Brien led the way, pushing the laundry cart in front of him. When Jerry made a sudden motion, we all stopped. He pointed to a sign I'd missed on the way to the supply room: "Service elevator."

When we entered it, "Penthouse" was printed next to a button on the panel. Once I'd keyed in our destination, we zipped to the floor we wanted in no time.

"Ready or not," I said when the elevator stopped. Bernadette pushed the cart into the hallway on the penthouse level. I followed her. Behind me, Kim and Laura pushed the laundry cart out while Jerry held the button, so the car wouldn't leave, and Tommy kept the door from closing.

"Which way?" A shiny bronze plaque was posted on the wall here instead of the painted letters we'd encountered in the basement. An arrow pointed right to the Palma Oro Penthouse and left to the Palma Diamante Penthouse. Before we could answer, an elevator somewhere to our right pinged. We froze. When it opened, a man in a resort security uniform stepped out. He headed right. Then, he stopped, turned, and walked up to us.

"We said no turndown service." His eyes swept over us, and as he counted heads, he became increasingly suspicious. When he reached into a jacket pocket, I felt sick. We were so close!

30 TRIPLE-CROSS

We're too close to stop, now! I thought as I rammed the housekeeping cart into him. When I did that, he folded in the middle. I must have hit him in a sensitive spot. A phone went flying from his hand.

"I thought he was reaching for a gun," I said as the guy writhed on the ground. I grabbed the phone he'd dropped and pocketed it.

"Don't worry about it," Brien said as he leaned down and gripped the guy's neck. He stopped moving instantly.

"Did you kill him?" Tommy asked.

"No, but he's feeling no pain." Then Brien picked the man up off the floor and placed him into the laundry cart. Kim flew into action and covered him with a comforter we'd brought along for Frank.

"Turn right!" I said and we all dashed down the hall that way. There was no turning back now. With his muscles bulging, Brien shoved the laundry basket as though it was still empty. When we reached the ornate double doors that led into the Palma Oro penthouse, I didn't hesitate.

"Housekeeping!" I announced as I rapped sharply on the door. I prayed that silence would be my response. No such luck. The doors swung wide open. The interior was dark.

"Housekeeping," I said less confidently this time. When I

pushed the cart into the foyer, I'd taken only two or three steps when someone grabbed me from behind. I fought to get the arm away from my throat before I passed out. Then the lights came on and my assailant released his grip.

"Jessica!"

"Peter!" I replied as I struggled to get off the floor where I'd landed with a thud. Bernadette shoved the housekeeping cart inside and out of the way, making room for Brien to roll his cart in, too. The others hustled inside and shut the doors.

"What are you doing here?" Peter asked. "I could have killed you!"

"Tell me about it!" I snapped. "Where's Frank?"

"I can't find him," Peter replied. He was here. I heard his voice. That el abogado character whose real name is Dugan, gave orders to someone in Spanish to do something with Frank."

"What?" I gulped.

"Put him away to keep him safe—seguro means safe or secure, right?" Bernadette nodded. "I checked all the rooms and closets—after I convinced those two to let me go." He nodded in the direction of the two security men I'd seen with Peter on the elevator. They were out cold.

"We've got one, too." Brien pulled the comforter off the body of the guard.

"We brought the cart along for Frank," I said. Brien must have thought I meant for him to empty it. He picked up the guy like he was hoisting a sack of potatoes and placed him on the floor next to the other two.

"Do you want us to go see if he's up on the roof?" Jerry asked. "We can probably get up there using the service elevator." Peter looked puzzled.

"How? You need authorization to do that."

"We don't have time to explain now. If you've got any secret assets, Peter, now's the time to put them to use." Peter nodded as Bernadette fixed her eyes on him.

"Give me a phone, and I'll make a call. I may not have found Frank, but there's plenty in Dugan's office that ought to interest the feds. The Mexican police won't be happy to learn the lawyer's been smuggling more than drugs across the border—counterfeit goods and other contraband, plus priceless artifacts. The Mexican authorities won't look the other way about that."

"Fine, Peter." I said.

"Someone also needs to come and roundup Mik and Eckhardt, and Dugan's other dinner guests who have arrest warrants waiting for them. I heard somebody made that happen."

"That's great, but please get your guys over here quick with the limos, too. Tell them to bring Anastasia. Frank's in here somewhere. Hidden, like the safe in his closet at home. A crook like el abogado must have a vault or a room-sized safe."

"Or a panic room," Kim offered.

"How will they get Anastasia in here? She's famous!" Tommy was distraught and out of breath. He'd already run back and forth in vain, searching for Frank, despite what Peter had said.

"Tell them to take her to the gated entrance of the parking garage. I'll be there waiting. Hurry, please! We need to get Frank and get out of here before the bullets start flying." Peter made two phone calls.

"My guys can have Anastasia here in less than five minutes. We've got fifteen, maybe, before the other assets show up." I checked to make sure I had a phone and the keys, and then rode the service elevator down to the first floor. With my heart pounding furiously, I hung back, waiting in the corridor near the service elevator until I saw headlights flash outside. When I opened the door and stepped halfway out, Anastasia bounded toward me. In less than two more minutes, we were upstairs.

"Where's Frank?" I asked Anastasia as I pulled his handkerchief from a pants pocket and dangled it in front of her. I'd brought it along for good luck. We needed that now, as the minutes ticked by. I ran to the large master suite down the hall from Dugan's office. Anastasia ran after me. She dashed around the room. Nothing. Nothing in the closet or master bath, either.

"Den! Let's try the den." As we reached the doorway to the den, Anastasia suddenly went on point beneath a large painting in the hallway outside the den. Peter and Jerry knocked on the wall around the edges of the painting. When he stopped, I heard a faint echo. Anastasia dug furiously. Peter took the enormous painting down and set it aside. Brien joined Peter and Jerry, exploring from the floor as high as they could reach, in a frantic search for a seam, a pressure point, hidden button, or panel that might trigger the entrance to a concealed space. Faint knocks came from somewhere.

When Anastasia ran around the corner into the den, I ran after her. She whimpered as she scampered to a wall with heavy wooden bookshelves that jutted out a foot into the room from floor to ceiling. The men filed into the room, running their hands along the shelves and pushing at books. An enormous desk dominated the center of the room. I scanned the surface of the desk and then opened the drawers looking for a panic button. When I reached up under the desk, I pressed a button and gasped. The shelves slid sideways, slowly, revealing a solid steel door.

Peter tried to open it using a handle on the outside of the door. The handle didn't budge. A keypad next to it suggested that we needed a code to get the doors to open. I was standing there trying to figure out what to do next when two things happened.

First, the door opened from inside and Frank Fontana stepped out and threw his arms around me. Tears streamed down my face as I kissed him again and again. More tenderly and less passionately than I'd imagined because his face was bruised and swollen in several places, his lips, too, and he had the worst black eye I'd ever seen. Second, I heard cries from the other room. Then a man's voice.

"Come on out, all of you, or la vieja gets it."

We made our way down the hall as fast as we could. Frank leaned on me. When he stumbled, Peter stepped in and put an arm around Frank's waist to steady him. Frank wouldn't let go of me, though.

The double doors leading into the penthouse were wide open. Harry Mik stood next to Dugan. Mik held Bernadette in a vice-like grip. Eckhardt and Jenkins, who were a little late to the party, entered the room seconds later. Their mouths fell open. Eduardo and Rikki were with them, too. Rikki shook her head. I swear, if I'd had a gun, I might have made a liar of myself after promising Bernadette I'd never shoot her.

When I heard the ping of the elevator, I wondered how many more rats could possibly have been up on the roof! The model was nowhere to be seen, so it must be her. As if he'd read my mind, Dugan issued a loud command.

"Hilde get in here. You too, Humboldt. We've got a mess to clean up." By mess, I figured he meant us and not the damage that had occurred when Peter wrestled away from the security guards who still dozed.

When Dugan didn't get an immediate response, he turned toward the door. Mik did, too, and released his grip on Bernadette. Rikki flew into action, yanking Bernadette free. That earned Rikki a punch in the face that sent her flying.

"I said, get in here!" Dugan bellowed again. This time the model and Humboldt stumbled into the room. That's when I heard the now all too familiar sound of guns being cocked. Half a dozen men stepped slowly and deliberately into the room, shoving those in front of them forward.

"U.S. Marshals! Nobody move!" The attractive man who issued the order held a badge in the hand that didn't already have a gun in it. The men with him, including two members of the Mexican police, also had guns and badges. "Hello, boss. Are you okay?"

"Yes, Austin. I guess I should feel lucky I'm not dead." Rikki glared at me when she spoke. Then Austin nodded at Dugan. Handcuffs appeared from somewhere and he handed them to Rikki. She cuffed the lawyer.

"Uncle Sam's been trying to figure out who you are, el abogado. I've been tracking you since you got caught smuggling wine and ran out on a promise you made to show up in court. You made quite a name for yourself after the fire you set in a vineyard turned into a firestorm. We weren't sure where to find you until we got rumors that el abogado was hard at work in the Inland Empire."

"The name on the penthouse purchase agreement ought to have been a big hint!" Austin smiled in a way that lit the entire room.

"We needed more proof than that for you to put him away once and for all. We didn't want him to come back to Mexico again. Peter tells me there's plenty of evidence in el abogado's den. Not to mention, the money." For the first time, Dugan reacted. It was as if a bubble had burst. Perhaps, he'd been holding onto the hope that he'd escape once he returned to the U.S. and could have another crack as a fugitive. "Rikki has done you a favor to offer you shelter in a U.S. federal prison. It may be the only safe place left for you."

Eduardo issued an order in Spanish, and two officers stepped forward with more cuffs. They stepped past the gaggle of IED members who hadn't moved an inch. The security guys who'd been out cold were finally stirring. They woke to find the police standing over them with cuffs.

Austin motioned to the two men with him to use zip ties to take the other IED members into custody. They briefly explained they were being taken into custody as fugitives from justice and would be returned to the U.S. to face charges being made against them. Dugan's girlfriend was being whisked off at the expense of the U.S. government, too—subpoenaed as a witness.

When Frank saw Kenneth Humboldt, he just shook his head. He had difficulty speaking. When he found his voice, it was filled with anger and bitterness.

"No wonder the promises Bill Mackintosh made went up in smoke. He sold me out to a member of the IED. Did you destroy the ledger?"

"I don't think Mackintosh did that on purpose. He paid with his life if that's the case." I explained what had happened to the man to whom Frank had passed the ledger and why it didn't matter anymore what happened to the ledger now that the FBI had taken the nineteen-year-old amateur accountant into protective custody.

"I bet Mackintosh was killed by the same guy who went after you, Rikki, if that's what actually happened."

"Sorry I had to lie to you. Once Officer Muñoz informed me he had located el abogado, I hoped if I ditched you, you'd give up and let us do the dirty work. Austin and I had to get down here quick before we lost the trail again. It took me months to root Dugan out, so I called in a little help and arranged to disappear."

"We figured you were a double-crosser, Rikki. We just couldn't tell what kind," Laura said. "Telling us the truth might have worked. Maybe you should try it next time." She glanced sideways at Eduardo as she said that.

"A double, double-crosser actually," Tommy added. "Or was this a triple-cross? I don't care! We're alive. Frank's alive." Then he broke down. "No more lies, okay, Frank?"

"I'm sorry, buddy," Frank replied. "I thought I'd be able to do this without hurting any of you. Thanks for not giving up on me— even when I left with these guys. I promise—no more undercover cop. I've got a family to care for…" He squeezed my hand when he said that, and I had to choke back the tears.

"I'm sorry, too," Eduardo added. "Lying is your duty when you go undercover."

"You didn't lie about being able to cook. That's a point in your favor. I'm glad you're not dirty. That would have hurt, man."

"Thank you, Brien, for the compliment about my cooking." Eduardo did his snappy little bow before stepping next to Laura.

"The money you alerted the feds about, Peter, would have set Dugan up for life. As I already pointed out, that might not have been a very long one, considering the money belongs to the cartel and other unhappy people he ripped off."

"You have Frank to thank for that—he's the one who left the information for us to find."

"Another one of those love notes, huh?" Rikki shook her head, and I stiffened—ready to smack her again. Frank's fingers interlaced with mine, and I relaxed. I suppose, in a way, they were love notes. The heart is a clever, indefatigable hunter as we'd all revealed to ourselves and to each other. Right up there next to justice as a reason to do whatever it takes to figure out who's an angel and who's a devil.

EPILOGUE

"You're it!" Evie shrieked as she touched her brother on the shoulder. He dove under water and streaked toward his target. Brien moved out of the way, but not in time, since he didn't want to lose the last bite of Eduardo's brownies.

"Muy bueno," Brien said as he swallowed and took off trying to find a target in the game of pool tag that was underway at my house in Rancho Mirage. Summer was almost over.

"Thank you," Eduardo replied from where he sat holding Laura's hand. I hadn't seen my sweet, forgiving friend as happy as she was now in a long time. Time is a great healer, especially with a little help from friends.

Evie and Frankie, who spend summers at their Mom's house, had spent more time than they usually do here in the desert. I suspected that had something to do with the fact they'd come so close to losing their dad.

Frank had moved in with his parents to heal while contractors repaired his house in Perris. Evie and Frankie were remarkably resilient, but Frank needed more time. The damage Mik had done was more than skin deep. Frank had a fractured jaw and a concussion, as well as a broken rib. His rugged spirit had taken a few hits, too.

They'd intended to make Frank pay for giving the ledger to Mackintosh, even though Kenneth Humboldt had retrieved it from his cousin before having him killed. Frank's death wasn't going to be a quick one, like Roberts, who Mik had shot because, in a moment of weakness, Roberts had second thoughts about murdering a fellow cop.

Rikki, who'd signed a year-long contract with the Sheriff's Department, probably could have gotten out of it, but with Frank on leave, she stayed put long enough for him to rejoin the force. Besides, she had a vested interest in making sure the IED rats were found and received what they deserved. Now, she was returning to her post with the U.S. Marshals in Northern California. The party today was in her honor.

Rikki's departure wasn't the only reason to celebrate. Jerry and Tommy's wedding went off without a hitch in June. Rumor had it, there was going to be another one before Christmas. Kim wasn't wearing an engagement ring, although Brien was carrying one around with him, making sure we approved of it, and working up the courage to ask Kim to marry him.

Frank and I hadn't really discussed what his love notes meant for us in the long run. I'd gone back to work where, fortunately, Paul was no longer running things. I was. Paul and I hadn't seen each other socially, either, except at Jerry's wedding reception. My heart and mind were too full of Frank to make room for him.

Paul must have realized that. Perhaps once Jerry told him what we'd done to find Frank and bring him home. He hadn't called to invite himself over or asked me to dinner. It felt a bit awkward, but I'd try to find a way to clear the air without hurting the wonderful man.

When Rikki slipped into a chaise next to me, I quit ruminating.

"Thanks for the great send off."

"You're welcome to visit anytime, although I can't promise the kind of feast you had today with both Eduardo and Bernadette cooking to impress!"

"What a team, huh?" She smiled at Bernadette, who was chatting with Frank's mom, while Frank and his dad were engaged in a serious discussion about something. "You and Frank will have to pay me a visit in wine country. I don't cook, but Napa and Sonoma are foodie capitals of the world. You've got to have outstanding cuisine to go with the world-class wine the vintners in the area produce."

"That's a great idea. I'd love to visit with a local to show us around." I scanned Rikki's face, relieved not to feel anxious and suspicious. I'm not sure I'll ever feel as close to her as I do to my Cat Pack friends. Trust is so easily damaged, especially early on in a relationship. I was willing to try given the overtures she'd made toward friendship.

"I hate to do this, but is it okay if we talk business a little since I'm leaving the area?"

"What kind of business?"

"A legal matter. I have an odd situation with a case I thought I'd closed. The whole case was a strange one from the beginning. There's a young man in lock up who's about to go to prison for murder. He was underage when he supposedly committed the murder. The evidence points to him, and his lawyer got him a plea deal that reduced the charges from first to second degree murder. Because he was a minor, the court also showed some leniency when he was sentenced." She paused and took a sip of the beer she was holding.

"Okay, what's odd about the case?"

"I got a call from the murdered man's aunt. She claims, we've got it all wrong—Louie Jacobs—the guy who's going to prison— didn't kill her nephew."

"It's uncommon for a relative of the victim to come to the defense of a convicted perpetrator, but it does happen."

"I know, but it's even odder than that. Auntie claims she knows who's really responsible for her nephew's death."

"Great! If she has evidence to back up her claim, get it, and haul the real killer in for questioning. Who does she say the guilty party is?"

"This is where it goes past odd to weird. She says it's 'The Cleaner Man,' and he's done it before." The skeptical expression I wore got a nod from Rikki. "That's exactly what I expected to see if I went anywhere else with this. I was hoping you'd keep an open mind and check it out before dismissing the woman completely. Given the way you found Scott Bender, I thought you'd have an inside track. The dead nephew is local tribal member."

Before Rikki could finish what she still had to say, a commotion broke out around me. A cheer went up. When I turned, Frank was down on one knee with a huge bouquet of flowers in hand. Anastasia sat next to him, holding out a small basket dangling from a raised paw. I recognized the ring box we'd found in Frank's safe. I knew it contained the ring Frank's grandmother had given him.

"Jessica, will you marry me?" An expectant hush fell over everyone.

~~~~

Thank you for reading *A Dead Cousin* Jessica Huntington Desert Cities Mystery #5. I hope you'll take a minute to leave a review on Amazon and Goodreads. Your feedback is important to me and to readers!

If you haven't already done it, I hope you'll sign up for my newsletter at https://desertcitiesmystery.com so I can send you updates about my books in the Jessica Huntington Desert Cities Mystery series including the release date for *A Dead Nephew* Jessica Huntington Desert Cities Mystery Series #6. You'll also get news about sales, freebies, and giveaways so please join me!

You can find all my books on Amazon at:

https://www.amazon.com/Anna-Celeste-Burke/e/B00H8J4IQS/

ANNA CELESTE BURKE

Recipes

Herbed Rice with Pistachios

4-6 servings

Ingredients

1 1/2 cups basmati rice, rinsed several times until the water is not cloudy
3 cups water or chicken broth
1 teaspoon kosher salt
1/2 teaspoon freshly ground black pepper
1/2 cup shelled pistachios, toasted
1/2 cup coarsely chopped fresh mint, cilantro, and parsley

Directions

Bring water or broth to a simmer. Add rice, salt, and pepper and cook for about 15 minutes, or until liquid level is even with the level of the rice. Turn off the heat and allow the rice to steam to finish cooking. [Be sure to use water and not broth if you want to serve this to vegans like Peter March.]

Toast Pistachios. Position a rack in the center of the oven and heat the oven to 325°F. Spread the pistachios on a baking sheet and toast in the oven until golden and fragrant, 7 to 10 minutes. Transfer the baking sheet to a wire rack to cool.

Roughly chop the nuts and herbs. Fold into the rice.

Sesame Noodles [Vegan]
Serves 8

Ingredients
1 16 ounce package linguine pasta
4 garlic cloves, minced
2 tablespoons sugar
3 tablespoons rice vinegar
4 tablespoons soy sauce
3 tablespoons sesame oil
2 tablespoons canola oil
2 teaspoons sriracha or chili sauce
4 green onions, sliced

1 teaspoon sesame seeds, toasted [Optional]

Directions
Bring a pot of lightly salted water to boil. Add pasta, and cook until al dente, about 8 to 10 minutes. Drain, and transfer to a serving bowl.

Meanwhile, place a saucepan over medium-high heat. Stir in garlic, sugar, oil, vinegar, soy sauce, sesame oil, and chili sauce. Bring to a boil, stirring constantly, until sugar dissolves. Pour sauce over linguine and toss to coat. Garnish with green onions and sesame seeds.

Serve hot or cold. Toss in veggies of your choice or tofu if you fix these often and want to change it up. Top with peanuts instead of sesame seeds.

Balsamic Roasted Vegetables with Feta Cheese

Serves 4-6

Ingredients
2 zucchini squash, cut into large chunks
1 large red onion, peeled and cut into large chunks
3 carrots, peeled and chopped
1 large sweet potato, peeled and chopped
4 medium beets, peeled and chopped
1/4 cup extra virgin olive oil
2 tablespoons balsamic vinegar
1/2 teaspoon kosher salt
1/4 teaspoon black pepper
2 tablespoons brown sugar
1/4 cup crumbled feta cheese

Directions
Preheat oven to 375°F.

Wash and cut vegetables. Spread them out in a single layer on a large rimmed baking sheet.

Combine the olive oil, balsamic vinegar, brown sugar, salt, and pepper in a bowl. Reserve 2 tablespoons for later.

Pour over vegetables and mix until all the vegetables are covered.

Bake for 30 to 45 minutes (or until your vegetables are tender, and brown).

Drizzle with the reserved vinaigrette, and sprinkle with feta.

Spiced Greek Lamb Patties with Pita

Serves 4-6

Ingredients

Patties and Pita
1 1/2 pounds ground lamb or beef
1 tablespoon minced garlic (about 1 large clove)
1 tablespoon coriander
2 teaspoons ground cumin
1 1/2 teaspoons hot paprika
1 1/2 teaspoons kosher salt
1 1/2 tablespoons extra-virgin olive oil
4 to 6 pita bread rounds

Yogurt Sauce
1 cup plain full-fat or low-fat yogurt
2 tablespoons fresh lemon juice
2 tablespoons finely chopped herbs, such as mint, dill or cilantro, plus herb sprigs, for serving
Kosher salt

Directions
Prepare the sauce by whisking the yogurt with the lemon juice. Stir in the chopped herbs, season with salt and refrigerate until ready to use.

Prepare the patties, mixing together all the ingredients, except for the pita. Form the mixture into twelve 3-inch oval patties (about 1 inch thick). Refrigerate for at least 30 minutes.

Preheat a grill for at least 10 minutes and prepare it for grilling over moderately high heat. If you are using a charcoal grill, leave one area where you can grill the pita indirectly.

Oil the grill grates and grill the patties until dark brown grill marks form on the bottom, 5 to 6 minutes. Flip the patties and grill for 4 to 6 minutes longer, until just cooked through.

Meanwhile, wrap the pita in foil and set the package on the top shelf of a gas grill or in the cooler spot of a charcoal grill and allow them to warm through, 8 to 10 minutes.

Wrap 2 or 3 patties in each pita, spoon some of the yogurt sauce alongside and serve with herb sprigs, passing the remaining yogurt sauce at the table.

Quinoa Tabbouleh

Serves 6

Ingredients
1 cup quinoa, rinsed well
1/2 teaspoon kosher salt
2 tablespoons fresh lemon juice
1 garlic clove, minced
1/2 cup extra-virgin olive oil
Freshly ground black pepper
1 large English hothouse cucumber, cut into 1/4" pieces
1 pint cherry tomatoes, halved
1 cup chopped flat-leaf parsley
1/2 cup chopped fresh mint
2 scallions, thinly sliced

Directions
Bring 1/2 teaspoon salt and 1 1/4 cups water to a boil in a medium saucepan over high heat. When it comes to a boil, add quinoa and reduce heat to medium-low, cover, and simmer until quinoa is tender, about 10 minutes. Remove from heat and let stand, covered, for 5 minutes. Fluff with a fork. Let chill for 30 to 60 minutes.

Whisk lemon juice and garlic in a small bowl. Gradually whisk in olive oil. Season dressing to taste with salt and pepper.

When quinoa is cool, add cucumber, tomatoes, herbs, and scallions and toss with dressing. Adjust salt and pepper to taste.

Salted Caramel Turtle Brownies

24 Brownies

Ingredients

3/4 cup unsalted butter
1 4 ounce semi-sweet chocolate bar, coarsely chopped
2 cups granulated sugar
3 large eggs, at room temperature
2 teaspoons pure vanilla extract
1 cup unsweetened natural cocoa powder
1 cup all-purpose flour
1 teaspoon salt
1 cup chopped pecans
1 cup semi-sweet chocolate chips
1 cup homemade salted caramel sauce

Directions

Preheat the oven to 350°F. Line a 9x13 inch pan with parchment paper, leaving an overhang on the sides to lift the finished brownies out of the pan to make cutting easier.

In a microwave-safe bowl, combine the butter and 2 ounces of chopped chocolate. Melt in 30 second increments, whisking after each, until completely smooth. Whisk in the sugar until completely combined, then whisk in the eggs and vanilla. The batter will be light brown and a little dull looking.

Add the cocoa powder, flour, salt, remaining 2 ounces of chopped chocolate, pecans, and chocolate chips. Fold it all together with a rubber spatula or wooden spoon. Batter will be very thick. Spread evenly into prepared pan.

Bake for 30 minutes, then test the brownies with a toothpick. Insert it into the center of the pan. If it comes out with wet batter, the brownies are not done. If there are only a few moist crumbs, the brownies are done. Keep checking every 2 minutes until you have moist crumbs. My brownies take 31 to 32 minutes. Remove from the oven and spread warm salted caramel sauce [see next recipe to make your own] on top of hot brownies. Sprinkle top with coarse salt [optional].

Place the pan on a wire rack to cool completely before cutting into squares. If you cover and store leftover brownies at room temperature, they'll be good for a few days—maybe even a week if they ever stick around that long.

Salted Caramel Sauce
Makes 1 cup

Ingredients
1 cup granulated sugar
6 tablespoons salted butter, room temperature cut up into 6 pieces
1/2 cup (120ml) heavy cream
1 teaspoon salt

Directions

Heat granulated sugar in a medium saucepan over medium heat, stirring constantly with a high heat resistant rubber spatula or wooden spoon.

Sugar will form clumps and eventually melt into a thick brown, amber-colored liquid as you continue to stir. Be careful not to burn.

Once sugar is completely melted, immediately add the butter. Be careful in this step because the caramel will bubble rapidly when the butter is added.

Stir the butter into the caramel until it is completely melted, about 2 to 3 minutes. A whisk helps if you find the butter is separating from the sugar.

Very slowly, drizzle in 1/2 cup of heavy cream while stirring. Since the heavy cream is colder than the caramel, the mixture will rapidly bubble and/or splatter when added.

Allow the mixture to boil for 1 minute. It will rise in the pan as it boils.

Remove from heat and stir in 1 teaspoon of salt. Cool before using.

White Chocolate Macadamia Nut Pancakes [vegan]

Serves 2: 6-8 pancakes

Ingredients

1 cup flour
1 tablespoon sugar
1 tablespoon baking powder
Pinch of salt
1 cup light vanilla soy milk*
1 1/2 tablespoons canola oil
2 tsp vanilla
4 tablespoons dairy-free white chocolate chips
3 tablespoons macadamia nuts, lightly chopped
2 tablespoons roasted macadamia, chopped for garnish

Instructions

Preheat griddle or skillet to medium heat.

Combine wet ingredients in a large bowl. Then add dry ingredients to a sifter and sift into the wet (excluding white chocolate and macadamia nuts).

Stir batter until just combined and no large lumps remain, then add white chocolate chips and macadamia nuts and stir. Let batter rest for 5 minutes.

Spoon 1/4 cup measurements onto a lightly greased griddle. Flip when bubbles appear on top or the edges look dry, then cook for 1 to 2 minutes more.

Serve with vegan butter and maple syrup, and top with a few more white chocolate chips and 2 T. chopped roasted macadamia nuts.

*choose another type of milk if you prefer

ABOUT THE AUTHOR

An award-winning, USA Today and Wall Street Journal bestselling author I hope you'll join me *snooping into life's mysteries with fun, fiction, and food—California style!*

Life is an extravaganza! Figuring out how to hang tough and make the most of the wild ride is the challenge. On my way to Oahu, to join the rock musician and high school drop-out I had married in Tijuana, I was nabbed as a runaway. Eventually, the police let me go, but the rock band broke up.

Our next stop: Disney World, where we "worked for the Mouse" as chefs, courtesy of Walt Disney World University Chef's School. More education landed us in academia at The Ohio State University. For decades, I researched, wrote, and taught about many gloriously nerdy topics.

Retired now, I'm still married to the same, sweet guy and live with him near Palm Springs, California. I write the Jessica Huntington Desert Cities Mystery series set here in the Coachella Valley, the Corsario Cove Cozy Mystery Series set in California's Central Coast, The Georgie Shaw Mystery series set in the OC, The Seaview Cottages Cozy Mystery Series set on the American Riviera, just north of Santa Barbara, and The Calla Lily Mystery series that takes place in California's Wine Country. Won't you join me? Sign up at: http://desertcitiesmystery.com.

CPSIA information can be obtained
at www.ICGtesting.com
Printed in the USA
LVHW09s2146101018
593201LV00001B/93/P

9 781723 817540